PEACHTREE

Lulu in Marrakech

LULU IN MARRAKECH

Diane Johnson

DUTTON

DUTTON

Published by Penguin Group (USA) Inc.

375 Hudson Street, New York, New York 10014, U.S.A.

Penguin Group (Canada), 90 Eglinton Avenue East, Suite 700, Toronto, Ontario M4P 2Y3, Canada (a division of Pearson Penguin Canada Inc.); Penguin Books Ltd, 80 Strand, London WC2R 0RL, England; Penguin Ireland, 25 St Stephen's Green, Dublin 2, Ireland (a division of Penguin Books Ltd); Penguin Group (Australia), 250 Camberwell Road, Camberwell, Victoria 3124, Australia (a division of Pearson Australia Group Pty Ltd); Penguin Books India Pvt Ltd, 11 Community Centre, Panchsheel Park, New Delhi–110 017, India; Penguin Group (NZ), 67 Apollo Drive, Rosedale, North Shore 0632, New Zealand (a division of Pearson New Zealand Ltd); Penguin Books (South Africa) (Pty) Ltd, 24 Sturdee Avenue, Rosebank, Johannesburg 2196, South Africa

Penguin Books Ltd, Registered Offices: 80 Strand, London WC2R 0RL, England

Published by Dutton, a member of Penguin Group (USA) Inc.

First printing, October 2008

1   3   5   7   9   10   8   6   4   2

 REGISTERED TRADEMARK—MARCA REGISTRADA

LIBRARY OF CONGRESS CATALOGING-IN-PUBLICATION DATA

Johnson, Diane, 1934–

Lulu in Marrakech / by Diane Johnson.

p. cm.

ISBN 978-0-525-95037-0

I. Title

PS3560.O3746L85 2008

813'.54—dc22   2008007700

Printed in the United States of America

Set in Galliard

Designed by Amy Hill

To the memory of Barbara Epstein,
Marie-Claude de Brunhoff, and Pauline Abbe;
and, as always,
to John Murray

ACKNOWLEDGMENTS

The Koranic quotations are based on a classic 1934 translation by Abdullah Yusuf Ali, widely available in many editions. The intelligence-related epigraphs and some of Lulu's references to CIA practices come from papers published from a colloquium on *Intelligence Requirements for the 1980s,* in several volumes, edited by Professor Roy Godson, of which I found "Analysis and Estimates," "Counterintelligence," and "Clandestine Collection" the most helpful. Many friends helped with special expertise, observations, and criticisms, especially John Beebe, Diana Ketchum, Robert Gottlieb, Craig Phillips, Sally Shelton-Colby, Marlise Simons, and Drusilla Walsh. Grateful thanks to my editor, Trena Keating; my agent, Lynn Nesbit; and as always to my husband, John Murray.

Lulu in Marrakech

How indeed is it possible for one human being to be sorry for all the sadness that meets him on the face of the earth, for the pain that is endured not only by men, but by animals and plants, and perhaps by the stones. The soul is tired in a moment, and in fear of losing the little that she does understand . . . she retreats to the permanent lines which habit or chance have dictated, and suffers there.

—E. M. Forster, *A Passage to India*

1

International terrorism may increasingly be a problem. . . . Better intelligence to counter terrorist activities cannot be based on technological intelligence (e.g. photography, radio, and traffic intelligence) but must be based on clandestine agents' activities, or what is called HUMINT.

—Michael Handel, "Avoiding Surprise in the 1980s"

During training for my present job, I had been particularly struck by a foundation document of tradecraft, "The Role of Self-Deception in Prediction Failures." It argues that Americans are especially prone to self-deception and that our ability to fool ourselves is greater than the ability of others to fool us. History shows plenty of examples, but it's my own that's made me understand the author's point. Am I myself more gullible than other Americans? Perhaps these are the very qualities I was recruited for: gullibility, and the rigidity of my belief in pragmatism—for I am determined not to let ideology, whether of love or patriotism, get the better of me again.

And when did the gullibility principle begin to work on me? Maybe not until I was on the plane to Marrakech, or even when I got the assignment to go there. Am I once again its victim? I still don't know, even now, how much of what happened had been orchestrated, how much was the collusion of unforeseen events.

But I should explain how I came to be involved in all this. I'm Lulu Sawyer—not my christened name, but it is now Lulu even in company records.

In our organization, we have foreign intelligence (FI), counterintelligence (CI), human intelligence (HUMINT), and communications intelligence (COMMI); there's covert, overt, clandestine, and paramilitary, and passive and aggressive in each category. I am FI/HUMINT/NOC. NOC means not officially connected to an embassy or government agency.

"Human intelligence," said my handler, Sefton Taft, in a regretful tone—I report to an insensitive and sometimes seemingly not-too-friendly case officer named Taft, who is stationed in Spain. "HUMINT. It must still be gathered. These Arabs are so backward; things like electronic surveillance, technical collection—these are useless. Knowledge is in someone's head, it's recorded in the knots of a camel's bridle, in certain passages of the Koran. The Russians, God bless them, at least had radio communications, listening stations of their own, cell phones we could intercept—those were the days."

"Human intelligence; an oxymoron," I remember saying.

HUMINT/FI had a basic mission in Morocco: to gather information intended to upgrade generally our database on the country, including information about the flow of money through certain Marrakech Islamic charities or, more startling, the European clubs and nongovernmental organizations (NGOs). It was the analysis at headquarters that it was the Moroccan NGOs, directed and mostly funded by foreigners, that formed the nexus of, or at least an important stage on, the money trail from Europe and America to various terrorist organizations, via Moroccan banking. It was important, because we had intelligence that the Islamists left over from recent crackdowns in Algeria had regrouped in the Sahara desert and were recruiting and attempting to radicalize everywhere in North Africa—Mali, Morocco, Tunisia, Algeria, and in the no-man's-land of the Western Sahara—and unless they could be impeded would have a powerful Al-Qaida-like base within easy striking distance of Europe, as the bombings in Spain had shown.

"HUMINT—it makes you long for the old days," Taft had added. "Satellite photos, listening devices, hard targets. You're well-placed, Lulu. No matter what happens with the boyfriend, you'll easily find a way of staying on in Morocco—a healthy, articulate, sociable girl like you."

Taft was briefing me: "Huge sums of money change hands in the souk, intended for jihad, never going near a bank. Who are the bankers? We think there's a network involving domestics, car repair guys, people who interact with Europeans every day. Waiters. We need a lot more information on them." It was from Morocco that huge sums of money were being distributed to radical Middle Eastern organizations and suicide bombers, and as reparations to their families. Terrorists were being formed there too—Moroccans had been among the bombers in Casablanca and Madrid, and were even connected to London. There is evidence that all of North Africa is home to rising numbers of fanatics.

"Remember," Taft said, "these people depend on a network of little shopkeepers, forgers, fishermen—sympathizers who can get a false passport, a train ticket, put them up for a night or a week, help them cross the water. These are people who won't themselves be planting bombs, but who indulge their convictions or ease their consciences by supporting the bombers. That's where we need information. Where are those passports coming from?"

I understood. I would not be Lawrence of Arabia. Mine was a frankly low-level and not very specific mission; but I was a low-level person who had happened into a potentially valuable cover, acquiring an English lover who lived in Morocco. Luckily our corporate ethic does not include celibacy, and though it was utterly unspoken, I sensed company backing for recruits who were also passable-looking and had a fair chance of going to bed with possibly useful men, and the willingness.

Beside this mission, other personal things drew me to the idea of Morocco—the warm weather, the fascination of a new culture, but especially my little love affair with Ian Drumm. I'd told my family and friends I was going to visit a lover in Marrakech, as, of course, I was, and it was a more-than-perfect cover for my real mission, which I couldn't reveal to them or to him. In my first post, I'd been attached to an international aid agency in Pristina, in Kosovo, where I had met Ian, and was now being reassigned conveniently near him. To spend a few months with him at his villa in Marrakech would hardly be work.

I'd never been to North Africa but had always liked travel posters of the mosques and domes, the salmon walls, the palms and donkeys and goats, all so evocative of warm sunshine and the melodic calls to prayer, and a dionysian miasma of goat and incense layered in the air. Islam drew me and repelled me. My misgivings weren't sectarian; part of my apprehensiveness had to do with the paradox that we are apt to fear most what we most want, in case when we get it, it turn to ashes. I wanted to succeed professionally—as predicted for the paradigmatic young person sought by the Agency (though I'm in my thirties)—and personally, with Ian, for I was kind of stuck on him.

2

Analysis may be the most important and is surely one of the most vulnerable components of the intelligence process. Analysts are required to answer difficult questions on the basis of usually limited data. Thus they are frequently tempted to accept data more or less at face value.

—Roy Godson, ed., *Intelligence Requirements for the 1980s*

Though I don't usually talk to people on planes, I had fallen into conversation with the woman in the seat next to me, a slender, tan, and well-dressed Frenchwoman in her forties. I'd stopped in Paris for a visit between posts and was flying out of Charles de Gaulle on Royal Air Maroc. The plane was crowded with merry Parisians making for their weekend places—their riads and condos in the warm, exotic desert.

"There's no problem in Morocco," she said. "It's the last place where Europe and Islam still get along."

"No one shot there, as in Egypt, or bombed, or kidnapped like in Afghanistan. Not yet," I said, for I had boned up on all this.

"Luckily, such things are impossible in Morocco. They are cultur-ally very French," she said, apparently remembering nothing about Algeria and the French experience there.

We were flying high enough that the whole contour of the northern coast of Africa was visible, a whole new continent, the dark continent, as it used to be called, though it lay beneath us as green and cheerful as one could wish—the strip along the coast at least—so lovely that I hadn't been able to keep myself from calling her attention to it.

This led to our introducing ourselves. She was Yvette Frank, and she dealt in real estate in Marrakech, but more interesting than that to me, she told me she worked as a *bénévole,* a volunteer, with a group in Paris that helped young Muslim French girls escape from the murder-ous intentions of their fathers and brothers: On the plane with us was a girl, Suma Bourad, whose father and brother had planned to slit her throat in one of the honor killings you read about, and which actually happen.

"We help these girls menaced by their families. Some of the *his-toires* are quite harrowing," Madame Frank had said, and told me what she knew of Suma's story, in a low voice so Suma couldn't hear. The girl was sitting two rows behind us in the first row of coach. They hadn't been able to get seats together, and I sensed that this was some-thing of a relief to Madame Frank, who, well-meaning as she was, probably didn't have a lot in common with a teenage Muslim victim. Or maybe the French charity wouldn't spring for a business-class seat. Anyway, luckily for the girl, she had eluded her family; at least, no mark was visible under the sedate fastening of her foulard, though one wondered what kind of mark it must have left on her soul.

Suma was a student, eighteen or nineteen, very pretty, with almond skin and large dark eyes shadowed by a sort of plum bloom around them, not quite bruised-seeming, but you looked twice to see what it was; it brought to mind the reason for her fleeing. Madame Frank didn't know if this was the first time she had been on a plane. She was born in France to Algerian parents, perhaps had never seen North Africa. Sumaya Bourad, Suma. She appeared such a model of Islamic decorum, I had to remind myself that whatever her religion, she was also a French girl, educated in dialectics and Descartes, hoping to be a doctor.

"It's not so common among Algerians, honor killing," said Madame Frank. "It's usually the Turks."

Suma's story, Madame Frank said, is not unusual among the daughters of immigrant families in Europe, when the old ways cherished by the parents conflict with what Parisian girls come to feel for themselves. For every one who accedes to the wishes of her parents concerning marriage or education, another rebels or—I don't really know the proportion of the rebels to the dutiful—but Suma was the former. She had embarrassed her family in some way, had believed her brother was going to kill her, and had gone to the shelter.

Apart from chatting with Madame Frank, I read and looked out of the window, but I was conscious of the young woman, who didn't seem to be doing anything. I would have expected a vibrant, rebellious girl, but she sat quietly the whole way, not reading, her hair covered in a dark blue scarf, eyes lowered, gazing at the seat in front of her. Several times I walked back through the coach section toward the toilets, which took me by her seat. She didn't give any sign of desperation, though I supposed she must be desperate.

I was glad she had the gumption to escape. The metaphor of flying contains the idea of flight from something, from danger or constraint, and it contains the idea of freedom. I supposed these were the things this trip meant to Suma, the opposite of what it meant to me.

"The brother is a fanatic, he's watched, the police have had him down for some time," said Madame Frank.

"It is almost too late to buy in Marrakech now," she went on, reverting to her favorite subject. "The beautiful old riads are mostly gone, though some remain, for a price. Currently I have a line on an especially good one, in a good location, completely *à rénover, naturellement* . . . if that should interest you."

"What will she do in Marrakech? Suma."

"She will work as an au pair for a very nice English family. They'll be meeting us, of course. I will present you. The Cotters. 'Sir and lady'!" She smiled the patronizing smile the French adopt when dealing with English titles and other vestiges of what they consider a backward political system they themselves had had the wisdom to ditch. "Maybe you know them?"

The French also always assume that all Anglo-Saxons know each other. "No," I said, "I don't know anyone in Marrakech except my host, Ian Drumm."

"But I know *him*!" she cried. "He is very known in the community. You must surely come to us during your visit."

I thanked her. I could see that Madame Frank, in Moroccan real estate, and Suma, positioned in a nice English family, could become useful sources for me; I hoped Suma and I would eventually become friends, and it seemed that Madame Frank and I were friends already.

3

Who stays at home during that month / Should spend it in fasting;
But if anyone is ill, / or on a journey, the prescribed period should
be made up by days later . . . and you may be grateful.

—Koran 2:185

"What may I serve you, Miss . . . Sawyer?" said the flight
attendant, glancing at her manifest. But when I asked for a
glass of wine, she said they couldn't serve alcohol during Ramadan.
"It is our sacred period, the Muslim month of fasting," she continued,
though I knew what Ramadan was, of course. We were now at the end
of September, and Ramadan had just begun. No food or alcohol all
day. Could they drink water? I suddenly wasn't sure, and this made me
doubt my general preparation, though I had read works of sociology,
slogged through the Koran, and learned the rudiments of the beautiful script.

The flight attendant was serving water, tea, and coffee, whatever the rule. Though most of the people on the plane were Western, drinking coffee and eating pretzels, some were sitting abstemiously. One or two hungry-looking people were standing in line before me waiting for the toilets in business class. Next before me was a beautiful, dark Middle Eastern–looking woman, her huge eyes kohl-lined, her clothes Armani. She took an inordinate amount of time in the *cabine,* and when she came out she was wrapped in a black chador, or abaya, as these garments are called in Morocco, an Islamic shawl over her hair, her body, the lower part of her face. I had heard that the abaya was not worn much in Marrakech, and in fact she was the only woman on the plane dressed in such a way, her black costume contrasting with the pastels and beiges of the Europeans and returning Moroccans, so that she stood out like the wicked godmother at the christening and was a powerful reminder of the strange fate of women in the place I was going.

We were flying a bit lower, so that now the cities of the northern coast were visible on the edge of the sea, arcs of settlement like white rickrack against the turquoise Mediterranean. Then we turned inland, south, toward the desert. We were too high to make out figures, but tiny towers rose here and there out of the chalky landscape. As we came down, the buildings resolved into apricot and beige, more nearly the colors of earth. Now from the sky, you were conscious of more desert lying to the south, the Sahara, a wasteland of hot sand and death, encroaching relentlessly on these human habitations and their precarious water supply.

When we landed, Madame Frank stood up to reach her carry-on, trapping me in my seat, but I could watch Suma follow the other passengers up the aisle. She carried a nice leather purse and one of those Chinese red-and-white-striped plasticized paper carrier bags. I noted these things, but mostly now that we were here, I had fallen to thinking of Ian and about whether a month or two with him would be wonderful or unwise. Thinking of sleeping with him caused an agreeable stir, but I reminded myself that months of sunshine and whatever you ate or couldn't drink in Morocco could also become as monotonous as the the limitless Sahara. If things didn't work out with Ian, my orders were to attach myself to an institution that I would eventually stay on to teach in or run.

There was nothing exotic about the brisk, modern airport except the costumes of the cleaners in their washed-out cotton smocks and backless slippers, in contrast to the smart European clothing of the arriving visitors and the people waiting for them. Otherwise all was potted palms and marble terrazzo, like airports anywhere. I looked beyond the passport line and was surprised that Ian wasn't among the group of excited locals waving to their families or Europeans waving at their guests. Instead, a man I didn't recognize, with a pudgy, cheerful face and a day's beard, wearing khakis and loafers, was holding up a sign that read MISS L. SAWYER. He saw my reaction, concluded I was me, waved from behind the barrier, and tapped his own chest to show he was meant for me.

I looked around for Ian again and couldn't see him. Though my tendency is to imagine that everything is okay, my training, and perhaps a trace of the slight paranoia that renders you suitable (as ascertained by batteries of standardized tests) for this line of work, spun scary explanations through my mind: Maybe this was Ian's driver, but he could be a kidnapper, an agent, the bearer of bad news. What should I say to him? How to get his credentials? Asking for a note from Ian was too dramatic, would suggest I had some reason to be fearful. Yet to go with some stranger would be an elementary mistake. I could refuse to go with him, I could say I preferred a taxi.

And, after all, how could Ian fail to come for me? What did this foretell? Indifference? Regret, perhaps? Yet probably neither—for him, Morocco was a normal place, with functioning taxis, well within the capabilities of a grown woman to negotiate; he would not think of kidnapping or robbery or indifference. This flood of thoughts occurred more or less simultaneously; meantime I smiled to acknowledge that I was L. Sawyer.

I found a cart and went to pick up my bags. The girl Suma had crowded close to the luggage carousel too. I held her eye for a brief instant and we exchanged the impersonal smiles of people who catch each other looking. Was there something uncertain and imploring about her glance? No lurking male relatives menaced her.

Madame Frank and Suma piled a suitcase and a box on a cart and began to push it toward the exits, it seemed without talking much to each other, but smiling, like two people of goodwill who didn't speak a common language. Madame Frank pushed the cart, and Suma walked behind her. I assumed I was seeing her off safely into her new life. My bags were the last, as usual, or so it always seems to me, and then I went past the barrier to where the stranger waited.

"Miss Sawyer? I thought it was you. Tom Drill. I'm supposed to take you to Ian's. He had to wait for his tree man," he said. "I said as I was coming to the airport anyhow . . . are these your bags?"

Obviously they were. I still hadn't decided whether to act on my mistrustful apprehensiveness. He seemed all right, American, familiar, but I couldn't judge the local context, the significance of his unshaven beard and rumpled khakis. And all the tales of kidnapped agents or businessmen began like this, at the airport, with an unfamiliar emissary saying someone had sent them. He's just near here, he wants me to bring you to him, he's waiting, was delayed.

So far, there hadn't been kidnappings in Morocco. But there hadn't been any in Beirut, in Peshawar, Cairo, or Athens, until the first one. Terry Anderson. Daniel Pearl. Thus did my inner discussion go. But if you make a fuss, express hesitation, they will see you have reasons, reasons an uncomplicated girlfriend ought not to have.

It weighed with me that this guy was American, but I dawdled, hoping Ian would appear, hoping Madame Frank would present me to Suma. They were standing in the lobby, maybe waiting for their own driver. As I watched, a tall woman wearing a yellow blouse walked up to Suma, smiling, welcoming, and they shook hands. A large, handsome woman around sixty, rather glamorous in the style of Mrs. Thatcher, with wavy whitish-blonde hair and a Thatcherian purse. Before I could catch Madame Frank's attention, Tom Drill greeted the woman in the yellow blouse, "*Ciao,* Marina." This was sort of a relief, that he was known to people.

Marina's Englishness was evident from her size and clothes, and no mistaking the plummy upper-class tones. While they chatted, I smiled again at Suma and said *bonjour.* "*Bonjour,* madame," she said. Yes, it was her first time in Morocco; yes, she was happy to be here. She would be studying and working.

"Suma will be staying with us," said Marina, or "Lady Cotter," in the terms of Tom's introduction. It was clear she and Madame Frank hadn't met before, but now they acknowledged each other enthusiastically, and Marina Cotter thanked her for the help of her group.

As we parted, Madame Frank asked me again what my last name was. "Sawyer," I said. "I'll be staying at Ian Drumm's."

"Yes, Lulu's here to visit Ian Drumm," Tom told Marina. Oh, how nice. Did their eyebrows raise slightly, did little smiles play across their lips?

"Yes, a charming man!" said Madame Frank. "I will invite you. I am always trying to get him to sell me his big Palmeraie tract. Maybe you will intercede for me. *Au revoir! À bientôt! À bientôt!*"

By now, it was starting to feel to me slightly too propitious that I should so neatly be furnished with all this local information; my arrival was sort of front-loaded with background facts, like the beginning of a play, and Tom Drill later gave me even more—that Sir Neil and Lady Cotter had a showplace riad, that there were a ton of Brits in Marrakech, that Marina Cotter was his own best pal, that she had recently been struck with tragedy: She had been saddled with her grandchildren after a daughter-in-law had died in Nepal. Their son, the father of the children, was in the military somewhere in Africa and couldn't take care of them. The little granddaughter played with Tom's daughter, Amelie, sometimes. Suma would be helping Lady Cotter. The Cotters thus had the satisfaction of rescuing a girl and getting a babysitter into the bargain.

Lady Cotter had given Madame Frank and me a knowing, complicit smile; we were all good people cooperating to help a girl threatened by violence. "And we'll be seeing a lot of you—we adore Ian, he is one of Neil's oldest friends, well, since he was a boy, Ian, I mean. Neil and Ian's father were friends in the Second War. . . ." She talked on.

Ian. In general I'm not attracted to Englishmen—too pale and pink, usually, and they smoke and drink too much. Ian didn't have these faults, but now, not coming to the airport was a fault.

4

Some qualities are directly related to the intelligence process. Curiosity is, of course, fundamental, as is a thoughtful turn of mind, matched with some humility against presumptions of infallibility.

—William E. Colby, "Recruitment, Training and Incentives for Better Analysis"

Soon after signing up for this life, my eye happened to fall on a manual used by Agency recruiters. It said that the type of young person they were looking for must be of above-average intelligence and intellectual curiosity, sociable and extroverted; good at both oral and written communication; have an interest in international affairs; be fluent in at least one foreign language; have "a preference for unstructured, even ambiguous job situations"; have a desire for leadership and readiness "to manipulate others to achieve legitimate goals," sound judgment, common sense, self-discipline, some experience living overseas, and "experience and ability in relating to foreign persons and cultures"; be good at role-playing; approve of what we would be doing; and not have too many ties back home in America.

To think that I might conform to that description gave me at least a moment's pause for self-examination and a stab of chagrin. While some of these are qualities I admire, some certainly are not, and some I know myself positively to lack. It's true, for instance, that I speak a little French by now, but leadership is the last quality I picture myself having. I had lived overseas and was free of American ties (I had stayed awhile in France after my junior year abroad, then came back to finish college in California and got an M.A. in international relations after, let's face it, various personal screw-ups and the terminal exasperation of my relatives). I was having fun, or thought I was, but I knew my life wasn't leading anywhere, and then, coming to the end of my rope, almost by accident I was recruited to my present job.

Though I should be too old to be a concern to my parents, I'm aware that I am one. They believe I should have found my way before this. Will she ever settle down? Will she marry? If only she would marry. If only she were happy. Their sweetness to me (when I was younger, they were firm, even harsh, about my mishaps) reveals their fear that they have a fragile being on their hands whom they must not challenge. But this is far from true.

Role-playing, manipulating others—I knew I was doing those when I agreed to visit Ian in Marrakech. I knew I planned to stay on. Ian's invitation was opportune—my rotation in Kosovo was finishing, it could not seem more natural that I should visit him before my next move somewhere. Of course I hadn't told him about my affiliation, if only for reasons of tact—if he knew I had other reasons for being in North Africa, that would certainly challenge the sincerity of my attachment to him. It was the one thing no one must know. Once in

Marrakech, I expected to find other reasons for staying on. It would seem natural that there would be interests and useful things in Marrakech to attach myself to—a museum or charity, certain people I would meet there.

As I said, I'd met Ian in Kosovo. After my training in Virginia, I'd been sent to work in Pristina with AmerAID, an international rescue organization. That was my first cover, but of course I also actually did AmerAID work, both overt and covert. Overtly, our office packaged the food donations, coordinated the medical volunteers from Médecins sans Frontières or the Red Cross, dispatched the bundles of cleaned and sorted secondhand clothes arriving from the World Council of Churches and American civic groups, and generally assisted things (despite the disillusioned air of apologetic self-sacrifice in AmerAID headquarters). And covertly I had a modest success, by having a correct hunch about the whereabouts of Vlad Janovic, a prominent second-string war criminal we'd been wanting to pick up.

Now, just as I'd worked in the aid organization in Kosovo, I had a cover mission here, evaluating and preparing a report on female literacy programs for the Middle Eastern Partnership Initiative, MEPI, an umbrella grants organization I had been working for after I was first recruited. As you would hope, in a country where only half the people can read, there were a number of recent programs devoted to women reading, and my inspection work would be expected to take some months. I expected this pursuit would in itself be interesting and useful; I'd majored in social work in college and was more than competent to do evaluations of this kind. I thus had a double feeling of self-satisfaction, serving my country and doing good too.

It had surprised my family and friends that I could stick at what they saw as drab humanitarian missions, as it surprised me. Still, as they saw it, I had little else to do, hadn't found another path, so helping others was my path; and at one time I too had really thought the secret of happiness might indeed be a life of service (though not of self-sacrifice; I had no taste for that). Service, a preoccupation with helping others, doesn't rule out personal happiness, and I had thought it might produce it. It doesn't seem useful to think about whether you are happy or aren't.

People my age were in general not brought up in a tradition of service, but I suppose I was. My father is a retired air force officer, now a professor. In his last post, he'd taught at the Defense Language Institute in Monterey, and then after retirement he took a civilian job at the junior college in Santa Barbara, where my mother is from. My grandmother was a candy striper at a hospital; a docent at the museum; a member of the Red Cross, the Altar Guild, and the King's Daughters; and an election official. My mother and stepmother both have been members of Planned Parenthood, Friends of the Earth, the Sierra Club, the League to Save Lake Tahoe, the League of Women Voters, and who knows what else? Was I not in a natural progression? (But, I have to say, most of the time, growing up, I thought all of that the most total, time-wasting, bullshit optimism.)

Strange to think that now if they knew about my real job, they would object—the danger, the distant postings, and above all the taint of patriotism and conservatism and clandestine assassinations and so on, for, paradoxically—given the military background—they were nice liberal Californians, horrified by all that. What they believed was that I had taken another job with AmerAID, and even that alarmed them with its smell of government. Californians, we lacked the links to good Eastern schools and Yale and so on that would have made a spy agency a more normal option. But AmerAID was an aid organization after all, and to some extent they were relieved that I had fallen into a respectable family pattern after those early false starts.

I actually did (do) believe in serving my country, even if I haven't lived there recently, not counting the months in Virginia. But it was there I had also come to see that it wasn't service I was really drawn to, it was adventure, and it was in that spirit I was off on this mission, a secret mission, as all would be, with a new name, a slightly altered biography, and, fortuitously, with Ian for cover. As to my employers, I didn't know what they saw in me, yet I was prepared to defer to them; I expected to discover, eventually, some property in myself that I would recognize as validating their view. Meantime I just felt like me, a little skeptical but willing to learn.

We had been taught that sometimes you must forget your personal history and come to live another. Sometimes you must learn not even to respond upon hearing your real name, not even by a tiny acceleration of your pulse. On the other hand, your new name must turn your head as if you'd been hearing it from the cradle. I had been given elementary Arabic, but here also with a cautionary injunction not to seem to understand it. I would learn that this injunction was not necessary: I would understand very little.

In some other respects, I can see now, I was going to Marrakech with a negative attitude. For one thing, I was a little frightened of Islam; after all that's happened, who isn't? Maybe Muslims themselves are afraid of it, disconcerted to find themselves prisoners of societies where even their families and people they know might turn on them and blow them up. Maybe they are too afraid to speak out, for fear of getting fatwa'd, or even beheaded, like Daniel Pearl. I thought of the many tales of girls killed by their fathers and brothers, and of how no one speaks of, or even bothers with the names of, those poor young boys strapping on their suicide belts—surely with some ambivalence? Salvation must seem so eventual when the world is here and now—what makes them do it? I keep thinking about them. Had they said good-bye to their parents? Had they recited special prayers? Did they believe them?

So now I was thinking of this poor girl Suma, who was fleeing some of the things her religion had brought down on her, oppressed like the erring girls in a film I saw, made to do laundry for terrifying, sadistic Irish nuns. Those nuns were ostensibly Christians. After what we had seen in the Balkans, I wasn't reassured about Christians either. At one point we were taken to see the bones of the Srebrenica victims, neatly polished and bundled to be returned to their families, Muslim boys killed by Christian men. Then there are the Hindu crazies, setting fire to trains and mosques to burn alive the nonbelievers. Are there any virtuous religions? It really doesn't seem so. It almost seems that religion makes you wicked.

5

KATOUBIA MOSQUE, MARRAKECH

A stunning example of how the Moroccan architectural artistry is particularly reserved for religious buildings. Though the dars and riads and kasbahs and nomadic tents (even) all provide the architecture nerd with lots of eye candy.

—Photo caption on *Political Stew* Web site

While Marina Cotter was helping Suma, Tom Drill was all helpfulness to me; he heaved my suitcase onto his cart and retrieved a few parcels of his own. "I co-run a tea shop, more or less an expat hangout, heavily patronized by Brits, so I have to send for certain things from London: demerara sugar, certain kinds of tea." He went on with these details, amiability itself, increasing my discomfort, my rising irritation at Ian.

The woman in the black chador I had seen on the plane, I now noticed, was being met by a man in the white robes and distinctive headdress of the Saudis (for I had studied the different tribal costumes, the headdresses and fashions); this explained her un-Moroccan way of dressing—they were not Moroccans. Possibly they were tourists like me. They were standing by the baggage carousel with a huge pile of fancy luggage—Vuitton cases and duffel bags of handwoven wool. I noticed his polished Gucci loafers.

Outside, the first gust of heat rising from the paved passenger drop-off road was agreeable. Tom Drill drove a nineties Peugeot 504 diesel. The road into the city was peopled by old beige Mercedes diesel taxis, fume-emitting buses, and carts drawn by donkeys or horses, driven by white-gowned men with skinny brown legs and dusty pink heels in heelless slippers. Of the women walking along the shoulder, some were veiled, some not.

My heart rose at the exotic beauty and inaccessibility—I was in North Africa! Mules and goats! Here were the waving palms! All buildings were of rust-colored mud or stucco, the walls polished and crenellated; the curious, beautiful color was the color, I supposed, of the local earth. There had been people walking along this road for a thousand years, or maybe two thousand.

But human history changes here only slowly. It had not been a hundred years since slavery had been abolished in this country, and it was said still to go on in covert forms in the recesses of the medina and in the camps isolated in the vastness of the desert. The black Africans from the south had been, and perhaps were still, enslaved by the lighter-skinned coastal people along the Mediterranean. Now, I had read, the king was trying to liberate women, but the women walking along the road didn't look liberated, just lethargic and timeless, with a calm that could be stupor or could be biding and waiting.

Tom asked if I'd mind if we stopped by his daughter's school to pick her up. We parked by a mud wall. He went on foot into a warren of stalls and buildings while I waited in the car. It didn't seem like a good place for a school. I felt my uneasiness deepen, but he came back in a minute or two with a curly-haired, dark little girl in a school uniform with an enormous backpack across her skinny shoulders. She clung to Tom's hand, or vice versa, and was called Amelie.

We drove back onto the main road, past the walls of the medina and the minarets of the Katoubia Mosque and the Mamounia hotel. I had studied these monuments and recognized them—the tower had been there for a thousand years and, like everything else, was a fragile pinkish ocher color, the color of white buildings seen at dawn. Islam, Islam, its beauty proclaimed, and I was thrilled to think of its permanence and grandeur. "The Katoubia dates from the twelfth century," Tom said. "You may find it hard to keep track of their Almovarid and Almovad history. They were all Berbers, not Arabs, exactly. Berbers, Arabs, and Europeans all have a history here."

In another fifteen minutes, we had left the main road for a narrower paved road. Now we had entered the desert. "The Palmeraie," said Tom. In contrast to the walled city, the Palmeraie was the ugliest place I had ever seen, desiccated and bare, dotted with stunted palm trees so attenuated they couldn't even grow their fronds, just emitted stubby shoots, or maybe these had been gnawed by animals. Gashes of dry creek, perhaps the vestiges of some primitive irrigation system, cracked open the stony ground. Plastic bags and empty containers lay in the ditches along each shoulder or clotted together in a wave rolling along in the light wind, a sea of plastic. The ugliness reanimated my fears, which had been lulled by Tom's good-natured tour-guide recitation of what the buildings in the city were called and where we were.

In the distance, a couple of shanty villages could be seen, and some walls that probably enclosed nicer places, houses or hotels. Their hiddenness proposed opulence, oases in the otherwise bleak desert.

I know there are people who find the desert beautiful but I wasn't finding it so. In a few minutes more we left this road and turned down a narrow dirt driveway, past a gated arch with a sleeping boy on the stoop of its little gatehouse, through thickets of bougainvillea trained up the walls on either hand, and through open gates.

Now we were inside a large compound, a garden enclosed by the thick, pink adobe walls. Ian's house stood in the middle of this space, which was perhaps as large as an acre. It was a two-story pink structure of the same adobe material, with onion-shaped Middle Eastern arches along the porch, which wrapped around the two sides we could see. The driveway led past the house through rather tangled, pleasant foliage, and gardeners pottered in a bed to our left. I couldn't help but think of the moment in *Pride and Prejudice,* a movie I'd liked, where Elizabeth says her love for Mr. Darcy intensified when she saw his beautiful house and grounds.

Despite my pique at Ian's absence at the airport, I felt excited to be about to see him. I had a clear memory, perhaps now somewhat idealized by distance and longing, of him in Pristina, his tall figure, wearing khaki work clothes that gave him a somewhat military air, and a baseball hat, like those generals who give press conferences on CNN. I had known his Kosovo incarnation was temporary, that really he was a British businessman who lived in Morocco and that he would seem different in a different context, the way people always do. But his love-making would be the same, presumably, and his ironical manner would be the same.

We parked at the apex of the driveway and got out. I wheeled one of my bags, Tom Drill took the bigger one, and Amelie carried my purse toward the house, Tom waving off attempts by one of the gardeners to help us. We stopped at a carved wooden door heavily studded with nails, and Tom pushed a button. "Don't mind the jungle out here," he said. "He's still got a lot of work to do here. Inside it's all beauty and repose."

After a time, the door swung slowly open and a dark head, wearing a crocheted skullcap, poked out.

"Hullo, Rashid," Tom said in English, "here's Miss Sawyer." The door opened the rest of the way and we went in, Amelie and I following Tom. Then Ian appeared in the dim foyer, arms outstretched. I felt a jolt of happiness.

Ian is very English-looking—a bit heavyset, lion-colored and handsome, hair worn longish—and his roundish face with its Byronic cleft chin in repose has an expression that can seem petulant, like that of the reprimanded soccer player who turns a suave and smiling face to the camera. To me he is always suave and smiling, but I have seen him snap at a messenger or office worker. He's well-off, or his father is, so I had extra respect for his dedication to the work in Kosovo, his zeal for it even. Despite his disguise as a soul weighed down with the tediousness of life, he'd worked tirelessly, staying up with sick people and driving long distances to get them this or that medicine.

We'd been lovers for some months. At first, by tacit agreement it was simply to sweeten our mutual exile, but since he'd gone back to Marrakech, I'd found myself thinking about him more than I had expected, and now the sudden start of joy at seeing him surprised me.

But it was followed almost immediately with concerns. I felt rather dazed. Part of this first reaction to seeing him was due to the fact that he seemed different, more imposing and in command; another part of it was due to my amazement at the grandeur and size of his house. He had told me only that he had a large old Moroccan house that he had restored. Here, away from the grim Balkan winter, he seemed more substantial and more genial, a master and host, relaxed, his collarless shirt untucked, wearing jeans. I don't know what I had expected.

He kissed me rather formally on one cheek in the English fashion, not on both in the French way as he might have in Pristina, nor the ardent way he would have kissed me in private.

"My dearest Lu, I'm so glad you're here. You've forgiven me for not being at the airport? At least I sent the charming Tom. If this dog of a tree man, who's stiffed me three times already, hadn't chosen the moment of your flight—you see how crucial is the tree." He was speaking of a gnarled, many-rooted cypress tree that dominated the space by the door. A brown man in a blue robe was painting a white ring around the trunk. "It's more than a century old." Ian kept my hand and slung an arm around Tom. "Thanks, friend, for fetching my fetching guest. Hullo, Amelie. Would you like to see the baby goat?" He smiled at Tom's little girl, who plainly knew and liked him. A little goat was tethered near the driveway, and Amelie ran to pet it.

A little farther off at the side of the house I now saw a swimming pool, with tables and lounges, and several people in bathing suits, seemingly dead, lying with towels over their faces. A very red man came to life, got up, waved cheerily, and crept off without coming over for an introduction. I was taken aback to see other people—was this a sort of hotel, perhaps not Ian's house at all? Its size, and the presence of strangers, violated my idea of the love nest I was looking forward to. I had imagined us in passionate isolation, interrupting passages of love at intervals for touristic expeditions during which he would show me the marketplace, the famous square of Jemaa el Fna, the museums and public buildings, the ancient mosques and tombs of the Safavid kings.

He kept one arm around me and with the other pounded Tom in a comradely way, and drew us farther into the hall, through a comfortable-looking living room furnished with several sofas and wicker chairs, and out into a vast inner court open to the sky, with another arcaded porch shading the walls of the enclosure. It was indeed a realm of beauty, pinkish ocher exterior walls decorated with blue and white tiles of intricate design, and another immense tree that presided over the space. Orange trees in huge pots and eucalyptus scented the air, and a little fountain plashed in the center, near other tables and chairs.

"It's all so much more beautiful than I'd imagined," I said. "So seldom in life do things exceed expectations." He laughed at this sententious remark and said I was too young to be so cynical. He's a decade older than I.

"I suppose it's the mark of an optimistic nature at that, always having expectations too high to be exceeded," he conceded. He took my breath away with the warmth of his smile.

I was a little off balance. I was prepared to forget my personal history, but I wasn't so sure I could obey the instruction about emotional involvement. Seeing Ian again, I knew I was emotionally involved with him. But I also knew from experience that I could handle it. The great love of my life was behind me; this was something lighter and more delightful. I had reasoned that if you're going to have a fling, a little respite from the gruesome realties in the Balkans, you had to be involved to a certain extent; your heart had to be in it, had to flutter a little. It remained to be seen whether the same attraction, the same fascination, would still be there in Marrakech, but from first indications, it was.

6

Michael Barclay did not think of himself as a spy. Nor would he even say he belonged to the secret service or the security service—though he'd agree security was at the root of much of his work. If pressed, he might nod towards the word "Intelligence." He liked the word. It meant knowing a lot.

—Ian Rankin, *Witch Hunt*

We sat for a moment near the decorative pool and were brought some tea. When Tom and Amelie had gone, Ian said he would take me to my room, his reference to "my" removing one ambiguity, for though we were lovers, I hadn't been sure what my new status would be or how connubially we would be living.

My room was as austere as a nun's cell, with high, whitewashed walls and a wooden ceiling. The ceiling was domed, with an open lantern that let in light, and a filigreed lamp, shaped like the inverted dome of a mosque, hanging in the center. A large bed festooned with netting was almost the only furniture—the netting a bad sign, I feared, thinking of mosquitoes and scorpions; there was a little closet and a table to use as a desk. A small bookcase was set into the wall, with a few English paperbacks on its shelves and a picture over it of a genie on a carpet floating above a pond. Heavy wooden shutters would close out the light.

This room led to a cavernous bathroom lined with marble and rustic tile, slightly musty, with a shower of stucco and a toilet with a chilly-looking marble seat set into a box. Ian's razor, shaving soap, and a bottle of vetiver eau de toilette were laid out on the marble sink. Ian's room adjoined on the other side. As we stood in the bathroom, he kissed me properly and said he was glad I had come. Then he left me to unpack and told me lunch was at two. It was a little abrupt, but I had seen that he was, here, a host responsible for more people than just me. Still, this casualness was slightly disappointing; I'd imagined a more rapturous welcome. But it was hardly important yet.

I unpacked my bathing suit, tennis clothes, paddock boots—for Ian had mentioned pack trips in the mountains—some low-cut dresses for dinner, covered-up dark dresses for public excursions, underwear. I arrayed my objects—my laptop; my ordinary-looking clock radio, so chockablock with useful capabilities; my clever James Bondish fountain pen; and bottle of secret ink. There were the versatile utensils in my writing portfolio—little sticks of wax made up like pencils, a supply of cellophane, my camera with its several lenses; all could be turned over by a maid without seeming to be what they were.

I plugged in my computer. I was working "bare"—if I got caught at something, my colleagues would deny knowing anything about me. No official status, no gun; I didn't need a gun. I have to admit I'm drawn to guns and have been since learning to shoot at the Stanford University summer camp I went to as a child. My parents were upset because we came home with National Rifle Association certificates at the end. They considered the NRA an institution of the devil. Here a gun would have to be hidden with particular care, so I wouldn't ask for one.

In time, if necessary, someone could bring me a "firearm" (as Taft called them), but this was not considered a dangerous or "wet" mission unless I somehow stumbled into narcotics or nukes. We don't usually concern ourselves with drugs, though.

Some of my equipment filled me with a special sense of unreality. Why would I, "Lulu," an untroubled Californian tourist, have a microdot reader? Why were the names of people I could just call on the phone encrypted? I knew why, of course. There were particularly ruthless elements in North Africa, there were corpses in doorways, throats slit, ears removed, whose errors might only have been letting it be known they had talked to one of my colleagues or had done a little business with them. I knew all this but never could help an innate feeling that the frankness I have always been criticized for was the better course. Secrecy was against the grain, but I also have heard that to go against the grain is to grow.

I couldn't resist checking my e-mail, in part to see how good the reception was and whether I'd need to dial up, but there seemed to be a strong signal. I've mentioned that I reported to this especially irritating man named Taft, who seemed to know nothing about the Balkans, and now nothing about North Africa. In part, I was to communicate with him by e-mail, in a transparent way. He was called Sheila ("Dear Sheila") with a simple AOL address and a fairly impenetrable set of code words by which I could alert him to look for an encrypted message online and vice versa.

He had already told me that in Marrakech I would meet another agent; that agent in turn would know our people in Casablanca and Rabat. That agent, I was told, would find me. Now, Sheila wrote, "Watch your purse in the souk. Is it called the Casbah? I know several people who were pickpocketed." That is to say, watch your back, there is danger, there is something afoot. With my heart excited by Ian, the message from Sheila acted on me like the chilling admonitions of my mother, recalling me to duty and common sense.

7

Emilia: How if fair and foolish?

Iago: She never yet was foolish that was fair.

—William Shakespeare,
Othello, act 2, scene 1

At two I went down to lunch, disappointed that there were other people staying, but was quickly brought out of that mood by the prospective comedy of house parties, with their tiptoeing, significant looks, and creaky doors. Maybe it was propitious that there were others here; maybe in the long run, love would thrive on stolen moments, and maybe the other people would help me find my way into Moroccan intrigue. Though I didn't quite see how. The other guests were a gangly British laureate poet named Crumley, a man in his fifties; his younger, pregnant wife, Posy, a sturdy girl with the English ankles, or maybe incipient swelling problems related to the pregnancy; another Englishwoman named Nancy Rutgers, a soignée blonde in her late thirties or early forties who worked at Sotheby's in London, expert on clocks and carpets; and her boyfriend, an American bookseller or antique dealer—one or the other—David someone.

"They're only staying a few days," Ian whispered, nodding toward Nancy and David, brushing the top of my head with his lips as he bent over me. Aloud, he said, "You've come on a Wednesday, Lulu, so you get the full shock of Marrakech life this very night—tonight's my turn to host the Shakespeare club. You'll have to take a part." He explained that members of the English-language community read Shakespeare plays aloud on the first Wednesday of every month, an inviolable date.

"I see her as Emilia, definitely," cried Robin Crumley, the poet, with a gallant gesture toward me that seemed to irritate his wife.

Lunch was a somewhat stringy chicken *au poivrons rouges*—I supposed there was a Moroccan name for this dish—served by the man who had answered the door, Rashid. Throughout the meal, I felt Ian's eyes on me, and when I met his gaze he gave a little smile, as if to affirm that we were a couple and that he was glad I had come. This made me unexpectedly happy; I was finding my whole reaction to Ian stronger than I'd imagined it would be, and I longed for the sex scene to follow.

It was a long lunch, with lots of a Moroccan rosé, and I was grateful when we rose from the table to take a turn around the gardens outside. Ian was extremely proud of them. "I was influenced by the Persian *chahar bagh*, a private and restful garden space, as you can see, but fruitful too," Ian had been saying. "The pools in the center and the *jub*—that ditch—running around the edge, are actually for irrigation, but strongly decorative, I like to think. Those are flowering cherries; they'll be beautiful in the spring, but these are lemons and limes. . . ." This new botanical Ian surprised me very much.

It seemed no time until the Shakespeare club began to arrive. Some of the members I had met already—Tom Drill came in with his partner, who proved to be a younger, attractive black guy named Strand Carter, with their little skinned-knee girl, Amelie, and the bony, imposing Cotters, Sir Neil and Marina, who were dressed as they might have dressed in England, in tweed and leather. They didn't have their new employee Suma with them.

"We have an apartment in London," Sir Neil found an occasion to tell me at once, in a confidential tone. "But as we spend a lot of time here, we sometimes let our London place on very reasonable terms— you must tell me if you ever want a stay in London." I was somewhat nonplussed to have this either invitation or commercial proposition put to me in Ian's house, as if I were a paying guest here whose whims might soon require her to rent a place somewhere else. I thanked him but said I didn't expect to get to London.

I did have a chance to speak to Lady Cotter—Marina—about Suma. "Yes! We're so pleased! She seems a charming girl," she said.

"How is it you are in touch with SOS Femmes?" I asked.

"Actually, I'd never heard of them," she said. "A friend in Paris knew how desperately I was looking for an au pair. It's a godsend. Of course, I didn't realize she'd only speak French."

"Does she speak Arabic?"

"Yes, I suppose it will be good for the children to learn both, since they have to live here. My daughter-in-law . . ." She told me something of the story, the tragic death of her daughter-in-law in the mountains of Nepal, leaving these young grandchildren. The daughter-in-law suddenly couldn't breathe, in her tent, lost consciousness and died before anyone could do anything, and was cremated on the spot. That sounded odd. I suppose it is what they'd been told.

"Didn't they try to take her down to a lower altitude?" I asked.

"Well, yes, I imagine so," Marina said, but looked dismayed, as if thinking they might not have. I suppose some people are more fatalistic about death than Americans are.

"Suma seems a nice girl. I don't think she'd done anything very shocking, dated a boy and went on his motorbike or something. She wears the head scarf. The brother tried to kill her. We forget how primitive some of these people are, even if they do live in Paris."

"I'll come visit her one day, if I may," I proposed, and Marina assured me she welcomed the idea.

"I'm sure you speak more French than we do. We learned it at school of course, and to speak to vendors and such, but not for proper conversation; how it fades over the years."

A former American ambassador to Tunisia came in—I wondered if he'd turn out to be my contact. One or two of the guests were Moroccans, whose unfamiliar names I didn't retain. I had worked on learning common Muslim names but found them elusive except for the main Koranic ones—Mohammed, Ali, and so on.

The most unexpected arrival was the same Saudi woman I had seen on the plane and again with her husband at the airport, only now we were introduced: Gazi and Khaled bin Sultan Al-Sayad. As they came in, she was still wearing a black veil—the abaya—though not over her face, but she whisked it off and was wearing a beige pantsuit underneath, with lots of gold chains that emphasized her dramatic sort of harem-slave beauty, like a concubine out of the *Arabian Nights,* maybe Scheherazade herself, and seemed to symbolize the enslavement implied by the veil. Her husband, Khaled, who had worn white robes and a red-and-white head cloth at the airport, now was wearing a Western-style suit and was a good-enough-looking man of maybe thirty, though with a remarkable nose that grew like a falcon's beak between his dark eyes. How I admired the way Ian had mastered their long string of names, laced with "bins" and "bints" like a refrain! They lived next door—that is, in the next nearest villa estate—and were apparently well-known to everyone else here and deeply admiring of Shakespeare.

"Of course. I went to Brown University," said Gazi to me. "And Khaled went to Yale. Not that we're pro-American particularly, it was just the only game in town educationally, though many Saudis go to the Oxbridge colleges instead. And who else but Americans can control Israel?" She made these somewhat disconnected observations with a provocative smile that seemed to invite some response or comment, but I had no idea what to say. I wasn't even sure she realized I was American.

"I know you must think it's odd for me to have a man's name," she said. "Gazi—it's more or less a family joke. My real name is Ghaniyah. We go to London and Stratford every winter to see the performances," she continued. It seemed to me that Shakespeare was as good a foundation for international understanding as any other—better, really—and I was glad to hear that educated Arabs admired him. Do we know as much about their great poets? I knew the names of two Persian poets, Hafiz and Saadi, and Omar Khayyám, but that was about it.

Waiting to begin, the party spoke in several languages—English, French, and what I took to be Arabic, lending an air of baroque multicultural sophistication I found thrilling. We sat in a ring of chairs, I next to Gazi, so I dared to ask when and how it was that she wore the veil, even here in Marrakech, where most women didn't appear to.

"Always worn at home in Riyadh, naturally, but here only sometimes—when I'm out with Khaled, who prefers it on the street.

He's not a benighted jerk, not at all," she said in her perfect but slightly odd English. "He went to Yale, after all. But it reduces the chance that someone from Riyadh might see me. There's a certain amount of resentment there of people who have homes elsewhere or send their kids away to school. They all would if they could." I assumed that Khaled must be rich, like all Saudis, but I didn't know enough about that to ask even an oblique question about his business or profession. I admit that I also thought, What good is it to be beautiful if you have to live in Saudi Arabia?

The guests, now fifteen in number, sat in the ring of chairs in the courtyard by the pool and studied their parts for a few minutes while a maid lit the hundreds of candle lamps that ringed the swimming pool. Ian's servant, Rashid, passed drinks—orange juice, whiskey sodas, and white wine. The evening cool was beginning, but the air was somehow dusty. There were no mosquitoes. In the distance, from somewhere, it was just possible to hear the sonorous drone of the evening call to prayer.

8

A man he is of honesty and trust.

To his conveyance I assign my wife. . . .

—William Shakespeare,
Othello, act 1, scene 3

I supposed that Tom Drill's partner, Strand, would be Othello, but I was made to face my own literal-mindedness, or whatever you would call it, to have assumed that because he was African American he would fit the part best. (Were the others mired in a retro form of political correctness that assumed it would embarrass Strand to be cast as Othello? I've been out of the U.S. for a while, uncertain about the changes in P.C. nuance.) After Strand, I would have picked Khaled for his fierce nose and warlike bearing. But I had forgotten that Othello is also the best part, and so it went to Ian, who I could see did have the best voice, a deep baritone, like Orson Welles, and the actorly English diction, being an Englishman.

Nancy Rutgers said a few pedantic words about the sources of Othello. "From the *Ecatommiti,* the sixteenth-century collection of tales by Giovanni Battista Giraldi. We don't know whether Shakespeare read the Italian or the French translation of 1584," and so on.

I was not Emilia, as someone had foreseen, but a courtesan, Bianca, perhaps because Bianca has less to say. There was some oblique discussion of American accents. Posy Crumley was Emilia, and Gazi was to be Desdemona, but she objected. "I've always hated her, so docile and trusting, stupid really," she said. "Make Mrs. Crumley be Desdemona. I'd rather be nobody."

"It's only a play, Gazi," said Ian sternly, seconded by her husband.

"No, no, no," she said.

Posy Crumley also refused, on the grounds that to be Desdemona might hurt her unborn child. In the end, Desdemona was played by Marina Cotter, whose incisive British upper-class tones, once she modulated them into a more pitiable sweetness, were not wrong for the part, any more than Ian's for Othello, and the two gave the whole production a satisfying sort of professional patina.

Wonderful it was to hear all our voices gain in resonance and confidence, reading out the immortal lines. It seemed that the theater, as a genre, fulfilled its real raison d'être in this situation, re-creating for English people, exiled from their native isle, the epitome of its genius, the language of its principal Bard. (As Americans, in Paris, get together at Christmas and defiantly sing "Rudolph the Red-Nosed Reindeer" and other songs the more dignified French don't even know the words of.)

Khaled, the Saudi husband, reading Cassius, said to me afterward, as we drank tea in the patio, "The language of your Bard and the language of the Prophet have something in common—could Shakespeare have been inspired by a reading of the Koran?"

"Do you think it's possible?" I said, not knowing if Shakespeare could have read the Koran. As Khaled spoke, I was wondering if he thought my sundress horribly immodest. I had read that Muslim men are offended by us. At the same time, I was telling myself not to be self-conscious, I am not immodest. Odd that the thought had crept in on me.

"Yes, yes! As where the Book says, 'Seest thou not those who turn in friendship / To such as have the wrath of Allah upon them? / They are neither of you nor of them, / and they swear to falsehood knowingly.' Cassius might have spoken those very words to warn Othello about Iago."

And indeed, at moments during the reading, as the horror of the story mounted, I had been seized by a sudden bleak sense of dislocation to find myself in this unexpected, faraway corner of Islam with strangers reciting poems, without any real sense yet of the warm welcome I'd been looking forward to. As happy and excited as I was to see Ian, there was a little stab of dismay at the impossibility of what I had to do, tasks that seemed as far beyond my own powers as flying a jet would be, in a land I knew nothing of firsthand.

A warm welcome was to follow in the night and went a long way to reassure me, though when Ian, so recently speaking in the tones of the violent, murderous Moor, came to my room wearing a red robe Othello might have worn and the lacy-patterned light from the swinging lamp shadowed his face with flickers of darkness, he was unfamiliar and disconcerting, large, even a little frightening, even for me, who am not easily scared.

"Really, hello," he said. "Rather stiff to plunge you into all this. Had you expected it?" Did he mean the size of his house, the trillion candles lit on the patio, Shakespeare, the other people, the general air of organization and ongoing life into which I would have to fit my-self?

"I didn't have much of a sense of your . . . real life," I said. "I thought . . ." What had I thought? Business interests, philanthropy.

"Is this my real life? I don't know," he said. "I suppose it is. Any-how, I hope you'll like it here."

"I hadn't expected it to be so fancy."

"As you'll see, it's relatively modest by local standards. But let me kiss you properly. I've missed you . . ." And so it went, the real wel-come. We were practiced lovers by now, smoothly suited, satisfied.

Yet there was, perhaps, a little distance between us. I told myself it was because we'd been apart for two months, since Pristina. Now Pris-tina was elsewhere for Ian, and he was back in a world more natural to him, where I must have seemed to him a little out of place, the way people seemed whom you had met at camp when you ran into them during the school year. He was always an ardent lover—it was some-thing else, a tinge of formality that disappointed. Soon, though, I was made to realize yet again, if I hadn't known already, how much our relationship meant to me, physically and psychologically, and how eas-ily sleeping with Ian returned to me the sense of love and ease that had been missing for the last couple of months, after he had returned to Marrakech and I was alone in Pristina.

My policy with Ian—though "policy" is not a very good word to use about someone you are in love with, too redolent of desperate an-cient female calculation—my rule is never to seem more in love with him than he with me. This requires some fine calibrations: What does he mean when he says "My darling Lulu" and "You are so beautiful"? Sometimes I'm not sure and don't know what to say back. I realize I don't know him very well.

9

Those who rehearse the Book / Of Allah, establish regular prayer / and spend (in Charity) / Out of what We have provided / For them, secretly and openly / Hope for a Commerce that will never fail.

—Koran 35:29

When I came down in the morning, no one seemed around. The sun shone, the pink walls glowed in the matinal sun, there was a bird somewhere singing in the shrubbery as if it were in a forest. It was hard to remember that we were in the middle of a desiccated North African desert suburb. Ian's vast house still seemed a little like a hotel surrounded by an oasis of flowering plants—the rooms on the main floor large and high, opening broadly onto the inner patio. Last night this inner courtyard had been lit by flaming torchères, though now morning calm had come over the building; a vacuum hummed somewhere, and there was the faint sound of a radio. Ian was gone.

It was nine. I was either early or late, but I had no idea which. Posy Crumley was the only other person there. A table had been laid outside, where she was just beginning her breakfast. I sat down with her. I saw she must only be in her late twenties, growing pudgy with her pregnancy, skin flushed.

It was reassuring and comfortable to have another woman to talk to. With the coffee and sunshine, the mood was one of friendly harmony; we admired the silent service by a housemaid all in white, pants and tunic, head wrapped, feet in the noiseless slippers. We admired the charm of the silver teapot with its pointy lid and the greasy deliciousness of some thick pancakes kept warm under a straw dome.

"How long have you been here?" I asked.

She sighed. "Three months. Absolute hell, actually. It's a sort of writer's sinecure. Ian invites writers and that sort of person to stay for a month or more, to work in ease and solitude. Robin, that is. We're to stay a full five months. I had thought there would be others . . ." Her voice trailed off hesitantly, an insecure young wife. "At Charleston, in England, there were plenty of people to talk to, but here, at first, when Ian was still away in wherever it was, Robin and I were the only ones. Of course that was nice, in a way, but it must have been hard on Robin to only have me to talk to."

"You must have learned a lot about Marrakech by now," I suggested, thinking that she too might turn out to be an excellent resource. I was also interested in hearing about Ian's generosity to writers, something he'd never mentioned.

"Not much. I wish I could admire the beauty and interest of this culture. Robin does," she admitted. "But I can't, because of their sexism. I know that sounds rather American—sorry, not that that's bad—" I could almost see her blush with her sudden perception that she had been on the point of saying something jocularly rude about Americans, something others say among themselves. I suppose my normal California accent has modulated now, from years in Europe, into a less distinctive mid-Atlantic speech, so that people can forget I am one.

"You know what I mean, Americans go on about such things. Those words 'sexism' and 'racism' are very degraded by now, but they do mean something—the way women are treated and thought of, the way the subject seems to preoccupy them up here. Of course I know they can't help it, it's the way they are used to thinking. . . ."

She talked on about the pitfalls for women here and the boredom of life in a compound in Marrakech where there was nothing to do until nightfall, when there were parties. She seemed desperate to have someone to talk to, American or not. We sipped our tea, we talked about the hard lot of Arab women. I told her about the literacy projects I'd be looking at. I thought of Suma, wondering if in coming from Paris to a Muslim country, she'd gone from the frying pan into the fire. I told Posy what I knew of Suma's story, ending with how happy I was that she was being protected by the Cotters.

"Of course Marina Cotter would need a little slave, now that she's stuck with her grandchildren; she's a busy woman. People who live here full-time have lives crammed with things to do, mostly silly. Marina volunteers at the British Consulate doing something; there are charities and the like. Oh, I'm so glad you're here!" she cried. "I can't even go out by myself—you feel funny walking alone. I don't know if it's safe, and we're miles from town. And you don't see anyone pregnant here. Maybe they stay indoors the whole nine months. But two women can walk around together. We'll go to the souk." This prospect seemed to cheer her so much that I agreed; of course

I did want to see the souk, the lay of the land, the nature of the tasks ahead.

"Don't worry, things will unfold," Taft had said. "Think of yourself as a woman in a window, watching, passive, part of the landscape. Your duty at first will be to build your cover. That will take months. Be nice to the Englishman."

"Have you seen Ian this morning?" I asked.

"Yes," she said, "someone called him earlier to say there'd been an explosion, and one of his factories was on fire. Robin went with him to see." I had a flash of irritation—we'd been sitting here for a half an hour and she hadn't mentioned this.

"But we must go see!" I said. "Don't you love a fire? Isn't there someone who could take us?" I had to see it, for to me it almost seemed owing to my presence that an alarming event should unfold as soon as I got here, and it gave me a pleasant sense of being in the thick of things already.

"I don't see how," Posy said, "but we can ask Rashid." She went off to find him; she had rapport with him after all this time.

"He says no, Ian said we were not to come to the fire. Anyway, Ian and Robin took the car, but he is to take us to the souk in a taxi; he can guide us around if you want. Let's do. I've gone to the souk a lot, but I still don't know my way around it without him." She was just bored, I supposed.

Presently, Rashid took us the few miles into the center of the city in a taxi. Rashid was a man in his forties, maybe no older than Ian, but already worn-looking, and he had a slight harelip. It was no more than a scar and the slightly flattened aspect of a repaired upper lip, but it caused a little lisp. He wore the tunic and the white skullcap most of the men seemed to wear, and performed the office of a tour guide, pointing out to us the houses of Yves Saint Laurent and some symphony conductor from London, and some shantytown villages whose corrugated metal roofs glittered in the sunlight.

"Moroccans," he said. "These villages spring up from nowhere like maggots from a rotting melon."

The taxi driver appeared to be his brother, at least so Rashid called him: "Turn here, my brother," etc. I thought they looked alike. The driver wore a dusty suit and a sort of military cap, and *tutoyer*-ed Rashid. It was odd that they spoke French instead of Arabic, perhaps to reassure Posy and me they had no secrets from us. I could see there was no use opposing Rashid and Posy, so I tried to submit to this expedition with some good grace at least.

As we drove, I became more aware of where we actually were when we were at Ian's—some miles out of Marrakech in an area made up of large walled properties, mostly owned by Europeans, according to Rashid. Fanciful names in French and English decorated the portals, of the "Sans Souci" variety, but some were in Arabic, which Rashid translated; things like "Perfumed Rest" or "The Pearl of Solitude." Luxurious vines bloomed on every wall, and all the walls were the same curious ocher pink, crafted from local clay; all the vines were intense fuchsias and oranges, ablaze in the dry landscape. I could see that our location so far out of town was not propitious for information gathering. The medina, the central walled part of Marrakech, was beyond walking distance, and a woman alone along the highway would rivet attention—every movement would be visible for miles.

We parked in a parking garage, a prosaic, rather jarring modern touch at the edge of the ancient enclosure of the medina. Posy and I followed Rashid, apprehensions coming back, into a dank alley lit by electric bulbs hanging from wires, though it was bright sun outside.

Orange halves and peels washed in a trickle of water down the center of the way, watched by a skinny cat, happy in her element of darkness, and two children splashed their feet in the water. From here we emerged into the great square I had seen the day before, and once again into a twisty maze of boutiques and hawkers. Fairy-tale carts were piled high with oranges and dates perfuming the air, wafts of incense and the smell of animals stung our nostrils, and the music of drums underlay the bustle with an exciting throb.

The narrow lanes of the souk were crowded with shoppers, mostly stout young women in long pastel robes and head scarves, carrying baskets and parcels, but also men, families, little kids skipping along, and many, many tourists, so we were by no means conspicuous. Occasionally a woman stood out because her face was entirely veiled with a black handkerchief; these seemed like veils of shame, some sort of stigma, or symbol of contagion, but Rashid said they signified extra piety. We saw one group of women draped all in black, and these had the air of being tourists like us, turning confusedly at the intersections of the alleys or peering where the doors of a mosque stood open.

At stalls suggested by Rashid, Posy bought a caftan, the ideal maternity garment, and I bought some slippers, more or less for verisimilitude, women shopping. Of course I hated to bargain, but Posy had already gotten rather good at it. Why do we hate to bargain? Westerners, I mean. I suppose because it implies that a falsehood is the basis of the transaction—the first asking price is a lie. Whereas we value candor and relying on each other's word, which would mean you state the true price right away. And there is an unpleasant metaphor of victory and defeat embedded in the bargain—you finally defeat your adversary, yet you really know you are defeated, because he is getting the price he secretly meant to get all along.

As we wandered the alleys of the souk, closely followed by Rashid, I began to understand even more about the limitations of my situation, a woman alone: first would be the simple difficulty of walking around unnoticed. I thought again of a discussion with Taft on the general principles of recruiting and getting to know the locals. What a poor choice he had made in me, an agent limited by social conventions. He couldn't ever have been faced with those particular disqualifications: Without Rashid I would be, geographically, lost in seconds in the winding labyrinth, and the idea of establishing any sort of rapport with any of the indistinguishable men and boys crowding the indistinguishable stalls of polyester fabrics and cheap underwear was beyond imagining, let alone thinking of prying into their ancient networks and bankless financial repositories, resources existing since the beginning of time and entirely male. What had Taft and I been thinking for me to have come here?

But of course it was not expected I would get to read the native secrets of the souk—it was the European community that was, for the moment, of interest. "Someone with Western connections is cooperating with or running the Islamists," Taft had said. "Nobody knows to what end, but there is chatter. Something may happen." Was it Ian's fire, was it happening even now?

10

Is it ye who grow / The tree which feeds /
The fire, or do We / Grow it?

—Koran 56:72

We stopped for a cup of tea in a little tearoom overlooking the edge of the square Jemaa el Fna and gazed down at the spectacle, storytellers and snake charmers, and native people coming and going on the errands of their daily lives. When we had drunk our tea, Rashid, who had briefly disappeared, led us down to wander in the thronged square. We stopped on the fringes of a crowd around a man telling a story, with a little drum he used to emphasize the thrilling parts—of course, we couldn't understand it, but Rashid whispered a translation.

"It is a poor widow, she is defenseless, her children are starving, but she has found a ring, left by a stranger to whom she offered the last drops of her poor soup. It is a jewel of indescribable value, and she will sell it. It means her children will eat.

"But soldiers have come and accused her of theft. She is dragged off to prison, and the children are left to starve. But now the story is over. People have to pay him more money. But they are walking away. Perhaps they have heard this story."

"Oh, no!" cried Posy bitterly. "How could they just leave it hanging?"

"Instead I will take you to the best saffron," Rashid said. Hoping to get to the fire, I would have said no, or "later," but Posy fell into smiles. He had told her that most saffron is false, people are fooled and disappointed, there is a trick to telling true from false saffron, and she felt she now had the confidence to buy. Saffron was the thing everybody back in England wanted her to send them. He led us into alleys we'd just been in, to a little stall we probably had passed without noticing, lined with apothecary jars and hanging bunches of herbs and peppers. It exuded the fragrance of lavender or thyme, and, if I was right—for I am only beginning to take an interest in culinary things—some sort of anise concoction resembling the odor of pastis, a nasty French drink I'd never liked. Bottles of rose water and *fleur d'oranger* lined the shelves, and little fragrant mountains of powdered cumin and turmeric were composed on a plank in front. Burlap sacks of pods and dried leaves were artfully opened to add to the richness of the array. A wind would have wafted the whole of his treasure into the air, but there was no wind.

Rashid saluted the owner, a fat, slow old man in a wrinkled polyester robe, and went to crouch against the wall opposite, watching us. In a droning voice, the old man began an almost mechanical spiel about unguents and remedies, especially directed at Posy, for an easy childbirth, for a beautiful child. Posy brought him back to saffron. I suppose my mind wandered, for suddenly Posy was counting out dirhams and he was pressing waxy balls of something wrapped in paper into our hands. After his effusive good-byes and bows, we stepped back into the lane and looked for Rashid, who was now talking in a group of men. He left them and came over to us, and nodded at the paper-wrapped balls we carried.

"You must eat them," he said. "To acknowledge your trust in his products. They are sweets, with your fortune inside."

"'Your thoughts are perfumed with the words of the Prophet,'" Posy said, reading the writing on the inside of the wrapper.

So I opened mine, and it said, "The Bearer Angel may safely communicate with Aladdin the Eagle through the trusted dealer in spices," and it contained some other words that must be mentioned in any communication of this sort, known only to my colleagues and me. Aladdin the Eagle, that is, some agent of that designation, was getting in touch with me, therefore knew that I am me, and that I'm the Bearer Angel.

Taft had told me that someone would be in touch with me, but I hadn't expected it so soon. He had said people undercover might go years without much or any contact; we were taught that our problem would be to keep up a sense of purpose and reality, except in the form of a generalized indignation fueled from reading in the papers about people dying at the hands of suicide bombers, car bombers, roadside bombers in Israel, in Cairo, in Rome, on sunny Pacific islands, with an increasing sense of disgust at fanaticism of any kind.

Of course I couldn't let her read my message, so I made something up—very ill-judged, exactly wrong, suggested, I suppose, by Posy's pregnant form. "This one says, 'The happiness of motherhood awaits you,'" I said, the first thing that came to my head, realizing only too late that she would think such a message was meant for her, that our fortunes had been strangely swapped, and that she would want to save such a propitious message. I stuffed it in my pocket, mind speeding up with the possibilities of who had sent it. Was it the old man himself or someone known to him? What was Rashid's role?

"Here, let me keep it," she said.

"I was kidding. Mine is too horrible, I just made it up. I'd rather think my thoughts are perfumed with the words of the Prophet," I said, and I hastily dropped it onto the filthy cobbles, where she wouldn't pick it up. "How stupid of me. Never mind." And I drew her along.

We walked on, and when Posy stopped to look at some brass trays in one of the stalls, I started back to retrieve the paper. But Rashid was already bending to pick it up.

11

During a journey, Mohammed found a man who started a fire and had endangered some ants. Mohammed was very disturbed to see this. "Who made this fire?" He asked. "I made the fire, O Messenger of Allah!" came a reply. "Put out the fire! Put out the fire!" was Mohammed's teaching.

—The Hadith

"You're right, I think we should see the fire. I love a fire, don't you? We should take them some food," Posy said, looking at the dates and mandarins. "Please take us to the fire," she suddenly said to Rashid, who as usual hovered near. He shook his head.

"It is dangerous," he said. "It is far. Monsieur does not wish it." Ian had said we were not to come, etc. Of course I was distracted by questions about Rashid—how had he known to take me to the saffron man, was he trusted by Ian, what did Ian know, and so on, an infinitude of questions raised by what had just happened. But Posy had taken up the cause.

"We wish it. We insist. Your brother can drive us." We were a tiresome chorus, and he had to agree, but from his surly expression, I understood that by defying Ian's instructions, we were making an enemy, or at least not making a friend. The problem was, I would come to understand, that women do not have wishes and the power to insist, at least in public. Yet we had power over him too, Western and spoiled members of his master's harem.

"Very well," he said at last. "We will take the truck from home." Another taxi took us back to Ian's; Rashid produced a small pickup truck from the garages at the back of the house, and we set out.

It took us about forty-five minutes to reach the foothills of the mountains, but we imagined we could see a plume of smoke high in the sky almost as soon as we left Marrakech. To a Californian the foothills of the Atlas range felt like a natural landscape; the rising ground, ravines, and scrub undergrowth looked like it does around Santa Barbara, still arid but at least not flat, and at the lower levels, there were gardens and vineyards, terraced and reassuring, with flocks grazing and all the lovely details of agriculture and husbandry one might also see in Italy or Spain.

The route was complicated and I could see why Rashid hadn't wanted to take a taxi, for he seemed to know the way perfectly. It was steep. In three quarters of an hour we'd climbed a thousand feet, passing occasional trucks and carts coming down, and the smoke and fumes had increased before at last we pulled off the road into a dirt track on the right and then across an expanse of hard ground for perhaps a half a mile. "God in hell," Posy complained of the bumpy, hard ride, "I'm sure to miscarry."

You would have to know where you were going to find the place at all. Up ahead a small group of men and a couple of vehicles were clustered some distance from the still-blazing building. A few other men, in work clothes or uniforms of the gendarmerie, had assembled at the edge of the road, gazing in the twilight at the spectacle. I had noticed in the square in Marrakech that people gathered together were noisy, but here they stood in silence.

As for the building, a huge, rectangular, cement-block industrial structure, there wasn't much doubt it was beyond reclaim. From the fingers of flames still shooting from every window, I could imagine the inferno earlier, and the metal roof began to buckle as we watched. The heat was too strong to allow us very near. A smell, very strong now, was getting worse. A white fire wagon was parked near us, with its hose coiled on the ground like a lethargic serpent; no one was trying to use it. There was no hydrant, there was really no way to stop a fire, and I was surprised that that there were so many people—I imagined the onlookers were workers in the factory. Another small, helpless-looking fire truck trailing a water tank arrived; two men unwound its hose and aimed a thin stream of water at one of the flanks of the building, but it was only a gesture.

Ian and Robin Crumley were standing by the side of the road, Ian with an expression of preoccupation, and both men smelled of fire and chemicals. They were amid a knot of men, perhaps seven or eight, all gazing with the eagerness that people always feel to see something burning. The men moved away from Posy and me. Ian and Robin greeted us perfunctorily, and if they were irritated that we'd defied Ian's injunction, they didn't say so. Ian said several times, as he stared, "Luckily there was no one inside."

It seemed odd that they were not worried about the fire spreading, but Ian explained that the dirt road, which led to distant buildings, created a natural firebreak. In the dry brush, there was nothing else to burn except the brush itself. Ian said again that there was no one inside—the explosion had come at a moment of a prayer interval and tea break, when people had gone outside. The main question was, how had it started? Ian's manner now was concerned but not surprised, was almost resigned, as if explosion and loss were overdue.

Later he explained that his factory was a building that, though he owned it, was leased to a manufacturer of fertilizer, a product by its nature explosive, and such an accident was always to be feared and provided against. I knew that Ian had a number of such projects; in Kosovo, he had talked about his four compact but efficient industrial buildings, built on tracts in the Atlas foothills with his own private funds and a development loan from the World Bank. These buildings were leased to Moroccan entrepreneurs for developing light manufactures of various kinds. In another place, he had built a coeducational school for young children of farmers, in practice attended by only a few of the more forward-looking locals in the area. He supervised and managed these properties—I don't know who had managed them while he was in Bosnia; it was strange that he'd go off and leave them.

"What exactly were they making?" Posy asked.

"Well, in effect, explosives. That is, fertilizer, ammonium nitrate, a perfectly stable compound unless it's set off. As it can be—one reason it's manufactured up here. There's a lot of security. Ammonium nitrate plants have been detonated a few times—in Toulouse in 2001, another once in Texas, with hundreds of deaths."

"I thought Toulouse was an accident." I probably shouldn't have known that.

"They would say that, wouldn't they?" Ian said. "The French authorities. They didn't want to give anyone credit, or cause panic either, so soon after 9/11. But it takes a trigger—a rocket or torch. They don't see evidence of anything like that here, but they haven't ruled it out. We won't know for days, till it cools down."

It seemed inappropriate to think of love in a violent situation like this, but my heart stirred with love to see Ian that day. Whereas in Kosovo he had been an attractive compatriot and confidant, in Morocco, in his own grand house, and even at the ruins of his factory, he was the personification of lordly colonial master, someone before whom a man asleep on a mat on the floor would leap up and bow, as I had seen with my own eyes. No different from other women, I liked this powerful, preoccupied Ian even better and, after the transports of last night, was prepared to be more deeply committed to him than ever.

Only one thing disturbed: From the perspective of my being here, now that I'd seen its comforts and luxe, in retrospect, it was Ian's sojourn in Bosnia that seemed slightly odd. He had always said he was "wanting to give something back," volunteering with Oxfam to do what amounted to rather simple work, loading and unloading things, passing out supplies, pretty much like the stuff we were doing at AmerAID. At the time, this had seemed a handsome, humanitarian thing for him to do, but now I could see that Ian was a highly skilled manager of things like factories—even if they did blow up—and had been considerably overqualified for his work there. I was willing to subscribe to theories about British eccentricities, however, and chalk his priorities up to those. But it was slightly odd.

As we stood there, faces flayed by the mounting gusts of intense heat, something unlikely happened to me. I had been thinking of horrible things I had seen on television as a child, a house burning in Los Angeles, with people inside, and the voice of the announcer at the scene, quivering and tearful. I also thought of a reality police show I'd seen, watching a meth lab go up. With these thoughts, at the same time, a rising smell of ammonia became almost intolerable. The others cupped their hands over their noses or fished for Kleenex, but I was all at once somehow unable to raise my arms. I had never felt so strange, leaden limbs and nerveless fingers. The flames were lurid colors of purple and green, dazzling my eyes, and the next thing I knew, I was lying on the ground, with the others bending over me, fanning me with Posy's scarf. People helped me up, me protesting that I was all right. Apparently I had fainted, with a sort of amnesia making me unable to remember hitting the ground and with no sense of how long I'd been lying there. Ian said, "We should get everyone away from here. There's nothing to be done here anyhow."

"Right," said Robin Crumley. "This can't be good for Posy, or any of us. The baby." They believed my fainting was some reaction to the smell, but as I thought about it later, I came to think I'd also fainted from from a sudden perception of the metaphorical significance of flames, the force engulfing the Englishman's building, the country of Morocco, the region of North Africa, as if the poisonous vapors were coming up through a chink from a terrible netherworld.

That seems melodramatic, but anyway, I now believe I was terrified at a sort of unconscious level, and I saw that I'd been scared ever since I got here, of something I couldn't exactly explain. It had been scary enough in Kosovo, where people didn't hide in baggy robes and veils.

Ian instructed Rashid to drive Posy and me back to the Palmeraie in the car. They were obliged to wait for some sort of bomb squad from Rabat. Robin Crumley, the personification of uselessness, insisted on staying with Ian, his gangly arms flapping with almost Victorian officiousness as they stuffed us into the car.

"You should both take showers; there might be fallout," Ian said.

So we left, worrying about Posy's baby and the extent of the toxicity and wondering what had made me faint. I had no way of knowing whether this fire was the thing that Taft had heard might happen or if it was coincidence, or even some projection of my own will for a dramatic event.

Posy and I had gone to bed before Ian and Robin came home, after midnight. I could hear their voices in the patio, evidently talking to Ian's other female guest, Nancy Rutgers, and her friend, David, who must have been getting home at the same time. Then Ian came up. I heard him showering for a long time. Eventually he knocked, so quietly it wouldn't have waked me unless I'd been awake. He came into my room and sat on the chair some way away.

"I'm worried there may have been someone in there," he said, his voice shaky with fatigue or emotion. "The watchman and maybe his little boy. No one has seen the little boy and he was there this morning." His face was drawn with horror. "It has to be an accident. We just don't have sabotage or arson in Morocco."

"Those bombs in Casablanca?"

"There's been no trouble in Marrakech. I keep asking myself, could it be personal, some revenge thing, but for what? It's important that it not be deliberate, not just for the insurance, but think of what it would portend. The Moroccan security people are all over it already."

"You think it wasn't an accident?"

"No, no, I think it was an accident, a ghastly accident," he said.

"I think Rashid was dismayed that I was defying you by making him drive us up there," I apologized. I needed to know if I was authorized to command Rashid or not.

"I don't remember saying he couldn't," Ian said. "Probably he just didn't want to."

"We met his brother, the taxi driver; he could have driven us."

" 'Brother' in a manner of speaking, probably. They often call each other 'brother.' Rashid's real family is still in the Western Sahara, in the camps. He's a Saharawi, poor bastard. He sends them all his money." I loved Ian's English pronunciation of "bahstard," one of those irrelevant stabs of love that would insinuate themselves at inappropriate times.

We talked a little more about this, then he said good night and went off to his own room. I stayed awake a long time, and when he had to have fallen asleep, I got up and Googled "Western Sahara" to learn more about depressing refugee camps where displaced Africans and Algerians have lived their whole lives, something like the Palestinians. Then I sent a message to Taft—"Sheila"—about the fire and asking him to confirm about Aladdin, asking for instructions.

12

Fight in the cause of Allah / Those who fight you /
But do not transgress limits / For Allah loveth not
transgressors.

—Koran 2:190

Two days later, Ian, Robin, and I drove up to the site with investigators to see the useless heap of ashes and tottering, charred rafters to which the strong smell, not quite ammonia, would cling forever. An investigation, or investigations, had been mounted at once into the causes of the fire, to figure out whether it was deliberate, an accident, or an act of terrorism—there were various scenarios. Ian walked around and around the ruin, like a dog getting ready to lie down, but the investigators only took a sample of rubble and some photographs. The Moroccans were determined to find evidence of arson or terrorism, and there remained a question as to whether anyone had been inside. It began to look like that had not been the case—they were reassured so far not to have found human remains.

The principal investigator was a Commissioner Doussaq, from the OCP, Office Cherifien des Phosphates—a stout man in khakis and the white cap of a camel driver, who drove a car without license plates. "The Moroccan police are much more sophisticated and competent than I may have expected," Ian said of Commissioner Doussaq at dinner later.

"Their history as a police state," said Robin Crumley. "In authoritarian regimes, the police are always efficient."

With Commissioner Doussaq I made yet another faux pas. I had come along for my own reasons and was dying to ask an expert about what they believed had detonated the ammonium nitrate. I had hastened to read up on the possibilities—it can be exploded by being mixed with fuel oil, put under pressure or confined in a close place, exposed to extremely high temperatures, or set off by a rocket or dynamite. Anyway, I asked the commissioner which he believed it was: "If the gas was only ammoniac, would anyone—as I was, in fact—be affected enough to lose consciousness?" I was saying. Standing behind the commissioner, Ian shook his head slightly, but I didn't immediately understand this was an embarrassment. The commissioner stared at me and then looked at Ian, as if to say, do I have to answer her? But, instead of knowing enough to shut up, I persisted. "But if oxides of azote . . ."

"Miss Sawyer has been following our talk," Ian said, smiling. "I've explained that she was probably not harmed by the ammonia smell."

The commissioner's expression turned almost to gladness; the little lady was only concerned for her health. Still too thick to understand that I was overstepping polite female behavior, I plunged on with questions about the storage conditions.

"Mademoiselle s'intéresse à la chimie," he said to Ian, approvingly, tolerantly. "They study everything these days."

Afterward, Ian said for me to meddle in the investigation was impossible; it was improper even to talk to the Moroccan inspectors. He used a gentler word than "meddle." He may have said "get involved."

"No matter how modern they are, or we are, or how foreign, there would be no way he would be friendly with—well, our womenfolk." He smiled, but it did cause me to wonder whether Ian had not absorbed some of the Muslim sense of the opposite sex (Posy and me) as being volatile and frail. Posy said later that I had blushed at Ian's reprimand, but my true emotion was not remorse but chagrin.

In the days that followed, the aftermath took much of Ian's time, with delegations of police and government officials coming to the house or convoking Ian to the prefecture almost daily. Whatever I'd known of him in Kosovo—that he was there to do good works and had a caring, charitable side—I hadn't before observed his uniformly excellent manners and consideration to everyone. Besides running his industrial park, I had learned that he did various good works; gave money to local schools, literacy projects, and public works; and was a hero to his valet. Anyway, though I say "managed," Ian micromanaged—he would troubleshoot a burst pipe or meet a need for more chairs; he obviously enjoyed his little empire and felt it to be a contribution to this beautiful and poor country. Of course I thought this bleeding-heart side of him was a strong point.

He was polite to the investigators and to his servants, attentive to his guests—but especially to Posy, whom he did seem to regard as delicate, though she was a strapping Englishwoman, and handed her up and down the stairs if he was anywhere near her with a sort of reverent anxiety her husband didn't show. (Though Robin Crumley was absentminded, he didn't seem indifferent to her; it was more that he seemed to remember her and their coming baby suddenly, from time to time, and snap into a solicitous mode. But not very often.) "Ian is very attractive," she once remarked in a somewhat wistful tone. "He was Robin's student when Robin was a young don at Oxford; that's how we know him."

There was a mechanism for my getting mail from people who would be writing me, my parents and siblings, my carefully maintained magazine subscriptions, etc., addressed to my real self, care of an address in Rabat. In Rabat, letters were opened, retyped to Lulu Sawyer, and sent to me at Ian's, with the names of the senders disguised if necessary. The path of my replies was the same in reverse. In writing my parents in California, I had found myself saying things I didn't know I felt, about Ian and Morocco: I loved it here, I might have met The One. Partly that was what they wanted to hear, but it was true too, as much as ever one can be sure that something is true.

One day, circling the ruins, Ian rescued a very young kitten, a creature of maybe six weeks old, with its eyes stuck shut from infection, at the site of the fire, not huddled in a bush as a prudent kitten should, but standing blindly in the middle of the road, hoping for the best. It was gallant; it would stumble around and purr when you held it. When we got home, we bathed its eyes and got some antibiotics from the vet. We decided to hold off naming it—him—till we were sure he would live, like people in the olden days with their children. I found Ian's way with it touching. "Good chap," he told it when it ate a little bit. Some people seem to disapprove of kindness to animals, as if it distracts from kindness to people; others feel there's nothing much to do for people, since they are so hopeless, and we should concentrate on animals. I don't see that one rules out the other—anyway, I found this yet another reaffirmation of Ian's excellent character. My love for him increased. So did my resolve to be better at dissembling for my job.

"I wonder what does the Prophet say," Robin Crumley had said at dinner that night, which we ate inside in the dining room, "about stray cats, for example, and animal creation generally?" His tone held in check a note of rising aversion to cats, or to the Prophet.

"Very little, I would imagine," said Ian. "Are there cats mentioned in the Bible?"

"I'm sure there would be the attitude that Allah, or God or Yahweh, created them for man's use," Robin went on. "Except, as is well-known, cats are of no use for anything."

"*Man's* use, that is," said Posy. "Not woman's. Women would fall into the same category as cats, just property belonging to men."

I thought this was probably true, but it didn't seem a fruitful topic. Later I Googled "cats in the Koran." The Koran tells the story of a woman condemned to eternal hell for starving a poor pussycat, while in the Christian tradition, cats are the agents of Satan and witches.

13

Who can have conceived, in the heart of a savage Saharan camp, the serenity and balance of this place?

—Edith Wharton, *In Morocco*

A few more uneventful days passed, with Ian busy most of the time with various activities—the fire and business affairs, leading the life of a husband: He had an office, a jeep that he drove to building sites in the Atlas mountains, and a secretary—an English woman, Miss Pring, who lived in the medina and, on some mornings, if Posy and I were to be allowed the car for our excursions, picked him up in the jeep to drive him to his office in the more modern part of town. He showed up back in the Palmeraie at lunch most days and played the host each night to people he had invited, or drove me and the Crumleys to some riad to visit other expatriates.

From our cloister, however, it was hard to meet Moroccans. "I wish you knew some," I had once said. Ian had looked puzzled, made a loose gesture around him to include the world.

"I mean socially," I had said, and I saw from his expression that he feared this was going to be a tiresome American politically correct discussion, and was about to say, "Oh, please, this from the citizen of a country where minorities are still one step up from the slave market?" I had learned never to bring up issues of fairness or racial integration with Europeans if I didn't want to hear about slavery, segregation, the American Civil War, Indians, Vietnam, the two Iraq wars—the whole panoply of reproaches our various leaders have let us in for. "I just wondered if you saw any socially."

"Of course," he said. "I'll invite some for you." After this, two plump, seriously urbane men would be included in many of the soirees—a military man and a doctor, Colonel Barka and Dr. Kadimi, who might be vying with each other for the mustache award. Colonel Barka's was flowing silver and Dr. Kadimi's a trim but wide reddish one. The former had an honorary title at the British Consulate, something like "Persona Grata." Both either were unmarried or their wives did not go out, and these were our principal Moroccans. Most of Ian's friends were other Europeans, especially other British people; even the great group of French were off our radar, except for a few, or when Ian made an extra effort to invite them. (I planned to invite my airplane companion, Madame Frank.)

I could see real Moroccans from the distance, on the road into Marrakech we traveled almost daily. Rising out of the desolate landscape were several villages, or clusters of houses of mud and tin, organized around unpaved courtyards, where children tumbled in the doorways and women, their heads covered, leaned talking to each other as they looked out at the stony ground where the goats wandered and all the little boys were always kicking soccer balls, dodging the plastic bleach bottles that rolled under their feet. I never learned what cultural practice demanded this massive quantity of bleach.

Ian's guest Nancy Rutgers was polite but seemed to have arranged many errands and activities apart from Posy and me. She and her friend, David Someone—for I was never sure about his name (Talbot, Talcott?)—pretty much led their own lives, visiting the many people they seemed to know or taking expeditions to Fez and Essaouira, never including Posy or me. I was not sure of their status—if one or the other was an artist, it wasn't apparent, and Ian was somewhat taciturn: "Nancy is an old friend" was the only explanation. David seemed to be staying somewhere else but was always around.

In just a few days roaming in the souk with Posy, we had nearly mastered its geography. I tried to learn all I could about my companions and wrote meticulous reports of them to Taft, in the guise of chatty notes to "Sheila," or, more usually, I reported that I had nothing to report. Sometimes I telephoned, often to ask how to proceed, but telephoning was cumbersome, involving pay phones and absences that must have seemed mysterious to the others. I couldn't believe that all I was expected to do was to be me, and yet that was pretty much all I was doing. Taft was probably used to people not having much to report; he ran a number of agents, and real information is rare even if you have much of an idea of what you are looking for.

As for Aladdin, my contact, I wished he would be in touch again, but as I had nothing special to communicate to him, I did nothing about contacting him. Nothing had changed in Rashid's manner to indicate he had any understanding of the little piece of paper with Aladdin's message on it.

Posy and I spent a lot of time together. Posy was the daughter of an

English publisher, now dead, and her stepmother lived in a castle in France, or something like that. Her background was not unlike that of Ian himself, whose father I thought I had heard referred to as a "press lord," though I was unsure if that meant he was called Lord Drumm or whether "press lord" was just a descriptive term, like "drug mule." I had heard that pregnant women think of little else but their pregnancies—my sister was like that—but Posy seldom mentioned her clumsy shape and swelling ankles. She had read literature at Oxford or Cambridge and preferred to discuss arcane topics like water imagery in Moroccan poetry; that topic sticks in my mind because it had occurred even to me that for a country hard up for water, there was everywhere an oddly ambivalent obsession with it. There had been, for instance, the strange reluctance to expend it at Ian's fire, yet there were fountains everywhere.

Water came up over and over in stories and poems (for, as an aspect of tradecraft, I was reading anything that would help me understand the Moroccan culture) as a distrusted force ready to overwhelm, drown, suck away, and engulf its helpless victims, beckoning the distraught to their fates, a *"mer dévoreuse,"* a metaphor for oblivion. These poems recognized that given the caprices of fate, you might be tidal-waved, rip-tided, broken in the surf: "The thirst of the sea was stronger than mine," sang the poet, though not the Prophet—he was a desert chieftain and maybe had never seen the sea, so he says very little about it. Their fascination or aversion to water was what probably made them have fountains and gurgling, trickling water sounds everywhere. For me, a conscientious Californian from the land of periodic drought, for whom even extra toilet flushes are slightly wicked, the constant splashes of some fountain somewhere in earshot wherever you went was a little distressing.

By now I had gotten to know a few of Posy's secrets: that she was not entirely thrilled to become a mother, and that she believed her baby had been conceived on the Eurostar—so that technically it might be either French or English—she would always wonder which. Robin Crumley, with his graying hair and pale eyes, was anyone's idea of a distinguished poet, but it didn't seem to me he would be a very satisfactory father, and it was certainly impossible to imagine him fucking in a train. He was always to be seen on the patio shifting cushions, looking for his pen or glasses, distracted by some poetical conundrum from the business of real life or even conversation.

Most evenings, Posy and Ian discussed books. (Robin, the professional man of letters, seemed to feel it was beneath him to join in those discussions, and I didn't know enough to.) During the day, Robin Crumley was generally in his element, with plenty of solitude for composition; according to him, perfect monotony was somehow a precondition of art. He was never seen before lunch, and after lunch he disappeared again, ostensibly to work—actually to sleep, Posy suggested.

Sometimes Posy and I, with Ian and Robin or not, were invited out to lunch—sometimes an English lunch of roast, potatoes, and gravy at the Cotters', sometimes American salad and quiche at Tom and Strand's, sometimes at a Moroccan restaurant hosted by a French or Moroccan acquaintance, for instance Colonel Barka, who always paid pointed attention to me. I chalked this up to my flashy blonde hair, something of a novelty here still—as it was for me, for I am not naturally blonde, it is part of my disguise. But it seems to alter the character too, just as people think it does. Required to be blonde, I just decided to go all the way with it; it's Hollywood pale, very showy, Swedish-starlet-colored, and I have indeed found that people react to it and treat me differently. I can't be precise about how, but it's that they take me for more of an adventuress than they would have with my nice-girl brown—and they aren't wrong. I plan to keep it this way.

Moroccan dishes are somewhat monotonous, lamb and chicken, at least in the hands of Ian's cooks. I found that I was putting more and more harissa paste, with its Mexican hotness, on all of the food I was served. Apart from this, though each new recipe or person brought the possibility of learning something, doing something, basically I learned nothing, did nothing worthy of reporting to Taft—except, of course, my cover interest in Moroccan literacy. Taft had at least seemed very interested in Ian's fire.

"Lulu, for the moment, stay in Marrakech, don't go to any outlying villages on your inspections," he had said on the phone when he heard about the fire. In our line of work, you don't challenge such orders, so I postponed a plan to go with a woman from the World Learning Project to a village in the desert to the south. Thus far I'd seen only one literacy project in Marrakech; it seemed to me an ordinary school, where girls of eight or nine bent over books in Arabic they were apparently reading. What did the books say? I couldn't read them of course. I smiled at the children, bent to look over their shoulders, nodded as I had seen Princess Diana or Laura Bush do in newscasts. Some of the little girls wore head coverings, some didn't.

"Oh, literacy," said Marina Cotter. "What good does reading do them? I think our project is much more useful. We teach them not to kill their donkeys. They beat them so, they starve them, and then when the creatures die, they bewail their misfortune. They have no conception of humane treatment or that it's in their own best interests to treat their beasts with kindness, for all that the Koran says you ought to treat animals kindly." She and a team of Arabic and

Berber speakers travel in the guise of veterinarians, offering to treat sick donkeys, which they do, then they slip in their lessons: "If he is in good health, Mohammed, he will serve you a much longer time."

"When their donkeys die, the women have to carry the firewood," said Posy. "You see women along the road here, little bent-over old ones, carrying as much as a donkey." Both Marina and Posy pronounced the word "dunkey," in their English way. Eventually I told one of the Moroccan literacy ladies about Marina's donkey rescue and asked her about the cruelty. She said, piously, "I am sure it is not true. Mohammed spoke of animals as God's creatures and said that they must be treated with kindness and care. 'Even looking after plants and trees is an act of virtue,' he said. That went for sparrows and camels and every animal." I found myself thinking that the sayings of Mohammed have a way of making him a whole lot nicer than his imams seem today.

14

In most of their secret talks / There is no good: but if /
One exhorts to a deed / Of charity or goodness /
Or conciliation between people / Secrecy is permissible.

—Koran 4:114

A few days after the fire, at the souk again, for no special reason, I left a message for my contact, Aladdin, suggesting a meeting the following day at the Jardin Majorelle, a botanical garden with paths and benches and enough tourists to render invisible two people sitting on a bench among them. It was public but discreet, and two people could talk there without seeming illicit or clandestine. I'd already noted which bench, secluded in a grove of papyrus, would serve best, just as I'd mentally designated other meeting places and dead-drop possibilities, at the airport, the Mamounia hotel, and a certain restaurant on the outskirts of Guéliz, where expatriates don't look out of place but no one goes. Ian and I had stopped there once while driving toward Fez.

Why did I hasten to meet Aladdin now? There had been nothing urgent in the summons, but I suppose I wanted some sense of collaboration, some verification of a metier that had begun increasingly to seem abstract, unimportant, slightly beside the point of my day-to-day existence. I hoped this secret contact would turn out to be Moroccan and could help me with understanding some things—Ian's fire, for example. If it wasn't an accident, what did it mean and portend? I'm not an analyst, but I was coming to see that the field agent has to be analyst enough to know what to report in the first place, what to take seriously, what to fear.

I went to the souk without Posy, sent Rashid away, and then took a *petit taxi,* the battered little vehicles favored by locals, from the souk to the Jardin Majorelle, a strange oasis in the north of the city. It had been created by the famous painter, featuring palms and cacti, and architectural elements painted an intense blue, called *bleu Majorelle,* I think, with pots of green and yellow set around, the whole vibrant palette at war with the dusty shrubbery. It reminded me of California motels when I was little, the strident colors and buzzing insects in the zinnias. Gardens are such symbols of transience and hope at the same time that I never know how to feel in them.

I bought my ticket and went in, inconspicuous, I hoped, among the tourists who walked along the paths and succulents and lurid bougainvillea. I followed a long, narrow pool toward a blue fountain that I'd designated as the spot for us to meet. Further along behind it was the bench where I would sit down to wait.

My first reaction to seeing Colonel Barka already sitting on my bench at the designated hour was one of panic, a sense of bizarre coincidence. I quickly realized, however, given that coincidences are rare, that the more plausible explanation was that he was Aladdin. We stared at each other, and then I could see he was more surprised than I. I had imagined that he knew that Bearer Angel was me—how else had he known to leave a message with the spice dealer? But he had not. I sat down beside him and uttered the phrase Bearer Angel should say: "Could Aladdin conjure up such a garden with his lamp?" His reply contained the correct words: "A genie is but a bearer angel."

Like lovers, we reviewed the steps that led to our meeting. He had been told to leave a message at the spice dealer's, but not who would turn up. Nor did he know, or he wouldn't say, who'd told him. Who was he working for? For us? That was my assumption, but for Colonel Barka to know my code name, Bearer Angel, opened up many other possibilities. Had someone else penetrated this mission? Even if my phone calls had been intercepted, I hadn't used my code name, nor was it written down or in my computer, even encrypted, so his information was very inside indeed, and I had to assume he was one of us, or of people we trusted.

Since this was my first such encounter with a person from the netherworld we both inhabited, I wasn't sure what questions were appropriate to ask. "Who else are you working for?" I asked eventually, though this is probably a breach of good conduct. I was assuming he worked for us, but maybe also the fabled DST—Direction de la Surveillance du Territoire—our analogous Moroccan counterpart. Our dictum is, in effect, that there are no friendly intelligence services, including the British, but that "a good partner withholds openly." He stroked his mustache with the suave gesture of a stage villain.

"I am a loyal Moroccan of course, and there are many instances of close cooperation. I can help you with many a little thing. Sometimes there are things I need to know—things I do not quite understand in the European community. You can help me with those."

This answer didn't enlighten me, really. He was obviously in contact with my employers, but he could also be a counterintelligence agent, "CI." Was I in turn being recruited as a Moroccan spy, a double agent of some sort? I hardly knew, but in any case, since I didn't know anything about anything, I couldn't see the harm in agreeing to keep in touch with Colonel Barka and to cooperate with him about "many a little thing." It made me feel, at least, a little less alone to see the conspiratorial spark in his eye. I also hoped to get an idea of whether he was a professional spy or a patriot. The manual says "the most effective spy is the ideological one. The mercenary or the person terrorized into spying will be much easier to turn and double." It made some difference into which category the colonel fit.

"I will leave messages for you with the spice merchant," said the colonel.

"Who is he?"

"He is reliable," said the colonel. "And I will take the precaution of asking Ian if I might have the pleasure of showing you some historic buildings of old Marrakech from time to time. How is he? Far too preoccupied with his fire to interest himself in tourism. He will appreciate my taking you and his other guests to see some of the more esoteric sights of Marrakech. Thus I can telephone you at the house. If I mention Miss Andrews, you will know there is something for you with the spice merchant. Here is a telephone number. If you call, leave your name—a woman will answer, either as Mlle. Sanyed or as Berna Andrews, in which latter case, I will leave another number with the spice merchant."

"What about the fire, what do you think?"

"Whether sabotage or accident? Sabotage, probably."

"Fertilizer is very volatile."

"If they were producing fertilizer." Colonel Barka dismissed this as a topic of interest with a wave of his hand, but to me it was a vital question; if it wasn't fertilizer, did Ian know it? Whose fertilizer—or Semtex, or whatever it was—was it? Ian's?

"Do you know for certain fertilizer?" asked the colonel.

"Not for certain. Ian said it was fertilizer."

"Rocket fuel is also made from ammonium nitrate," he said. "Ammonium nitrate is a principal product of Morocco. Rocket fuel is a popular commodity in this region."

"You think Ian is involved, don't you?"

"Evidently our people think so, yours and mine," he said. I'd thought about that, of course. Was it possible I had been set up, in a way, by Taft et al., by their putting me in a useful position to observe Ian without telling me all the implications? Their reasoning would be: Keep her in ignorance so she'll be completely natural. We won't corrupt her mind with suspicions.

"What about Rashid?" I asked.

"He has the soul of a courier and will accept a few dirhams for any little task, without question. Withal, I think, loyal to Ian, as he understands loyalty."

"Loyalty" was not a word I wished to examine. We talked about some other recent instances of arson in the suburbs of Marrakech. As we parted he said, "Perhaps, inshallah—God willing—we will come to mean more to each other."

This meeting with Colonel Barka gave me much to think about, not the least this last remark. Was it a suggestive personal or a political remark? He had seemed to me a little like the suave eunuch counselors in Montesquieu. But perhaps that was to underestimate him. If personal, it seemed insulting, unprofessional, and wrong in the old-fashioned way for someone who often accepted Ian's hospitality to hit on Ian's girlfriend, though maybe that compunction was itself old-fashioned. Was his an Islamic idea that Western women, particularly those living in sin, were loose and didn't mind who they slept with? Would I sleep with the colonel if I perceived a way to, say, break a dangerous arms smuggling ring? Sure.

I was more preoccupied with the colonel's hint about Ian. It was true he hadn't seemed that surprised at the fire. Allowing suspicions of any of Ian's movements or attitudes always brought up the curious fact of his volunteer work in Kosovo. It had seemed natural and virtuous at the time, but it continued to seem suspicious. I thought over all our talks, fishing for a time he might have expressed some pro- or anti-Islamic feelings, or special British patriotism, or any ideology at all. He never had.

Later, I had to accept that I was unequal to analyzing Colonel Barka's motives and connections. Besides being my appointed contact, was he Moroccan counterintelligence, sent to block my activities? To cooperate? Neither of these? Was he some sort of double agent on our side? With no way of knowing—a condition of bafflement endemic to our business; I would try to keep all of these possibilities in mind. After all, double agents are doubled, treacherous by definition. I reported fully and dutifully to Taft, who seemed unsurprised by Barka but didn't identify him either.

The colonel's and my relationship developed collegially. I liked the colonel better than I liked Taft. Though in his chatty e-mail persona of Sheila, Taft could be nice and even funny, the colonel and I had a certain level of trust: If he couldn't answer my questions, I trusted him to say he couldn't answer for reasons of policy, instead of lying, and I did the same. In answer to his questions, I was always having to tell him I didn't know, for instance about Ian's businesses, which he clearly suspected and about which I truly didn't know anything beyond what Ian had said about them. Now, I'm not sure why I was so obtuse about Ian. Because I loved him?

15

And familiarity with the subject language must be insisted upon, despite current American disdain for such studies. Idioms, expressions, and even pronouns reveal most of the culture in which languages flourish, and help in the deduction of attitudes and motives in many situations.

—William E. Colby, "Recruitment, Training, and Incentives for Better Analysis"

Part of my task was to recruit informants (we were told to use "informant," which was more polite than to refer to "informers") and create a network of "pickets"—storekeepers, waiters, and the like whose opinions could be useful; and finally, to monitor and transmit any political and/or weapons-related information that might drift my way. For this purpose, I made two important recruits. Pursuing my literacy evaluation task, one day we had an encounter that could have been awkward, but which luckily I was prepared for. Rashid had brought Posy and me to the headquarters of the Near East Friendship Foundation, where I had an appointment with the local director. Though this was a Moroccan-run charity, when a woman in

Moroccan dress came in to greet us, I could see that she was American. How could I tell this? I have no idea, something indefinable in her walk. The women I saw moving along the roads walked slowly, in a certain way, perhaps because most of them were stout. Or was it her expression, or her sunglasses? The Moroccan women didn't have sunglasses, and eventually their faces would become squinted and lined, just as our dermatologists would predict.

Anyway, we could see that this woman was not Moroccan; she had light gray eyes and pale, soft skin slightly wrinkled in a Western way, graying hair just showing under the hijab, and when she spoke, it was with a perfectly normal American accent, a woman of around sixty, maybe older.

"This is Habiba Al-Hayek," said the secretary who had let us in. "Madame Crumley and Mademoiselle Sawyer."

"Nice to meet you," she said in a businesslike way. "Let me tell you about Moroccan illiteracy."

Eventually, talking, it emerged that I was from California, and she said she was raised in Palo Alto. It was then I realized why she bore the trace of a memory or intuition for me—this would actually be a sort of relative, Alice Mott, a cousin of my stepmother, a person fabled in my family for having run off to Mecca during the sixties with her then husband Bob, both of them Ph.D. biologists who converted to Islam about the same time as Cassius Clay did. "It only happens in WASP families," I remember my father saying, not remembering Cassius Clay. "People of other religions take religion too seriously to do anything so silly."

I had already prepared myself to run into her, had supposed I would. We had heard that Alice had left Mecca, years ago, for the more welcoming atmosphere of Marrakech, and my parents had instructed me to call her when I got to Morocco, but of course I couldn't because of my new identity. I had thought about it, had weighed the possibility of carrying on an acquaintance without acknowledging our connection, and had decided on the course to follow should I meet her. Faced with dealing with it now, I admitted to enough familiarity with Santa Barbara and Palo Alto to enable us to play whom-do-you-know. I even admitted to knowing my parents, as if they had been pleasant friends of friends. I was not surprised that we should meet, since the foreign community, above all the anglophone community, is small, and most of the foreigners there were French. It was even predictable, and I could see that she was the perfect person to be an informant, connected to both the Muslim and American communities.

I'd absorbed Ian's reminders that any access to Moroccan culture must come either from inference, from him, or through some female network—the Moroccan male world was closed. Here was an entrée into a female network, though much would depend on her attitude to America. Sometimes people long-expatriated were nostalgic and positive about their native land, but sometimes they had retained whatever bitter conclusions had driven them away. I was more or less the former, but Habiba's attitude wasn't clear. In the meantime, she was very much the director of this branch of the Near East Friendship Foundation.

"We can go visit some of the schools next week. I have a driver—my programs are mostly in the villages." Her voice took on a tone of professional recitation, of a presentation she had often given, of facts and figures, funding sources, results. "We've seen the enrollment of girls go up from eighteen to nearly forty percent. Believe me, this is fabulous." The most intriguing thing she said was, "I'm committed to girls reading. Not everybody agrees." I wanted to hear more about the people who, like Marina Cotter, didn't think that girls should read, but just then someone called her away. She stuck out her hand, said how glad she was to meet me, and glided away in her robes and hijab. Cousin Alice/Habiba. It was odd but not unpromising.

It was hard to imagine a life without being able to read—the situation for three quarters of women and girls in the rural areas of Morocco. If you couldn't read, you'd have to wait for people to tell you things—how unreliable that would be! The little girls I'd already seen in the city school I'd visited (most aged about ten, wearing head scarves) seemed to be following a more or less modern curriculum. Thinking of the people who disapprove of female reading, I also thought of Posy, with her Oxbridge degree and views about water imagery and scansion and the rest, lumbering around, pregnant, waiting, and fretful, and I could imagine what the naysayers might say, that reading was wasted on Posy too, on all women, they should just get on with their baby-having.

As to recruiting informants, I had hopes of finding one in Habiba, and I also had hopes for Rashid. Though he hadn't gotten over his dislike of me, over the incident of being made to drive us to the fire, on our daily outings he had become almost garrulous and didn't disguise his outrage at things that were happening in Morocco, above all at the increasing despotism of the new king and especially his secret service. These groups had been appalling instruments of the torture and disappearances rife under the last king, Hassan II, elements the new one, Mohammed VI, had promised to control. Instead, they were active again; people disappeared or were imprisoned. The press was not free, and two French-language papers had recently been shut down.

"What are we doing about it? Nothing, madam. We are dogs. If we had the tails of dogs, we would trip on them between our legs," Rashid said.

16

Most of life is so dull that there is nothing to be said about it.

—E. M. Forster, *A Passage to India*

Ian had a leading and visible place in the business community, among both Moroccans and expatriates. I went with him several times to hear him address investors or bankers. His talks, adjusted slightly depending on the audience, were entitled such things as "Morocco, Land of Possibilities" and were about the potential in the sector of light manufacturing, focused on the availability of space, water, and labor. "The present business climate is the result of a favorable tax structure, generous financial incentives in terms of loans, mortgages, and exceptions for foreign investments." I usually tuned out after too many paragraphs of this, but his audiences seemed upbeat and responsive. I recognized that his English witticisms and his clarity about money made him a sought-after speaker. When I went to hear him, I didn't go with him as his companion, but went instead in the role of literacy-program examiner, separately, driven by Rashid. Ian had suggested this discretion.

The frequent visits of the Cotters, and ours to them, gave me a chance to get better acquainted with Suma Bourad, whom they often brought along to social events. She was lonesome, I thought, and seemed happy to speak of Paris, which she wasn't able to do with Marina Cotter or her grandchildren, who didn't know Paris and didn't speak much French. I also saw Suma from time to time if I happened to be at Tea Cosy, Tom and Strand's tea shop, when she brought the Cotter grandchildren to play with Amelie. Other times she took them to play with the two Al-Sayad children, and sometimes Gazi's maid brought them to the Tea Cosy. The Al-Sayad kids were pudgy, olive-skinned, normal-seeming kids, jabbering in Arabic and capable of polite phrases in English: "Sank you, madame," and so on.

Soon enough, I had gotten friendly enough with Suma to ask her about the murder attempt in Paris.

"That is not the real Islam," she said. "My brother was misled is all." I could see that she didn't especially want to talk about it with me, an unknown American.

"But what happened?"

"He said I was not a virgin and that he'd tell people that, so I was afraid, of course. Horrible things happen to girls when people think that. So I went to the shelter." I supposed she meant by "people" Muslim and unreconstructed people in the suburbs. I knew what she meant. I'd read about the horrible things—rapes, disgrace, disfigurement, and one girl in a Paris suburb had been burned alive.

"Do you hope to go back to France?"

"I am not at home here," she said vaguely. "Though in some ways it's better, because no one insults you for wearing the veil. I like it that everyone is a Mussulman. I'd be comfortable at the Al-Sayads', where pork isn't served and prayers are offered, all that sort of thing. Inshallah!

"Well, the Cotters are nice. I have nothing against Christians, I was raised among them after all. But I've come to see it isn't my path."

I asked her if it had often happened in France that people insulted her for wearing the veil. "Oh, yes, waiters absolutely shrink if you try to come into a restaurant. They pretend you aren't there. They think you're a fanatic." She laughed bitterly at some memory and added, "My parents didn't like it either because they thought it wasn't sincere. Sincerity is important in our religion, believe it or not." I believed it, since you would have to be sincere to blow yourself up. I would have asked her more, but she seemed to want to talk about cinema and the recent French literary prizes—stuff suitable to her age—instead of her future, and she claimed to be perfectly happy with the Cotters for the moment. The Cotters, I'm sure, were pleasant enough—large, British, distant, and cheerful, though they'd been stunned by the death of their daughter-in-law and the subsequent arrival of little Freddie and Rose, and worried about their distraught son, who was now away in the Lancers or some such British regiment. I liked them, at least at first.

The Al-Sayads, though they were Ian's neighbors, didn't mingle much with the European community, but they often sent their two fat children over to play with Tom and Strand's Amelie as well as with the Cotters' Rose and Freddie, and often whoever was in charge would bring them to swim in Ian's pool. We thought it odd they didn't have a pool. I was at Tom's once when they came there. Marcia, the Filipina maid, brought them in and then waited outside. Tom and I had studied her for signs of the famous abuse the Saudis are said to inflict on their foreign help, but she seemed fine. We speculated about the Al-Sayads' social life—they knew mostly Moroccans, but they also seemed to have a lot of Saudi visitors, judging from the black abayas their women guests wore getting in and out of white limos.

They didn't invite us to their house, which was named Garden of Harmony, in Arabic of course; but if Gazi or Khaled was in their driveway when Posy and I began one of our walks outside the walls, they would wave in a friendly way, and their visitors, implacable behind their veils, still somehow, by their stares, gave off an air of surprise that such an acquaintance was possible. For all their talk of Yale and Shakespeare, it was plain that the Saudi couple were ambivalent about socializing with the boozy Brits next door; in part, they seemed proud of it, or rather of their ability to mingle and be accepted among Westerners as if there were nothing odd about them. (I could not forget the sight of Khaled at the airport in his white robe and checkered headdress with its crown-of-thorns circlet around his brow. I was never to see him in those again—he must have laid them aside during his Moroccan visits, though Gazi kept to her black shroud disguise.) I also saw her once unveiled in public, at the Mamounia hotel, in a lime-green Armani jacket.

But with us they were always uneasy or on edge, as if at any moment they expected something to happen that would tax their ability to comprehend or stand it—some cultural absolute, some blasphemy that might really damage or appall them. Of course we were all careful not to tread on their beliefs, religion a subject never mentioned even when, as occasionally happened, world troubles or Arab unrest were discussed. Then they disclaimed any admiration for Osama bin Laden, or rather, they claimed to hate him. Gazi was outspoken about the lot of women in Saudi Arabia, and Khaled had the air of nodding in agreement, but more in the role of supportive husband than from conviction. I believed that at home he'd be a traditional Saudi husband, whatever that involved. In Marrakech, Gazi drove—I had seen her behind the wheel of a BMW—but I knew it was against the law in Saudi Arabia.

I thought about Gazi and the other Muslim women in their cloisters—in former times in actual purdah—and could imagine the desperation and intrigues that must have festered there. I pitied them, but I couldn't scorn them, since I was in thrall myself, to my "job," and sexually, to Ian, an enthrallment of my own making, dictated by nature, maybe, or a response to the loneliness of my role.

Once, I'd said something critical about Gazi—for I didn't really like her, there was something about her resolute gaity, her jewels, her air of crazy, madcap heiress so at odds with her black abaya, and her reputation (I imagined) for mistreating her servants; I had called her "the princess," sarcastically, and Ian rebuked me.

"Think of what she has to bear in Saudi Arabia. Think of the lives of women there."

"I meant it in the sense we say 'Jewish princess,' or 'Japanese princess,' to mean a spoiled, demanding person who spends a lot of time on her nails," I explained.

Ian gave me a long look and said, "What do you think of yourself as, Lulu?"

This was said lightly, affectionately, but though I'm not a sensitive person, it stung me, for its justice. As far as Ian could see, I was an indolent and sheltered American, who, apart from some harsh scenes witnessed in Kosovo, had not much experience with anything grim and had well-tended fingernails. And given that I hadn't produced anything much in the professional line, that was truly about all there was to me.

Once or twice I had caught Gazi in the act of hating Posy and me, mostly me, as Posy, married and pregnant, had already compromised the freedoms Gazi could see I still had and she could never have. Her feelings were seen in no more than a fleeting expression, and I couldn't blame her for them. It was no wonder she often mentioned her years at Brown University, which must have been the only time she wasn't constrained by her culture; her only act of defiance in her own country was the drive-in, the demonstration she'd been a part of after the first Gulf War in 1991 and the retributions afterward.

Gazi had told us about being a member of the Saudi drive-in, when a number of mostly foreign-educated Saudi women got in cars and drove up and down the main street in Riyadh to assert their right to drive. "I was not the leader," she said. "My older sister and her friends were. They suffered more than I. Really, the women did not suffer, for they are not responsible agents, after all, just suggestible sillies. Our husbands suffered. Khaled was put on leave of absence, and people—men—called us in the middle of the night, and sometimes there was just a voice uttering curses. And one girl committed suicide. My sister's friend Leila disappeared after the drive-in. She was never seen again."

"The men are afraid of women, I suppose," Posy said, voice dripping with scorn for Islamic manhood.

"Our husbands tried to help us, by and large. Khaled was wonderful. One group that was afraid we would succeed, though, was the drivers. What would become of them if women could drive?"

"Are the drivers the only men you are alone with?" I wondered.

"Do women have affairs with their drivers?" asked Posy. Gazi stared, disconcerted.

"No," she said. "I've never heard of that." By her expression, you could see she'd never thought of drivers as viable men. "We have to be careful, after all." Her sisterly expression seemed to imply that they were as frisky and prone to adventure as we Westerners.

I admired Gazi for the strength of character that drove her perfect poise, her perfect grooming, though in Posy's opinion this was just self-preservation.

"He might take a second wife at any time, remember," she said. "Then a third and fourth . . ." I couldn't help but remember that Gazi was one of the luckier Saudi women, relative to the poor village women, even in Morocco, who were like beasts of burden, limping down the road under their bundles of sticks—little, invisible, bent, disposable.

All the while, I myself was feeling a little like a harem girl—sex in exchange for, in this case, the right to be here, to snoop into Ian's affairs and those of his friends. I told myself that I'd be here anyhow, because of being in love with him, or as much in love as I could allow myself to be.

As a younger person, in Paris, I had plunged into all that you're supposed to do there—lose your head completely over a man, learn how to read a menu, muster a barely passable French, etc. But here, now, in my new situation, I had no sense of the expectations and whether I was living up to them, and no sense of self-improvement.

And also, frankly, when he reproached me about Gazi, this admonitory side of Ian was new to me. Was it because I was now in the position of chatelaine of his household that he scrutinized me for perfection? Alas, I was/am so far from it. My ambivalence about Ian was complicated—as I guess ambivalence is by definition. The more I felt myself in love with him, the worse I felt about my exploitive double life, using him as cover. Thus I didn't allow myself to be as nice as I wanted to be, or as in love as I wanted to be.

Trying to be nice, I began to interest myself in the details of managing the meals and the gardens, knowing little about either, but this wasn't received very well by the competent employees: Rashid, Aisha, Miryam, and Mohammed. ("You can call anyone Mohammed here and have a fair chance of being right," Posy Crumley had told me. "They're all called that or Ali. Oh, don't rule out Ahmed and Hassan, but that's about it." To me she sounded exactly like colonial Brits in novels by Kipling or Maugham.)

"I think that's rather a good thing," said her husband, "very leveling and democratic, the way Koreans are all called Lee or Park, or Kim."

"The African way of giving everyone an absolutely unique name makes it very hard to remember what people are called," Ian had agreed. "Is she Taisha or Kimmet or La Donna? . . .")

In fact I had begun to realize that Ian's staff mistrusted me or resented me. They bowed their heads or looked away when I came into the kitchen or asked questions about cooking or produce. Only very slowly did I begin to get the sense that it was moral contamination they feared: I was the unmarried mistress, the concubine, not at all the sort of person they should associate with. Of course this surprised me very much. Was it too late to redeem my character? The more I became aware that the household staff, especially the maids in their nurselike white head scarves and long, modest tunics, didn't approve of me, the more concerned I felt to convince them of my goodness, my devotion to Ian (whom I presumed them to love), my standards of housekeeping, my knowledge of gardening, my charm to his friends. But I could tell it wasn't working. Their impassive faces, their politeness, the remarkable slowness of their movements conveyed their mistrust.

I discussed it with Posy. The cooks liked and talked to her, especially one, Miryam, a middle-aged woman who seemed to represent wisdom to the others. "They wonder about your relationship with your family," Posy said. "They asked me about it. They think that having lost your virginity, you've been cast out by them. They notice that you seldom get letters."

"How do they know I've lost my virginity? They must have been snooping in my pills." I didn't like them snooping in my stuff.

Posy laughed. "I've tried to explain our general indifference to virginity, but they don't believe me. How could we be indifferent to losing our sole possession, the entire determinate of our value? Not its moral symbolism, either, they mean the actual membrane."

True, of course. Western young women had never been taught to think of the hymen at all. It had been explained to us in gym class that with Tampax and horseback riding, we probably didn't have one. Whatever we had experienced of unconscious denigration, to a person of my age no one had ever been so derisive, so condescending to women, as to imply that our value lay solely in our virginity.

"Let alone expect us to bleed like a sow," Posy said. "It's the most offensive thing in all Islam." That was saying a lot in Posy's book, since for her it was a religion full of offensive ideas. I was still trying to focus on its beauty and antiquity.

Posy said, "It's not such a big deal after all, to have a man poke you in that particular way. Enjoyable of course, but I mean, it doesn't change your essence, it doesn't change *you*."

I agreed. I tried to remember being a virgin and I couldn't. That is, there was no difference in me either way; it was exactly the same, and it was terrible to think there were whole continents of poor girls for whom that inconsequential poke might mean life or death.

After this conversation, it came to me that if I were married to Ian, all would be well. In the ritual duties of wifehood, in the possession of silver and china, I would be redeemed and safe. I wish I hadn't had that thought, for it stayed with me; what a reasonable thing it would be to marry Ian.

17

. . . The central riddle of the mysterious North African civilization: the perpetual flux and the immovable stability, the barbarous
customs and the sensuous refinements, the absence of artistic
originality and the gift for regrouping borrowed motives, the
patient and exquisite workmanship and the immediate neglect
and degradation of the thing once made.

—Edith Wharton, *In Morocco*

After my rendezvous with Colonel Barka, I had lunch with
him from time to time, usually along with Posy, in the guise
of being shown some tourist attraction, to establish the normalness of
our relationship. It was known that the sociable and urbane little man
often showed European friends through palaces and restored riads in
the medina, or drove them to charming oases or even to Fez or Essaouira. I knew now that this was part of his mission, but he had a
streak of the natural tour guide and a real relish for the details of Moroccan history and architecture, and it allowed us to meet more or less
freely.

"What have you brought me?" he would ask while Posy went to the ladies' room—oftener and oftener as her pregnancy advanced. He would gaze into his tea as if to read the leaves and I would whisper some tidbits, never anything much, for I didn't know anything much. I could tell him how the fire investigation was going or some details of Ian's business plans. I saw no harm in this, because Ian was plainly not involved in anything, or so I came down on the side of thinking. Colonel Barka in turn would give me some Moroccan names, people who went to Casablanca or supported certain charities, for me to pass along to Taft. It was enough for me that he had come recommended by those above me, trusted if not altogether ours; I was allowed to trust him, and I did.

With Posy present, the colonel would discourse on world events. "There is a systemic American blindness—your intelligence services failed to notice the Berlin wall was coming down, that Russia would implode, that your enemies in Islam were at your door. You believe the myth that you are the most fortunate country—I don't say the best; Americans are too modest to say that. But fortunate, that is, with the happiest way of life—this is a serious error, for it prevents you from achieving a more cheerful and pleasant society, like some others."

Since I've lived abroad since my twenties, I had sort of forgotten that myth, that we had the best way of life; I liked where I grew up, Santa Barbara, though I remembered some bad things about it. "You shouldn't say 'you,'" I protested, "as if you mean me. All Americans are not alike." For I knew, now, that ours was not the best way of life, that there were many countries with higher standards of living—though there were also many worse.

Talking of Islamic radicals, "I am no ideologue," said the colonel. "I do not pretend to understand our passionate young men. But I half admire them for their puerile focus, their energy."

"If women led more normal lives, the men would be less angry," I said.

"You see—you have an American view of what is normal." He smiled. "To us it is normal for women to be busy perfuming themselves in the hammam and waiting for the caresses of their husbands." Posy and I laughed.

These lunches were fun because Colonel Barka, without ever mentioning our mutual profession, was a fount of lore about the history of espionage, especially as it related to Morocco, in the days during World War II when spies congregated in Casablanca. He could quote long sequences from the film of that name and had memorized the works of John Buchan and the more recent Ian Fleming and John le Carré. Often he said, apropos of almost anything, " 'I am shocked, shocked.' "

I was able to firm up my recruitment of Habiba. Whatever her attitude to America had been during the sixties, now it was friendly, even nostalgic, and so I hinted to her that I knew people who would appreciate insights about the Islamic world and would make donations to her literacy program. Whether the payments I made ever got to her programs I never knew, but she would give me little lists of donors and officers in other charities and of any Europeans she was aware of who made donations. I passed these along to Taft, but her usefulness to me was often just as an interpreter of events. She hadn't lost her ability to respond like an American, but she understood the Moroccan perspective too.

"They are obsessed with the safety of their king," she said. "He is universally loved. As loved as his father was hated. I remember the days of his father."

"What was that like?"

"The people suffered. Everyone knew he was CIA. My husband's brother was in prison for nineteen years, just for being against him. No trial, just a sort of cursory process. But the present king is loved."

Tom and Strand were my other "pickets." Sometimes I gave Posy the slip, figuratively speaking—she would nap or be reading, and I would ask Rashid to drive me to Tom Drill's tea shop. There I had discovered, over the weeks, that Strand smoked a lot of dope; maybe someone not Californian wouldn't notice the unmistakable, rather delicious smell, the bright eyes, the mellow welcome. I was actually thrilled to find something vaguely criminal going on, for if he would tell me about his dealers, I would finally have a sense of the intrigues and betrayals that I was supposedly looking into. Another consequence of my supposedly privileged and isolated situation was being remote from the fast, racy, drug-sniffing, opium-smoking world of the prominent French fashion and English film people. This world was said to exist, but I never saw it. Ours was the staid world of whiskey and soda, business, and diplomacy—the very world we believed was implicated in money laundering and support—but any depravity was invisible. The sole outward sign of the secret life of Marrakech was the flock of little boys at every corner, alert to guide the traveler to some den or other. But never me.

Tom was no help; deploring Strand's life in drugs, he refused to know about his sources. "It's just easier for some people in this household to get stoned than deal with things," he said snappishly when I mentioned, in a nonjudgmental way, that smelling marijuana made me nostalgic for California. I figured Strand needed to be stoned to get up at four every morning to do the baking, as he did, which Tom had rather unfairly forgotten.

"Morocco is all about drugs," he said. "Why do you think people come here? All those English directors, all those French dress designers, it all goes up in smoke." It was clear that he was worried about Strand's habit, if only because it meant that with Strand so laid back, he, Tom, did most of the work around the house and the tearoom, and most of the parenting. Tom didn't smoke, or only rarely, but this was my introduction to the subject of drugs in Morocco, not at all the focus of my presence there, but of interest, linked as they often are to politics, as a source of money to support political, i.e., terrorist activities, and as an expression of general defiance and disillusion—philosophically linked.

Tom and Strand thought I was just trying to put together my sense of where I was, and they liked to be of help with information and analysis of their tearoom clients, who came in with whom. Strand told me about his buying expeditions, how you shouldn't buy hashish from the little boys who proffered it by the side of the mountain roads and were in league with the police, who'd arrest you soon after.

"You have to get it in the restaurants," he said.

"What an experienced drug dealer you are," I said.

"Well, don't laugh, I *was* the drug dealer when I was at Berkeley High, but now I just buy a little for my own consumption."

18

For the prohibited month / And so for all things prohibited / There is the law of equality. If then anyone transgresses the prohibition against you / Transgress ye likewise / Against him.

—Koran 2:194

Sometimes, fed up with company, I'd go to my room after dinner, leaving Ian to his guests. I would write my e-mails to "Sheila," and I'd read. To tell the truth, I'd never been much of a reader. One reason I never liked to read is that I early discovered that in stories, the female character you were supposed to love and admire was expected to make choices of the heart instead of rational choices. She was supposed to be buffeted by her emotions, and that was what made her lovable and womanly. True, in *Little Women* you liked Jo, the most intelligent one, though my secret was that I didn't like the little women at all; Jo was only the best among them, but even she, swayed by her emotions, sold out for the ugly, bearded, older professor, a repellent choice for lots of reasons.

I had really taken up reading when I went to work in Pristina, where, unlike here, there was nothing to do in the evenings; so before I met Ian, I'd begun to form the habit of going to bed early with a book. In Marrakech, first I read the supply of miscellaneous paperbacks and old Tauchnitz editions to be found on the bookshelf in my room—one volume only of the Forsyte Saga (*Indian Summer of a Forsyte*); *Mr. Midshipman Easy*, which was a sea story; *The Man in Lower Ten;* the collected writings of Max Weber (English translation). Then I began to bring home books from the informal lending shelf at Tom and Strand's tea shop, the Tea Cosy, old paperbacks people would leave for each other. It would be this that led to a useful development, the library project.

I was reading Montesquieu's *Persian Letters,* in which the traveling Persian bemoans the vengeful behavior of the vindictive women in his seraglio back home. I couldn't help but think that my situation, at the moment, was not so different from theirs. Well, it was totally different, of course, for I could always leave. Instead, with the perfectly truthful excuse of feeling guilty at having so much free time, apart from my modest expeditions on behalf of female literacy, I had suggested to Ian that I needed to find something else useful to do, and he had suggested volunteer activities for both Posy and me, an idea we had had ourselves, of course, but, given our unfamiliarity with the way things ran there, needed his help to set up.

On the nights I went up early, Ian often didn't come in at all, as if to punish me for my lack of sociability. I wouldn't give him the satisfaction of admitting it was punishment, so I pretended not to notice and didn't complain—though it was punishment. I feel positive about sex and have since I began it, and it was certainly part of what I'd come to

Morocco for. It was after those nights of no love, in the morning, that we nodded a little guiltily and avoided each other's eyes.

Posy shared my restlessness, and I felt much sorrier for her than for myself. I had my secret job and my overt one, while she was stuck there with no useful occupation, newly married to a vague, fluttery, older husband, not really ready for motherhood, and perhaps (my secret vanity) less endowed than I with inner resources. When I suggested she throw herself into the world of poetry, she indignantly pointed out she had a good degree at Oxford in English poetry and the like, and must already know much more about poetry than I, which wouldn't have been hard.

"I meant the politics of poetry," I said. "The critics, the patrons, the competition—helping Robin with his career."

"Oh, Robin is deeply attuned to that," she said.

"I'd like to read Robin's poems, if you have a book of his," I suggested. To my discomfiture, several copies of slim volumes by Robin Crumley were sitting reproachfully next to my breakfast plate the next day. However, I liked them, short witty lyrics and soulful evocations of green English scenes, and even the tongue-in-cheek parody of older English subjects, on the line of "Where is the ploughman / poor bastard / who used to slog along this lane?"

We had begun our researches for a useful project. As I had been briefed before coming here, Marrakech was crawling with NGOs devoted to all kinds of worthy things—literacy especially, but also there were other aspects of the advancement of women, public health issues, historic renovation and beautification projects. Some of the expatriate women were involved in such causes, but most groups were nonetheless run by Moroccans, or by people from other parts of the Muslim world, who with their colonial memories were not really receptive to Christian Anglophones.

At first I volunteered to teach women how to read, along with evaluating the various programs. Besides her donkey rescue, Marina Cotter was involved in a teaching program, but she and her friends were teaching English to only a handful of Protestant Christian children, for the simple reason that most children's families had no use for English. However, it became apparent to me that teaching reading in any language demanded patience and special techniques I didn't know.

Once we started seriously looking, Posy and I easily found something more suited to our skills to throw ourselves into: There was one glaring lack in the Christian/English community that struck us as a way of doing a real service, and coincidentally might give me an entrée to a variety of new places; apart from the single shelf at the Tea Cosy, there was no lending library, either British or American, for books in English. The idea of founding one hit me with a rush of excitement, for it would give me the perfect reason to go around talking to people, Moroccans as well as foreigners, snooping into things, soliciting funds, and getting to know the power structure, at least in the expatriate community. And Moroccans would use it too, and be exposed to the benefits of the best of Western literature (fatuous assumption). It seemed strange, even slightly shocking, given that Europeans had been here for centuries, that no one had thought of a library before—or maybe they had.

The location for this library was easily found, in a dusty two-room storefront annex adjoining Tom and Strand's Tea Cosy in Guéliz, a modern section of the city where a lot of foreigners live. Tom was delighted and supportive, for what could be more compatible than books and tea shops, and he had already operated as librarian, by default, of the informal library shelf of paperbacks his patrons traded and helped themselves from.

Acquisitions would begin with a book donation drive, which I began to talk up in the course of the active nightly social life around Ian, and everyone volunteered to donate books. I also began to search the Web for lists of books basic to any library—reference works and classics to start. We ordered things from Amazon to be sent to Ian's address in London, for it proved complicated to import books directly to Morocco. Morocco put maddening obstacles in the way; every book ordered from abroad had to have a certificate of importation and get past a censor. Each book had to be cleared of being offensive—no Salman Rushdie, not even any Zadie Smith, as the censor was unable to feel sure about the tone of her presentation of Muslim characters. The library project thus tallied nicely with my clandestine interests, since it turned out that a lot of intrigue was required—asking people who were going to Paris or London to smuggle books back, for instance.

All this library activity gave me the feeling I was doing something useful, even though I made little headway on my covert mission, and only slow progress on the lumbering report I was drafting on the literacy programs, though I'd become passionately committed to them at the sight of little girls laughing at stories they were reading, about bunnies and such. The river of money flowing through Morocco to the benevolent imams of the suicide bombers, the opium producers of Afghanistan, or the arms dealers of Bulgaria did not abate, but it was an underground river. Patience, said Taft/Sheila. Sometimes you wait for years.

Nor was I proving to be a good judge of the Morocco I was seeing. In a village: Were these people the desperately poor or were they the relatively well-off? Was there worse, in Tangiers, in Casablanca? Was the water clean? I didn't know and couldn't find out. The girls who came in to wash the dishes in Ian's kitchen came from such villages—what did they say when they went home? Did the lavish hot water amaze them? I didn't know and couldn't find that out either. It was as if the Europeans and the Moroccans were each afflicted with an eye disease that prevented them from seeing each other—it was the perennial eye infection of colonialism. The girls in the kitchen played the wailing music of popular songs. Tuneless and anguished, it drifted through the gardens, its passionate rhythms suggesting that frenzy lurked beneath the placid surface of comfortable daily piety.

"In Ramadan, they don't eat all day. They're preparing our food but they can't eat it themselves," Posy said. "I'd poison us if I were them."

I had noticed too that they cooked for us without complaint pork roasts and wild boar, forbidden in Islam.

Apropos of the kitchen girls and the maid who did the rooms, Posy told me in a low tone one morning, when Ian had left the table, "It's so awkward. I don't quite know what to do. I'm pretty sure I had a hundred and forty euros in my suitcase—I don't know how I happened to remember the amount. But now there's only eighty. Robin says just forget it, but I tend to think someone should tell Ian that one of his people is—can't entirely be trusted. But what if I'm mistaken? And it means so much less to me than to some poor person. I'm not sure what to do."

Of course I sympathized, but it seemed hard to imagine that the silent maids in their nunlike white wimples, white pants, and tunics would risk their jobs for sixty euros. In the end, Posy decided just to watch for a while. "They must imagine we don't notice, rolling in it as we are," she said with an ironical laugh. From her tone, I guessed the Crumleys could be hard up—that must be the poet's lot; people won't pay much for poetry.

I was shocked that the maids would steal from Posy, as if she were made more vulnerable by her pregnant state, though I knew she wasn't; I made a great mistake though, in thinking Posy had mentioned this to me as the de facto mistress of the place so I could deal with it. Dutifully, I asked to have a word with Miryam, who was in the kitchen. We stepped outside by the pool.

"Mrs. Crumley has lost some money," I said. "Perhaps you could help, if you have any ideas . . ." As soon as I began, I knew this was sounding tactless, hopeless, accusatory. She looked at me with fathomless eyes and said, "No, mademoiselle, how could I?"

Not wishing to ruin Posy's good rapport with the maids by suggesting she had complained of or accused them, I ended by practically begging Miryam to forget the whole thing. So much for my qualities as a law enforcer.

For my Taft reports, I spent a lot of time with the newspapers. I read two French-language ones, *Libération* and *L'Opinion,* carefully, all the way through, including all the ads, and still couldn't really tell what their politics were. I took note of odd events in my reports. Looked at in a certain way—with paranoid vigilance—there was a surprising number of possibly interesting events: small fires, assaults, explosions, even car thefts that could indicate the presence of terrorist cells or training facilities. I began to think of this as the meth lab or firework factory effect, inadvertent explosions. You never knew but looked for patterns. For instance, apart from Ian's explosion, there had now been two others—the first mentioned in news accounts of the fire in Ian's building, the second a few days later in a small sewing factory where the employees escaped unharmed. Was this a lot of fires for a small desert city? The analysts would know that; I didn't. I would also ask Colonel Barka.

Then there were a number of rather fascinating items too trivial to report, for instance that Marrakech was being visited by a party of Austrians fathered by Moroccans during the Second World War, now here trying to discover their roots. Also, in 1976—only thirty years ago!—in a small city near Meknes, a soldier noticed his mother "among the slaves of the mayor" and had to be restrained from trying to liberate her. He was sent to another city; the fate of the mother wasn't reported. I had to read this several times, trying to understand if *"esclave"* meant what we mean by "slave."

On the whole, with the library project and our social life, I was learning more about the dimensions of the international community than about the Moroccan. We belonged to the British part, but most of the foreigners in Morocco were French, Lebanese, or Egyptian, either businesspeople or the idle rich, and most of them had real lives in big cities somewhere else, usually Paris or Bordeaux, or London or Beirut, with Marrakech as their playground. There were a few Saudis, like the Al-Sayads. The French and British didn't seem to mingle much with each other, and there were very few Americans. Tom, Strand, and Habiba were about the only ones I knew.

I had several ideas about who among the people I had met could be involved in dark activities worth reporting. Khaled Al-Sayad was an obvious choice, if only because I started out with a built-in reflexive dislike of a man who would make his wife wrap up like a funerary statue. He also had a bank account in Morocco, was connected in the business community there and in the U.S., and had the ostensible front of an expensive second home outside of Saudi Arabia. I asked

Taft for information on him, but I didn't yet know much about the nature of his business; his card said he was in the Saudi Ministry of Defense and Aviation, rather chilling, considering 9/11, but he didn't seem to realize this. He talked of his indignation and of how, though the other bin Ladens were nice, no one in the family approved of bad seed Osama.

The other person I knew who most fulfilled the general conditions of having Western and Eastern contacts, Moroccan bank accounts, etc. was of course Ian. I couldn't imagine either of them abetting suicide bombers, but one thing you are taught is not to trust what you can or can't imagine; you learn that intuition has a role but does not replace facts and may mislead.

My intuition didn't mislead me, I think, in showing me how stupid I'd just been with Ian, despite my resolutions. He was in my room; we'd made love after a party in the medina and had lapsed into a kind of dreamy, erotic conversation afterward; and I found myself telling him how much I'd fallen in love, how much I loved him—stuff that was in my heart just then, fervent and surprising even to me.

He was sweet, of course, and, without saying he returned these sentiments, was reassuring about how delightful it was of me to say them.

"It makes me so happy to have you here, Lu. I'm so hoping you'll see the excitement and importance of this country. Our future—yours and mine—could be wonderful here. You'll see how you'll like it. I think you like it at moments already, right?" He smiled with this reference, I supposed, to our lovemaking.

But there had also been a moment of startled panic in his eyes—I don't think I'd imagined it.

19

Take a little dainty, hot, full-breasted thing, and you get all kinds of good information from her. You know—a tiny, soft little mouse. You can stretch your arm a long distance, through a woman.

—Maxim Gorky, *The Spy*

When I telephoned Taft, it was usually from the Mamounia hotel, from the public pay phones in the corridor outside the ladies' room, one-time events less traceable than cell phone records. I used a prepaid phone card and a different line each time, but we kept the conversations ambiguous in the assumption that all of them were tapped all the time. Posy and I had taken to going to the Mamounia for a drink at the end of the afternoon. Though I was always slightly bothered that Posy would drink alcohol in her condition, I was glad of a companion, and I somehow had the idea that if I was seen here on a regular basis, someone would eventually come up to me, or pass me a note, or I would see something revealing. I took to drinking tea instead of wine, for the sake of Posy's baby.

The Mamounia hotel is a venerable old place and a haven for foreigners, an open city where ethnicity is put aside and people of all religions suspend their antagonisms and even their dress codes in return for an ambiance of Europeanized, tranquil self-indulgence. The clientele was agreeably cosmopolitan and also neutral sexually: Pairs of people of any sex, women alone, men alone, mixed groups—all were perfectly proper, even in categories that might be viewed askance outside these walls. The hotel lay within the walls of the medina, in its own gardens of palms, magnolia, and hibiscus bushes where one might walk along the paths or sit on benches. Musicians in tuxedos, with the slicked-down hair of the lounge lizards in thirties movies, played Western music on the patio, and alcoholic drinks were served. Beyond the perimeter of the grounds or at the edges, the real Moroccans in their drab native costumes might have been hired to provide regional color.

Occasionally, Ian would meet us there, or perhaps Strand or Tom would stop in, taking turns away from their own place, and perhaps bringing the poised, serious little Amelie for an ice cream or lemonade. I also invited people to meet me there to discuss library development matters. I have mentioned that one day, from afar, Posy and I saw Gazi Al-Sayad, not wearing a head scarf, and for once without the black covering she usually wore in public. She was leaving in a rush, so we didn't call to her.

Gazi fascinated everyone—her beauty, her outbursts, the mystery of her willingness to wear the abaya, even of how she managed to keep the thing on, amazed me. Yet, over the weeks, I had grown used to seeing her in it, the way you get used to the green coat a friend always wears or a characteristic hat, and I stopped seeing it. She would come into a room and take it off, whereupon, instead of a symbol of female oppression, it became a limp square of black rayon, lying over the arm of a chair like a shawl, curiously inadequate to symbolize subjection or anything else.

Once she was unexpectedly sisterly and told Posy and me a little about her life. Posy had washed her hair—Posy has wonderful, long chestnut hair—and was drying it on the patio, and Gazi said, "Our mothers, or more our grandmothers—in their day the hair wasn't washed, it was oiled. By some strange chemistry, their hair was long and lovely, and not oily." I wondered if it was rude to ask whether her mother and grandmother had been plural wives. Probably they were. In the Louvre, I looked a lot at a painting by Ingres, of odalisques in their harem baths, with their jars of oils and myrrh. How sad to remember that the sultan was probably fat and ugly. I did think Khaled was better-looking than most Arab men, and better-looking in his tennis clothes than in his tablecloths. Probably that's just cultural conditioning, but Ian is still my idea of a handsome man. I wondered if Muslim men worried about whether they were attractive or not. Attractive from our point of view, I mean, of course. Probably they don't care, for their dominance is so total, they don't need to care. Looking at television of sheiks arriving at conferences or whatever, you can see they don't spend much time at the gym.

"It's funny, but she's actually a lot less conspicuous without her abaya," Posy observed later. "Maybe she wears it to get attention. The first time I saw women from Yemen—they're the ones that wear all black with the plastic mask like a beak; it was in Marks & Spencer—anyway, I screamed. They scared me."

We talked about how the horrible imams who made these poor

women dress in dismal black probably didn't realize how menacing they look to us, programmed as we are by the iconography of witches and Dracula's black cloak. Does Islam know that for us, wearing black is associated with crime and sluttiness? Might they really believe that wearing black is purer than pink or blue? I think you might arbitrarily adopt the custom of wearing black, but could you really believe it made you a better person? I see how you might believe that obedience makes you a better person, though. Nuns used to wear black in that spirit, I guess.

I have a belief problem of my own: I have trouble believing that people can really believe what they say they do—can they really believe, in their hearts of hearts, for example, that short sleeves showing a bit of elbow, or part of a lock of hair, can drive men mad and draw the wrath of God? In your heart of hearts would you feel purer wearing a head scarf? Eating fish on Fridays? What does "heart of hearts" even mean, except to acknowledge the secret reservations that lurk at one's center, unexamined, often not even by oneself?

Maybe skepticism is just a matter of temperament and blind faith does exist in some people, but I don't believe it, and I think if I could just believe one thing fervently, I would understand other people better, or at least I would know how it felt to believe in God, for example. But I never can seem to.

Poor Tom Drill, his was the lot of a wife. It took a lot of time, I could see, just organizing Amelie's social and educational life. Tom and Strand had been in Marrakech for eight years, all of Amelie's life. They had gotten her in Alabama as a newborn, from a private agency, and she was now eight.

"In those days, gay adoption? There was no way."

"Especially gay interracial adoption," Strand added.

"Nowadays it's probably easier in the States, no one thinks anything of it now. Here, though, the other kids still say things, like '*Regardez, Amelie et ses deux papas, hee hee hee.*' Amelie and her two dads. We make a point never to go to her school together."

I wondered what Amelie herself thought. "She thinks it's cool to have two dads," Tom said.

Most days Posy came with me to the tea shop or the hotel. A little tea and the reassuringly European ambiance of these places seemed to relax her. Apart from concern about Posy's reaction to the fumes of the fire—she was nauseated for several days afterward, whereas I felt fine—I had been worried about her general state of mind. At first I'd dismissed her as a regular, complacent English wife, but over the days, I'd gotten to know her better. I'd seen English wives, for instance at French ski resorts (for I'd had a season as a "chalet girl," that is, a maid, in Courchevel). Plumpish, with their beautiful skin, eyes trolling for different husbands—this more or less described Posy, though she was too pregnant, and too amazed by her status, to flirt with anyone but her husband, whom she was valiantly trying to interest.

I might have thought, if I'd met Robin Crumley without Posy, that he was gay, but often these things aren't quite one thing or the other. I had a feeling he was happy to have resolved his marital status and happy with impending fatherhood, but these states didn't interest him really. Marriage was like having your wisdom teeth pulled, just one more grown-up thing out of the way. He did sort of flirt with me, in the fashion of husbands of pregnant wives, but it was more out of a gallant, guestly commitment to general festiveness than anything personal.

But I had come to see that Posy was unhappy, or was beginning to be. Not a year ago she had been a husband-hunting yuppie with a boring job in a lingerie boutique in London, slightly in love, I gathered, with her brother-in-law, and depressed. Now she finds herself an in-cipient mother, married to a major English poet, marooned in Islam, and depressed. A strange progression of events, and some might have thought an improvement—I would, I think. But I wasn't sure she did, in her heart, though she said she did.

She didn't complain—it was her quality of inner restlessness that belied the stolidity of her expanding body. From one day to the next, she seemed to change dimensions, and her ankles were now the cir-cumference of Perrier bottles. She didn't ever even look at the baby clothes in the souk and seemed to make no plans, didn't have a list of names, didn't know the baby's gender. "Robin's in charge of naming it," she said, as if they'd never discussed it. "Being a poet, he'll have some lovely ideas."

She deferred to him, yet Robin didn't seem overbearing. In public, he was solicitous and fluttered around her. He did seem more inter-ested in Ian's social set and its doings than in the coming baby, but I have heard men only have a limited ability to empathize with gestation issues. I often sat next to him at dinner, where he was always vivacious, and once he startled me with an ambiguous brush of his hand across my thigh, probably accidental. He flirted with everyone, even Ian, so I told myself it was no more than his social manner.

One morning he emerged from his workroom, blinking slightly, as if the light of the patio hurt his pale eyes, and, seeing me, came and sat next to me at the breakfast table. Posy was not there, so he could talk about her. "It's nice of you, my dear, to spend so much time with Posy," he began. It irritated me to hear his patronizing tone about her, so I responded somewhat brusquely: a pleasure, Posy is so nice, so intelligent, etc. "Yes, she is, isn't she?" he said, in such an amazed way that I forgave him; he was just a somewhat obtuse man who was trying to do his best. "It's nice of Posy to spend so much time with me," I said.

I had considered whether it could be Robin Crumley who was some sort of spy or mole, whether for the British or an Islamic cause wasn't clear. He had exactly the educational profile of Kim Philby, and I had imbibed the institutional bias of my employers, that Brits were apt to be spies; it was they, after all, who had invented the term "double-cross" and its practice. But apart from the odd break during the day, he spent all his time in the workroom Ian had put at his disposal, writing poems, not out spying. In the few days that followed the fire, he was solicitous enough of Posy to satisfy even me. For, as I said, I had become fond of her, and protective.

Even though the shock and adjustment of marriage and motherhood, added to the culture shock of Morocco, had depressed her, even panicked her, at the Mamounia, diverted and away from the villa, she was calmer. We had long talks. She was interested in my affair with Ian—"He obviously is mad about you," etc. I loved Posy, but sometimes I envied her outspoken candor and her literary education, and sometimes I pitied her insecurity and restlessness; some inner instinct in me predicted that things would get worse for her when she had a baby and Robin was off giving readings and being lionized, and she would have to stay behind because it had chicken pox or something.

She must have sensed this herself, because something was still bothering her about her own life, and this was the day she brought it out. She told me with heavy sighs the one thing that had her very frightened about approaching motherhood: the fear that her baby would not have blue eyes.

"Blue eyes are recessive, you know. Any baby of Robin's and mine would have blue eyes. But . . ."

But she had had a little one-night stand just before meeting her husband, with a brown-eyed guy.

"It's awful, when I look back on it. It was a frantic period in my life, I was just bloody out of control."

I didn't think she should worry. "What are the odds?" I said. "These things aren't so cut-and-dried. A brown-eyed man could have had a blue-eyed parent. . . ." We contemplated the dismaying Mendelian absolutes.

"Sometimes I see it so clearly, I've ruined my life, and there's no way out of it," Posy cried.

20

Besides Posy's despair, another domestic drama manifested itself, chez Sir Neil and Lady Cotter. We had been seeing a lot of the Cotters. There were slight tensions over this. I had realized that Posy Crumley didn't much like them, but I did. I liked their utter willingness to behave like caricatures of English people abroad, complete with big sun hats, murmuring the expressions "I say" and "Jolly good." "I say, this modern music, yes, I'm talking about Berg and Webern, it's rubbish, no one likes to say so, but we all know it's rubbish."

I thought of Posy's attitude toward Marina Cotter as some sort of British class thing not apparent to me, though Posy was herself a perfectly upper-middle-class girl who had been to Oxford or Cambridge—I immediately forgot which when she told me and now of course couldn't ask. These lapses of attention reflected poorly on my abilities as an observer and cost me much private shame.

It became clear soon enough that the Cotters didn't really like me. Maybe they just didn't like Americans—that was bound to be part of it. But there was something personal that surprised me, since I am pretty harmless, I would have thought. To me they imputed all the faults of my nation, made explicit by assuring me I didn't have them: "Oh, you've read Lytton Strachey? Really! Do you read much of our literature? That's unusual for an American! Good for you!" And they seemed to find quite a few faults of my own, for instance with my clothes: "One day we'll have a shopping day in Guéliz—I know it's hard to find suitable clothing in the souk. I admire you for being so relaxed about dress." I pretended not to notice these criticisms, but I did notice them and hoped they didn't say things like that to Ian about me. What was wrong with my clothes?

"I don't know if Suma is going to work out," said Marina Cotter one day out of the blue. We were at our library, pasting little registers in the backs of books, for checking them in and out. (This was to be on the honor system, though, as we didn't envision having a librarian. Honor had worked well enough for the bookshelf at Tom's Tea Cosy.) "She seems so unhappy. It would help if I could talk to her, but my French is idiotic, it's not up to a heart-to-heart talk. Neil's is better, he can talk to her a bit, but he has so little insight into a young Muslim woman."

I was curious to know what the problems were.

"For one thing, she doesn't seem to know a thing about children. Rose and Freddie, our grandchildren, are traumatized, of course, after their mother's death; they need understanding and consistency. But she doesn't really interact with them. It could be the language, of course. And she is unduly hard on Rose, makes her do this and that, and then lets Freddie get away with murder, and I can't seem to make her understand that we treat all children the same in a Western household. It's like a story: Rose is Cinderella or something, and frankly, Freddie is a bit of a little beast anyway; he doesn't need more spoiling."

"But what happens?"

"For instance, though Rose is older, she is sent to bed first and Freddie can stay up, usually till I come in and send him to bed. You can imagine how this goes down with Rose. Or if they're playing a board game, she makes Rose clean it up and put it away. He gets first pick of things to eat—so many of our ways are unexamined till you see them done differently."

I had suggested that Ian, with his diplomatic manners, be the one to explain Western child-rearing practices to Suma, or at least to charm her out of her reserve, but that had been vetoed, on the grounds that she would be wary of a man. She avoided Neil Cotter very pointedly for the same reason. "She won't even be in the same room. It's hard to believe she went to a French lycée," Marina said. "And she makes everything stop while she does her praying, and she always has her nose in the Koran, but I think it's a way of getting out of helping."

But as events proved, Ian's intervention wasn't necessary anyway, because a solution was already under way.

There was far more difference in age between Marina and me than between Suma and me, and Marina must have thought Suma and I had become friends, though we hadn't, really. I had talked to her often, and even heard, more or less, her life story, after she had settled in and become more comfortable with the strange adults who now made up her circle of protectors. But she was always reserved. I now resolved to be nicer to Suma and make more of an effort to find out her thoughts—which is what I think Marina was hoping for. But Suma appeared to mistrust me—maybe it was my American accent.

"I think of myself as Algerian and French," she had told me once. She'd been born in France but then raised until the age of twelve in Algeria, after which her parents came back to France to escape mounting fundamentalist violence down there. Her father was retired and wanted to be a security guard, "but you would need a dog.

"My mother wouldn't have a dog in our small apartment, it's forbidden where there are prayers. So he doesn't work."

She had two older sisters and two brothers—an older one and the one who had not believed in her virginity. "It was Amid who watched us; my older brother was in college."

"Watched you? Babysat?"

"More or less. *Plus ou moins.* Protected us and kept us in, or went with us when we went somewhere."

"As if you might lose your virginity on the way to the store?"

"*Plus ou moins.* But you don't really understand," she said. "It's also about what others will think. If you just come and go, and no one cares what you do, how can they be sure?"

"The wedding-night bloody sheet?"

"Voilà," she said.

I tried to imagine how she, and families like hers, negotiated the difference between the freedom and autonomy of French girls and an adolescence spied on by your brothers. The idea of your virginity being of public concern I found odious, even upsetting, though I know hers is, worldwide, the most common view, bowing to some sort of testosterone-driven instinct of men to want to know their progeny is theirs. That hardly excuses it though. Especially now with DNA tests.

"I don't believe in making women stay in," she said, "but unless you have someplace you have to go, it's just easier than fighting with your brothers or whoever. It doesn't hurt you to tell them where you're going."

I tried to imagine telling my brother whenever I went someplace; how irritating he'd find it. My conversations with Suma had all broken up like this when I couldn't believe girls would put up with the kinds of restrictions she described, and in Paris, France, at that, and I would begin to wax indignant. I don't think she herself believed in purdah, but it was a sort of family defensiveness—a group that didn't like outsiders and Christians saying the things they could say privately among themselves. Yet it was a fact that there were women kept in purdah in France, here, everywhere.

"My friend Fatima was married, and once she was married she never went out. This is in Marseilles. She has to peek out through the blinds," Suma said.

We soon found out that Suma's situation at the Cotters' was resolving by itself—that is, by herself and the Al-Sayads' Filipina maid, Marcia. The two girls often met to allow Rose and the Al-Sayad little girl to play together, and apparently they talked, in what language I can't imagine, with the result that Suma eventually proposed to Marina and Gazi that she, Suma—who had passed the bac, was Muslim, and liked office work and computers—go to the Al-Sayads' to work as their secretary, and Christian Marcia, who was fond of children and child care, would work for the Cotters.

There was much discussion over several days and a sense of astonishment that these docile girls would initiate such a proposal. But it was fine with the Al-Sayads, who had other servants to look after their kids and were happy to have an educated assistant who could type and speak Arabic and French. Marcia was delighted to be in a Christian household, and the Cotters were delighted to have a more experienced nanny, especially one with the legendary Filipino warmth.

"Suma is fine, at least for the summer. I doubt she will want to go with us back to Riyadh," Gazi had laughed.

Until this happened, Posy had been apt to go on about how Suma was being exploited by the Cotters, though Suma didn't seem to feel injured and was evidently being included in family outings and doings, like a *jeune fille* au pair is supposed to be. Now Posy began to speculate on Suma's fate at the hands of Khaled Al-Sayad. I did wonder whether the Al-Sayads had mistreated Marcia, but presumably if so, they wouldn't have relinquished her so easily to tell the tale.

21

The tale goes, that on a certain day, Abd-el-Melik ben Merouane went to see Leilla, his mistress, and put various questions to her. Amongst other things, he asked her what were the qualities which women looked for in men.

Leilla answered him: "Oh, my master, they must have cheeks like ours." "And what besides?" said Ben Merouane. She continued: "And hairs like ours; finally they should be like to you, O prince of believers, for, surely, if a man is not strong and rich he will obtain nothing from women."

—Sheik Nefzaoui, *The Perfumed Garden*

These days, also colored in ways I have merely touched on by the long, drawn-out aftermath of the explosion—investigations, reports, assessments, papers—coincided with the visit of Ian's father, Lord Drumm. Posy was excited. This person, well-known in England, had a reputation, apparently, for thunder and mischief, which she hoped to experience or see. From Ian's apprehensiveness, I thought it might be true that we were in for an upheaval—or was it just that Posy and I, like long-term prisoners, were thrilled by the arrival of anybody new? Nancy Rutgers and her David had left, and we expected a new artist, a French painter, whose works were fiercely scorned by the Crumleys. Nancy left a blank, because she was always opinionated on bookish subjects or art and could argue vigorously for or against any particular work. "*Gone with the Wind* is a great masterpiece," she might say, and give her reasons, and would always prevail, because Robin, Posy, and Ian wouldn't have read it. One of our fiercest arguments concerned her pronouncement "The Islamic world is backward because it has no art."

Robin Crumley said, "They have poets," as if poets were a precondition for civilization and sufficient unto themselves.

"But all those poets lived five hundred years ago."

"So did Homer, Shakespeare, and Milton," said Robin.

"Homer lived five thousand years ago, not five hundred," said Posy, closing the matter, though we wrangled on.

Ian clearly dreaded his father's visit but in another way was really into it. For the first time since I had come, he took to hanging around the kitchen, talking to Miryam, who ran it, I suppose about menus. I'd been so rebuffed by Miryam I no longer tried to venture into a discussion about *poulet muhammara,* or lentils versus tabbouleh, or which lamb dish should be served, but of course Miryam had to listen to Ian and I sometimes gave him my views. I was wounded but not surprised when he once said, "Dearest Lu, don't worry about the food, the menus—these people love doing it and they are really competent."

We went to a restaurant one night to listen to the wild music of a group that played there so Ian could decide whether to hire them for his banquet. He wondered if he should find a belly dancer. Apparently this was not a common Moroccan dance form, but he had fond memories of it. I soon realized this must be because it was associated with a family time, before the divorce of his parents.

"He took Ralph and me—oh, and Mother was there too. We went

to see a belly dancer, when I was about eight; we were in Beirut. Of course I've never forgotten it! He was a passionate Arabophile in those days. He might get a kick out of remembering that. We'll look for a nice fat one—a sweaty, wriggly, real one."

"It's a fad among wives in England to take belly dancing lessons," Posy said. We had seen the costumes in the souk, spangly bras and low-rise shimmering skirts, bringing the vision of a nation of tourist ladies covertly undulating in the privacy of their homes.

"Don't think of it, Lu," he said, smiling, though I found it a somewhat wounding caution.

"You have to be fat," he added. "I'm sure you'll like him," he said grimly, thinking of his father again.

When I saw Ian's father, I had the impression I knew him already; he looked exactly like an Ingres portrait I'd often seen in the Louvre, of a nineteenth-century person named Bertin, a short, stocky man in a waistcoat and watch chain, strangely small hands ranged on his knees and a confident, cynical, wily expression—a twentieth-century face, unlike the usual faintly period faces surmounted by strange locks of hair you see in old portraits. I've heard the Ingres described as depicting "the triumph of the bourgeoisie." Bertin was a publisher, which I had understood Ian's father to be, but it turned out he was in hotels and freeway restaurants, a triumph of the bourgeoisie.

Ian was the second son of Lord Drumm's first wife, who got dumped along the way, with the usual repercussions for the children of first marriages, technically in the loop but removed from their father and made to listen to many recitations of his weak points: bad temper, imperious and controlling nature, coldness, etc. None of these qualities was noticeable during the visit.

After university, Ian, like his older brother, had gone to work for their father, but it didn't suit Ian. His brother has risen to vice president of the thriving empire. Ian was staked to another start in life, made conservative investments and bought property in Morocco, a place he'd been taken on vacation as a child by his father. It was an irony that now he ran his villa like a hotel and was even building a small, ritzy guesthouse in the Atlas Mountains. Lots of people have had worse starts, but there was friction, and I supposed Ian had good reasons to dread his father's visit. It was almost endearing to see his nervous concern.

One of the first things we did was take Lord Drumm—Geoff ("Do call me Geoff, Lulu")—to see the site of the fire. Why dead embers should have fascination I don't know, but I have heard that people went to see the ruins after 9/11 in the same spirit, hoping somehow to feel the impact of a mighty event they suspect has not really touched them enough. As we had seen several times, the factory was completely destroyed, and a question remained about the cause.

"The insurance was ruinous, but it was insured, at least. It remains to be seen if they'll pay," Ian was saying to his father. Whether insurance would pay or not would depend on the nature of the explosion—an act of terrorism would not be covered, falling into the same category as an act of God, or, I suppose, Allah. Negligence would also rule out payment of the claim. Ian didn't think the fire was an act of terrorism, but Rashid did, talking to Posy and me.

"Moroccans are like chickens, we cover with shit every branch we roost on." He was speaking French, so it didn't sound as strong a way of speaking to two strange ladies as it does in English: *"Nous emmerdons nos nids."*

Ian's father reproved him for being in the factory-leasing line. "Was it wise to lease to these people? They don't have the same business ethics we do. That's a nice site, lovely view—you'd have done better to stick with the hotel idea."

"Too isolated for a hotel," said Ian defensively. "Originally there were to have been better roads up here, but the ministry stiffed me there."

If Ian deferred to his father, it was interesting to see how Lord Drumm in turn deferred to Robin Crumley, talking to him, or, more noticeably, listening to him, which he didn't appear to do to anyone else. It made one aware of Robin's stature in England, and this pleased Posy, as if she needed reminding that her hero retained his fame even if, pale and blinking in the strong Moroccan sun, he had lost some glamour in her own eyes.

"What do you say, Crumley, about the schools' bill? It sounds like bringing back the eleven-plus to me. Is that a good thing?"

"I was a lad who benefited from the eleven-plus," Robin said. "People forget about the boys that were saved by it. What was nonsense about it was its inflexibility, not taking into account the late bloomers."

"Hmm. I was a late bloomer, Ian also." Ian looked surprised at this, either that his father thought him a late bloomer or that he had bloomed. For me, seeing Ian in this family context was endearing, or at least revealing, a strong man disconcerted by his father. Ian's mother lived in Cannes. I wondered if I'd ever meet her. Normally I don't daydream, but it did cross my mind to wonder if Ian had mentioned me to his father as someone he might marry.

With all the preplanning, the banquet went off without a hitch, the epitome of sultry orientalist glamour. All the torchères on the patio were lit, and also on the paths in the garden. Low glass lanterns with candles in them flickered under bushes, servants stole silently around with trays, and the musicians crouched in the driveway waiting for their cue to come in with the wild music. The air was perfumed with cumin and coriander, the characteristic smell of the whole country. This was a theatrical side of Ian (if not the advice of some interior decorator; I would later find out it was Nancy's friend, David) that I hadn't guessed at. The atmosphere of performance was enhanced by a troupe of drummers and dancers, who throbbed and spun at high volume. They seemed almost unendurably loud, so I was reassured my ears hadn't been damaged by my teenage disco years after all. The thirty guests, French, English, and Moroccan, were dressed to the teeth in silk and jewels.

Lord Drumm—Geoff—stayed only two days. On one of them, the Cotters had a dinner for him, with several Moroccan dignitaries—the honorary British consul in Marrakech, the ubiquitous Colonel Barka, us, the Crumleys, and a French diplomat, M. de Fruiteville, who sat on Marina's left. Ian's father was on her right, and I was next to him. Though heretofore I hadn't had any extended conversations with Ian's father, now I could not avoid it. Almost immediately, he turned to me and said, "This president of yours is a fine fellow!" The intonation of his voice, exactly neutral, with not a trace of positive inflection or of sarcasm, left me uncertain of what I ought to say—for I was never going to quarrel with Ian's father.

"Our presidents are uniformly fine fellows," I said. He probably didn't understand my tone any more than I his, for he dropped the subject of American presidents and went on, "Met Ian in Kosovo, he said."

"Yes, in Pristina, when he was working with Oxfam."

"Social worker you are, I guess."

"Not really," I said. "I just wanted to do something to . . ." Absolute silence, a remark to Marina on his other side, then back to me:

"Do you plan to go on in that line? Have you moved here permanently? Lots to be done here, I'm told." I told him about female literacy and the library, which obviously bored him utterly, but careful to preserve his reputation for great charm, he managed to make me feel it was fascinating—quite a reverse of the usual dinner table pattern in which the young woman would be fascinated with the important older man. He was apparently beyond susceptibility to the flattery of young women, his mind in some realm of megaplayers and world profit. So far was he above this present scene that his squat and bulky little presence seemed incorporeal, his merely material paternal incarnation, with his real self off in some archetypal boardroom. I could see why Ian was daunted by this frightening parent.

When he gave me his actual attention, I sensed it was because he was wondering about my relationship to Ian. Was I just a hot number? A serious candidate for Ian's wife? A good future mother of his grandchildren? I felt the intensity of his unacknowledged scrutiny; so unlike that by a potential mother-in-law, it seemed to include a fertility assessment, an I.Q. test, and, possibly, a sort of sexual scoring system, checking out the bosom, thighs, etc.—all this without there being anything rude in it. At the same time he was taciturn and lordly. Over dessert, he said, "Do you like Morocco, Miss Sawyer? Could you envision living in London eventually?

"I nourish the hope that Ian will come back to England someday," he added.

I thought about this a lot, later. It could have been a question that took for granted my involvement with Ian in the future and implied that he imagined my feelings for England would have some weight or importance. It made me almost sure, but not quite, that I was being looked over as a wife.

What would it be like to live with Ian in England, not a country I know much about except as a tourist? Would he be different? People often seem different when you meet them in a new place. They seem different in the night too. Ian, in his villa, distracted with projects and the duties of a host, and, this week anyhow, a son, was different from the more physical and more carefree Bosnian aid worker.

I would always look forward to the moment at night when Ian came into my room, so that the twenty-two hours of the day and night seemed to hang on two, a sequence that seemed badly askew; and yet I accepted this rhythm. We didn't always make love; often we just gossiped about the others and talked over the news of the day, almost as we used to do. After we had made love in Pristina, we had often talked into the wee hours, gossiping about colleagues, with recipes to remedy the world. Now he tended to go to his own room, mentioning things he had to do in the morning or the narrowness of the bed. His ardor was there but confined to our lovemaking itself.

I'm not among those women who regret that men don't share their feelings—I appreciate it, mainly (declarations of love excepted). I prefer third topics when they're interesting, on the subject of art or Moroccan development. But now I did wish he weren't so reserved. He wasn't reserved in bed, of course, but full of affection that seemed not to influence his conduct at other times or soften his demeanor of stiffish charm to one and all.

Sometimes, awakened by the first calls to prayer at about four, lying uneasily awake, I could hear that he was up too, but he never came in at that time.

But in truth, I found myself wishing we were back in Pristina, where we were both hardworking volunteers and we conducted our trysts in one or another of our uncomfortable quarters and ate the bad food at the one restaurant we could stand, snatching at moments of pleasure with a sense of gratitude. Here, all was pleasure, or at least leisure, almost cloying in its abundance.

Of course it was often on my mind how Ian himself was well-placed to be the conduit or recipient of knowledge, or of money to launder. Who better? He knew everyone, had a big safe in his office, and came and went mysteriously. But it was inconceivable that he could be connected to a terrorist network or an ideology of any kind, and withstood my disloyal scrutiny perfectly.

On the nights I went up early, skipping the long after-dinners, I had also read *The Perfumed Garden,* which was among the books on the shelves of the main living room downstairs. I was familiar with this work, because in Kosovo I had read Ian's complete series of Anthony Powell's novels *A Dance to the Music of Time,* wherein Jenkins, the hero, reads it under its subtitle: *The Arab Art of Love.* It made me laugh to think that Ian had acquired the original work itself, and of course I was interested to see what it said. It says such things as, "Thus it will be well to play with her before you introduce your verge. You will excite her by kissing her cheeks, sucking her lips and nibbling at her breasts. You will lavish kisses on her navel and thighs, and titillate the lower parts. Bite at her arms, and neglect no part of her body; cling close to her bosom and show her your love and submission." Of course I did wonder if all this was happening in all the nuptial chambers of Marrakech. Do the tired-looking donkey drivers remember all these steps? Do they apply to Englishmen? It did seem that, while perfectly done, Ian's version was quite a lot plainer.

22

Inside its cocoon of work or social obligation, the human spirit slumbers for the most part, resisting the distinction between pleasure and pain, but not nearly as alert as we pretend.

—E. M. Forster, *A Passage to India*

I had been in Marrakech three months, though it seemed in some ways longer. Because of the utter strangeness of the culture, I still had so much to learn—to bargain, for instance. I still felt impatience and resentment, but at least now I had learned to do it, the head shaking, the little movement as if to walk away, the proffering of a ridiculous price. At Ian's villa, we continued the routine of days occupied in visits, banal conversations, tracking the little vendettas (as between Posy and Marina) that seem to animate any small community. It did seem that the Europeans there lived in a parallel universe, served by under-beings in caftans who consented to cross over into ours, as in the time of the raj, or maybe it was like a film, with costumed extras bringing tea and speaking among themselves in a secret dialect.

In my role of tourist, I photographed groups of people at the Mamounia and people sitting alone or walking in the gardens. No one seems to mind you pointing your little camera at them, and if they did, or ducked their heads, I made extra sure to get them. These photos I sent to Taft/Sheila. I also photographed extensively in the souk, especially groups of men if they were young. Some of these photos I sent home to my real family too, who enthused about the exotic sights I was seeing, could imagine camels and sand.

I had had tea at the Mamounia regularly with Cousin Alice/ Habiba, to hear about Moroccan literacy and suspicious donations, and on these occasions she had talked very willingly about how she had run away to Mecca, now thirty-five years ago. She was a Sufi, and when she explained Sufism to me, I understood it; it was all the things people believed in at the time of my birth—hippies, and people going to India to find enlightenment, LSD and such—people you still saw in Santa Barbara bookshops, wearing love beads and mandala pendants, and now white beards. My stepmother, according to her, had been a hippie. How odd to think that she and my father, who'd been in the ROTC and then the air force, were now a harmonious couple with congruent worldviews.

"Islam is the most beautiful of all the major religions," she said. "Sufi prayers are incomparable." She scorned my questions about dervishes but offered one standard explanation of the basic beliefs of this sect, about a flame. You can be told about the flame, or you can see it, or you can touch it and be burned. "The Sufis seek to be burned, to have direct experience. I'm afraid I'm not as involved as I once was, but we do pray. Real life impedes mysticism. My husband is more pious than I." In fact, she seemed the soul of piety, with the fussiness of the convert, making sure that the sandwich was halal—from an herbivore slaughtered in just such a way, a way you didn't like to think of, actually, like kosher—and never having a drop of alcohol.

I asked about her husband—he worked as a biologist for the Moroccan government.

"We were impressed with the accuracy of the Koranic cosmology," Habiba said. "As early as the seventh century, there was an accurate description of the origin of things. The sky: 'We built it with might and we cause the expansion of it.' All the Koranic ideas are more or less confirmed by modern physics. Unlike those of the Bible. Since we were both scientists, that was important to us." I wasn't informed enough to conduct much more of a discussion about this.

"The Koran has a more intelligent idea of God," she said. " 'He begets not, nor is he begotten.' No nonsense about 'only begotten son' or the Trinity. God is a first principle, not a person."

"What about Allah? They imagine him smiting and so on. 'Inshallah.' He has views."

"Unfortunately it's a human tendency to reduce things to a level we can understand. I've never liked it," she said dismissively.

Habiba ran a large literacy program to teach adult women to read. I got the impression that non-Moroccans, especially the French, ran a lot of things in Morocco. It was hard to imagine back to the days when the opposite was true, when it was Islam in power and resplendent Moroccan pashas were waited on by European slaves snatched by North African pirates from the decks of English ships or even from the streets of European cities.

The second time we visited her program, a woman from the Moroccan government came with us. We drove about forty-five minutes to a village, watched some stout, beaming women pore over their books, smiling with vast friendliness and passing over their notebooks for us to see. When we left, the government woman said, "I will tell you my point of view, and you can report it. I see no reason at all to teach these women of forty or more to learn to read. It's a waste of resources—of money and teachers. What are they going to read? How will it change their lives? Don't tell me it will help them know their rights. We have the Moudawana theater for that, and most of them aren't interested anyway. They've raised their children, their daughters are long since married. Teach the grandchildren, start there."

I couldn't see any arguments on Habiba's side, except the vague philosophical one to do with the richness of life experience, and felt the harshness of the government lady's judgment that an older woman couldn't be made happier by knowing things, by finding new things to know, even practical things—remedies and crafts. In Santa Barbara, my stepmother and her friends are forever enrolling in new classes and they get very excited. But I know it isn't the same here. Half the men here can't read either. Why shouldn't everybody learn?

Suma Bourad, at the Al-Sayads', moved back and forth uneasily between the European and the Moroccan worlds. She found she was too French for some things, and she stopped making an effort to make Moroccan friends among most of the girls who came to help in the kitchens or with the gardening. For one thing, they were too ignorant and lazy, as far as she could see, and they described outrages, such as sisters or mothers kept in purdah, that were worse than anything in France. On the other hand, our world was strange because it wasn't French, and above all it was adult. We were not her nationality or religion or age group. She did have one sort of sidekick, a Moroccan girl of about twelve or thirteen, in school clothes—long socks and pleated skirt, and a navy scarf on her hair. It was her job to run after the children for Suma and the nanny. She was called Desi—I never heard another name.

Since Suma had been with the Al-Sayads, I'd noticed a change in her clothes. Where before she had worn a simply tied scarf over her head, this headscarf was now black, with a blue one worn underneath, tucked up under her chin, though she didn't wear an abaya as the Saudi women did. No doubt the scarf was in deference to the Saudi customs in the new household, but it made her seem to be sliding toward Saudi fundamentalism, though I had never detected any religiosity in the Al-Sayads. (The nanny wore a full Islamic costume of black.)

Suma's manner, however, was normal. We'd discuss things—whether it was hard to be a Muslim in France (sort of, or no, if you didn't make waves), or her plans to go to medical school in Montpellier in the autumn next year. She worried about this. She would ordinarily have been in a preparatory class for the entrance exams. The odds against succeeding were huge. A thousand people would start in the freshman class, but only two hundred would finish, and she would have to work at some part-time job to pay her room and board. "My parents will help if they can," she said, "but they aren't really in favor of women's education, or only up to a point, and being a doctor, horrors, what intimate, nasty things will be required of me?" I planned to speak to Ian about us possibly subsidizing Suma a little bit.

Conscious of educational hardships, Suma interested herself in Desi's schooling. "She can read," she told me. "She's been to school, and I hope she can go back. She's from a village where she was the only girl in the school, and the reason in her case is that someday she'll have to take care of her mother, who has some kind of wasting disease, and no one will marry her, given the handicap of her mother.

"The Al-Sayads don't pay the help when they're away in Saudi Arabia, and the Moroccans think that's normal," she added. I could imagine how shocking that was to someone raised in France.

"What about you? What about your brother? Won't you be in danger if you go back to France? What's to stop him from going to Montpellier and tracking you down?"

She shrugged. "I've written them the truth. I think they will hear it." I wasn't sure; we all know that abused women often give the abuser the benefit of the doubt, frequently to their cost. It made one think about the head scarf issue too; odd that it has to bear such a lot of symbolic freight, for Suma perhaps symbolizing piety, for Posy (and me) female submission. Suma said, "I'd never be submissive to a man, never! It is a sign for God." With nuns, no one thought about the veil, and now it was a principal article in dealing with vast political questions, such as Turkey joining the European Union.

"I think getting out of Paris is the most important thing," she added. "Out of sight, out of mind. Maybe I will find someone to marry on my own, and it will be a marriage of love."

Apropos of intimate nastiness, I suffered the eavesdropper's fate for the first and less important of the two occasions that were to shock me. One day, coming down from my room, I paused in the open arch of the stairwell to gaze over the gardens, and voices drifted up from the patio, Posy and Marina Cotter talking, not about me but about Nancy Rutgers. But the implications were for me.

"It can't have been easy for Nancy—the arrival of Lulu," said Marina. "She couldn't wait to get out of here."

"I think Lulu is the better suited to Ian, don't you?" said Posy. That, at least, was a response friendly to me.

"No, I don't think mixed relationships work out in the long run. Nancy is Ian's nationality, religion, and, frankly, milieu. And I don't see Lulu as a wife and mother. And, after all, she's American. I think that was his father's view too."

"Did he say that?"

"Not in so many words. I could see he didn't quite approve. He seemed quite affected by the situation."

"Luckily, whatever his father ordains, Ian will be sure to do the opposite," said Posy, as if she'd known him a long time. They both laughed. Mentally thanking Posy for her loyalty in not endorsing Marina's views, I waited a moment or two on the stair so that I couldn't be thought to have heard them.

Actually, I was startled. Nancy Rutgers a former girlfriend or pretender to a place of some kind in Ian's life? I had seen nothing of this, obvious though it now seemed. There had been absolutely no detectable behavior, of Ian toward Nancy or vice versa, that could have hinted at anything between them. No glances, not even any particular familiarity—that I'd noticed. What shocked me was my own failure to pick up anything. They had never even seemed to speak, and Nancy was always dashing around with David. Yet again, I was stupefied by my own deficient powers of observation, or the power of my hopes to drown out common sense. But this was a mild shock compared to what was to come.

23

One day soon after this, I was to meet Colonel Barka at the Sidi-Ali Restaurant, which was far out of town but had, he said, a special almond soup, *luz shorba,* and was in an eighteenth-century palace well worth seeing. The Crumleys were not coming, and they needed Rashid to take them to some social engagement, so I went by taxi, deeply preoccupied by the literacy situation, barely noticing the route, into an area of increasingly squalid houses—more washing hung outside, more animals in the street, the air of real life far from the detached remoteness of the Palmeraie.

"You get out here, mademoiselle," said the taxi man, pulling into an alley piled with cardboard boxes and cartons. "The boy will conduct you." This disconcerted me, but it was true that someone from the restaurant, carrying a staff like a tour leader and wearing a tall fez, was waiting in the rubble of a vacant lot, with two other Western-looking tourists, who smiled at me, plainly relieved that other Europeans had made their way to this forlorn spot. We waited in silent collegiality until three more plump, pink Europeans were delivered by taxi, then we all followed the fez into the warren of tiny streets too narrow for cars, exchanging pleasantries.

The restaurant, in an old palace, was furnished in the Moroccan style with low tables and chairs, rugs, decorative hookahs and brass vessels and drums, and elaborate tiles in a beautiful design without beginning or end, to illustrate the infinitude of Allah's will or being. There was the inevitable plashing of a fountain. Someone immediately stepped up to me and greeted me with a bow—Colonel Barka, who had been waiting just inside the door, his wonderful silver mustache larger than ever.

"So nice to see you, my 'Angel.'" He smiled. "I've asked for a little niche to ourselves. I hope you won't feel too compromised." I did, slightly, as this was our first public meeting without Posy or someone else present, and his tone was suddenly intimate and melodious. We were taken to sit on divans at a table in a curtained alcove of a balcony, with a good view of the main room below. With great deliberation, Colonel Barka settled us, deployed social pleasantries, ordered a bottle of Moroccan wine, and suggested several items from the menu. I accepted his suggestions with my usual passivity when faced with Moroccan dishes.

"I have a little something for you," he said at last. "As you know, we are most vigilant here. The attempts to kill the present king's father, Hassan II, can never be far from the mind of loyal Moroccans.

His precious son is well-protected, as you can imagine. But it was his own officers that conspired against Hassan II. Chased his airborne plane with fighters . . ."

"I've read about it, of course," I said. I took him to mean, probably, that they, and perhaps we, were anticipating some attempt on Mohammed VI, or else they were planning to do it. Or they were thinking we were planning to do it—we have a certain track record. When he said, "I have something for you," he of course meant, what did I have for him on this subject?

"The new king is much loved, I gather."

"The military—the air force—is no longer a problem."

"Purged."

"Yes. And of course the climate is different today. This king is a reformer." I had heard that this king was growing harsh, and even, as a symptom of covert antipathy, rumors that he was gay, but it didn't seem tactful to ask about that.

"Basically they're all gay—that is, there's a cultural difference about it," Strand had said. "As long as you're the active one, you aren't really gay."

Just then, as the waiter came in with the wine, he drew the curtain back in such a way that we could for a moment glimpse into a curtained niche opposite, across the well where the balcony continued on the other side, draped in its turn but open enough to reveal an unforgettable tableau: Ian and Gazi Al-Sayad having lunch and looking at each other with the limpid urgency of lovers. They were laughing, and as I watched, before the curtain fell back to hide them again, Gazi touched her fingers to her lips, then pressed her fingertips to the palm of Ian's hand and twisted them, with the action of stubbing out a cigarette.

At this astounding sight, I had the visceral feeling of dread you have at a doctor's office when you just know he is about to announce you have leukemia, or in the rising headlights of a car in an intersection, or at the moment of falling, a sickening moment of fear when doom is imminent. Why hadn't I seen this? How was I to get through life when I hadn't understood the slightest things?

Another line from the manual: "Intraspecific deception is generally observed in connection with the reproductive process." I have often wondered about that. I suppose the translation is: Fucking and lying go together. Colonel Barka saw Gazi and Ian too. He touched my arm and gave me a pitying, surprised look and said, "Hmm." Later I would wonder how surprised he could have been, how unlikely that we should just happen upon this by accident.

"I am at your service," said the waiter. "Will the lady also have wine?"

"Did you know about this?" I asked.

"Yes," he said to the waiter. "No," said the colonel, looking pityingly at me. "I brought you here because it is a place nobody goes." He laughed at the irony of this, and his hand on my arm became a restraint. "This is not the place, perhaps, to enact the scene you may envision." But I wasn't envisioning a scene. Did he expect me to fly like a tiger at Gazi? My mind was still ricocheting among explanations, all of them terrible.

"Give us a few minutes before bringing the wine," said the colonel to the waiter, and to me he said, "They must not see us." This was the first time I realized that the colonel must have thought I was stupid. Of course they must not see us.

Like lovers; that was my first impression of them, but less painful explanations soon began to line up in my mind: It was possible they, Ian and Gazi, might be talking about Suma. I had never discussed

Suma with Colonel Barka; I knew the Suma situation had no bearing on the funding of a ring of martyrs or saboteurs or whatever we found in that line. Yes, they were there to talk about the Suma situation, Gazi's little gesture was of solidarity, sealing their determination to protect the girl.

Or she was planning a surprise for Khaled's birthday. There was probably some simple explanation.

"I think Khaled is having a birthday . . . ," I said. Gazi's little gesture seemed to make believing that impossible, though, paradoxically, it was the gesture, thinking about it later, as the burning sight eased from my memory, that reassured me. It was the gesture of a conspirator; it wasn't erotic.

One of my manuals advised "studied unconventional thinking" for perceived events. It advised trying to look at things as would a cryptologist or game theorist, as would paranoids, confidence men, magicians, and financial swindlers. I tried to explain Ian and Gazi from these other points of view. But paranoids (me) and confidence men (Colonel Barka?) seemed apposite. A confidence man might try to convince me they were discussing ways of hiding Suma. A paranoid would suspect an affair.

Second thoughts: I should have gone to speak to them. To have been there without showing myself was sneaky and wrong. Gradually, these self-reproaches began to damp my indignation, though I knew it would flare up and change to fury if I let myself think of, for instance, *The Perfumed Garden*. Arab women must read that book too. I thought of the ugly parts that show how Arab men hate women, hate women's anatomy and hate their own need for women. Such thoughts led back to the natural fact that a Saudi wife would value an English lover, someone who liked women (though misogyny is relative, and Ian was still an

Englishman, thus slightly less convinced than, say, a Frenchman of woman's worth). Still, judging from its place on the bookshelf, Ian had also
read in *The Perfumed Garden* such things as remedies for a wide vagina
(the "greatest of evils") or "Things That Take Away the Bad Smell from
the Armpits and Sexual Parts of Women and Contract the Latter." Naturally, my mind did not rise to extensive quotation at this moment; too
much was spinning through it. Perhaps Ian partook of its sentiments.

"The beautiful Mata Hari," said the colonel, who saw spies everywhere and could not be talked out of his belief in Ian's involvement in
something sinister. Now he had Mata Hari to add to his pantheon of
conspirators.

I believed in the unlikeliness of an Arab wife being a spy: She
wasn't enough in the world, would never meet anyone; how could she
operate? But I agreed I ought to be thinking clearly about what aspects of this new situation might bear upon Taft's projects or upon my
own reports, or upon the whole question of who were not what they
seemed. I tried to separate the professional from the personal concerns, but it was hard just then.

"The Saudis come here to find the freedom they do not find at
home," the colonel remarked. "We welcome them within the more
comfortable precincts of a moderate Islamic society. We encourage
them, for eventually it will lead to more liberal ideas of toleration and
plurality for their own society."

"Or else the example of Saudi piety will shame the Moroccans into
fundamentalism," I said. "Isn't that what usually happens?"

"Sometimes, temporarily, the two forces struggle," he admitted.
"The secular will win eventually. The path of least resistance."

"Or else the worldly people, like the Al-Sayads, will be thrown out,
as happened in Iran."

"*Che sera,* as the Italians say."

I wondered, as usual, if the struggle within Islam was Colonel Barka's struggle, or if he was a patriot, or just an opportunist. It was all the same to me, but I wished I knew which. I had assumed all along that he was a Moroccan intelligence agent, but what did it matter anyway? At this moment I had eyes and thoughts only for my lover having an intimate lunch with the undeniably beautiful Gazi Al-Sayad.

24

Visionaries work everlasting evil on earth. Their Utopias inspire in the mass of mediocre minds a disgust of reality and a contempt for the secular logic of human development.

—Joseph Conrad, *Under Western Eyes*

When I got home, I felt foolish to have had these extreme feelings, for everything was normal. Ian was there, drinking stingers on the patio with Robin and Posy. I had finally mentioned her drinking during pregnancy, and she had retorted that it was only harmful to excess, except during the first month, and during the first month she hadn't known she was pregnant, so what was done was done. Stingers, and the day was sunny and cool, and the shadows of the palms were long and dark against the gleaming tiles, with their flowery ornament with endless entwined repeats. If they had been delft tiles, say, or Portuguese, there might be a little figure, or figures— lovers or sailors or gardeners on each tile, something to connect the artist to human life; but the Muslim designer was denied that impulse. Maybe that was what was wrong with them, I found myself thinking, that they were forbidden to represent humanity.

For in my heart, I did think there was something wrong with Islam, and this led me to a renewed commitment to what I was doing. There are born fanatics, I guess, but I was not one; still something flamed in me. Maybe I was just upset about Gazi and Ian, that they were having lunch, that her fingertips had stroked his hand.

That evening we dined with the Cotters. The other guests were a British film editor, the headmaster of the English school and his wife, and Dr. Kadimi.

We sat on the Cotters' roof to have cocktails. Ian seemed himself, expansive and cheerful. I almost thought I was wrong and could not have seen him that afternoon. If I met his eye, my brain swam with confusion, because he seemed the same—serene, guiltless, fond. I thought, I shouldn't be thinking "traitor." But then, I was never far from the thought, also, that when he looked at me, he could be thinking, Agent of a foreign power.

The Cotters' riad, in the medina, is an old and beautiful one dating from the eighteenth century, three stories high, with carved shutters of dark wood, and dramatic palms in pots, and floors of ruby mosaic tile. From the roof you see across the roofs of other buildings, shaded with canvas awnings or gauzy curtains, washing hung out, TV antennas, satellite dishes, and deck chairs. This is the universe for many Moroccan women, who escape up onto the rooftops, some perhaps forbidden to go out into the streets. I had heard that the men couldn't come up to these sacred female precincts and that foreigners like us staring at them ruined it for them, disgusting them with our sunbathing flesh and alcohol-fueled revels. It made me sad to think we were spoiling their roofs; but I couldn't help peering into these exotic worlds, if only for clues into their lives. We watched a woman hanging out clothes, a funny hour to be doing that. Cases of Coke bottles and an old T.V.s were stored up there.

"Oh, the poor things," Posy said, apropos of Moroccan women generally. "Some day they'll rise up."

"The Moroccan woman is light-years ahead of Algerians and Tunisians," said Marina Cotter. "The poor *Algériennes,* when they marry, they are locked away for life."

"Islamic men should just be nuked, or put on a desert island, and all the children raised by English nannies with sensible views, to start them out on a better footing," Posy commented.

As we sat in the light breeze of this attic veranda, we became aware of bustle and raised voices from the ground floor; the sound rose up two stories through the well of the courtyard; Neil leaned over the parapet to peer into the space below. "What is it?" he shouted down at the maid, Aisha.

"This man," she said. A man gazed up. "I want to see Suma," he said in French. We all crowded at the railing to see who was shouting. A young man, maybe in his twenties, angry and ruddy with emotion or exertion, arms waving up at Neil.

"Hold on," Neil said, and headed down the stairs, the rest of us waiting politely above. Presently Marina went downstairs, then almost immediately reappeared and beckoned to Ian.

"It's Suma's brother, and he wants to see her," she whispered. "Only speaks French."

"Ma soeur, ma soeur," he shouted, so we understood it was probably the one she was afraid of.

We watched like an audience seated among the gods, watching

the action on the stage, while Neil and Ian calmed him; then they all sat in wicker chairs below, discussing Suma. The brother was a compact, curly-haired man in his twenties, with the long head and good teeth you often see with North African men. I could see the family resemblance to Suma, a handsome family. Of course he didn't look like someone subject to murderous rages or calculated killings; you would say a graduate student. He wore a jacket over a T-shirt and Dockers, and carried a gym bag that he had stowed under his chair. He stood when the rest of us came down, as we soon did, and shook our hands. Marina was wearing an alert expression and a fixed hostessy smile. Posy and I greeted everyone in what must have seemed an insensitive interruption and were introduced. The brother was named Amid.

Amid and the Cotters sat down again, the rest of us drifted into attitudes of noneavesdropping at the other side of the loggia, and Marina rang for tea for this visitor. He went on with an explanation in progress. Marcia, the Filipina nanny, came in with the children, then backed hurriedly out.

"It's all a misunderstanding, a mistake," Amid was saying. *"Un malentendu."*

"Mistake, *malentendu?"* cried Marina, obviously upset and mistrustful behind her fixed smile. "The girl was terrified. She is in our care."

"My sister is *nerveuse.* She is intense and pious," he said. *"Pieuse.* I think myself that she must have had a sexual experience with her boyfriend, then internalized a feeling of guilt, hence of jeopardy. She believed she would be punished for the loss of her virginity, so she ascribed to us the intention of punishing her. Of course there was no such intention. We are not Algerian villagers. We are not Turks. I suppose that something I said might have caused her to fear reprisal, but I can reassure her. Our father is calm, my brother is calm—I am the second brother."

"We can tell her all this, or let you talk to her by telephone, but obviously Sir Neil and Lady Cotter are responsible for her and couldn't betray her whereabouts. It has to be her decision whether to see you," Ian said in French. The Cotters nodded in support.

"I have a right to see her," the brother began in a hot tone, then changed it. "It is a mercy she is in your care," he said, with a bow of his head. "I suppose there is no question of a child?"

"A child?"

"A pregnancy?" he explained.

"Certainly not, good grief, man," said Neil. "She's a lovely, pure, young girl, we've all become very fond of her." Marina didn't echo this, but she did nod.

"I am certain she wants to come home. Her letter to our mother says as much."

"You didn't bring it, I suppose," Ian asked.

"Non, non."

"Are you in town for a few days, Mr. Amid?" asked Marina, rising to her feet to receive a tray of tea glasses from a maid.

"Mr. Bourad," her husband corrected.

"Mr. Bourad," she agreed.

"As long as necessary," he said with a wave, refusing the tea; his tone once again had begun to leak exasperation. He appeared to decide that the visit was over and stooped to recover his bag. A bit more conversation followed, but he had stood up again and began to move toward the door.

"I want to see my sister," he said, his tone still seeming to risk betraying his anger. Then he again changed tack and modulated his tone: "I will so appreciate . . ."

"We'll tell her you're here. Tell us where she can get in touch with you," Ian said.

"I will let you know," said Amid, his face flushed. "I know she will want to see me. As it happens, I have business in Morocco. I may be here for some time—I will settle in and let you know where she can find me."

Marina and Neil moved toward him with polite good-byes, and promises to help, and qualifications, "in accord with Suma's wishes," etc. "I'll call tomorrow morning," he said. "I understand, of course, and I honor your respect for your promises to my sister. I wish you would tell her I am here, I'll telephone to let you know where. It's a shame to lose her studies, her life in Paris; she needs to come home. I honor you for sheltering her, however." This final reasonableness seemed to weigh with the Cotters and Ian.

"He seemed all right," Ian said when Marina had come back from seeing him out. "It's hard to know." We all agreed that Suma herself was the one to decide on whether to see her brother or not, though Posy feared the authority this brother had over her. We went into dinner, lamb and red lentils, with a cucumber soup to start, discussing her fate.

"It's true," Marina agreed, "battered women are notoriously apt to put themselves in jeopardy a second time." But I couldn't believe Suma would be that dumb.

"If she did lose her virginity, it's all up with her," Posy said. "They have to have their hymens surgically put back before they can marry. You can't believe the horrors the Islamic girls have to go through."

"After all, virginity is easily determined," said Dr. Kadimi. "Or, at least, approximately determined. Our young men would I think be shocked to know of the possible physical ambiguities. We in the medical profession tend to tactfully glide over them."

Neil and Ian didn't seem interested in this detail and went on discussing the probable character of the brother. Ian went to telephone the Al-Sayads and warn Suma. I wondered if he'd speak to Gazi and what they would say.

"It's incredible," Posy kept saying, "someone ratted her out, as you Americans say."

But I was in a state of extreme shock, because I thought I had seen the logo on his gym bag: Olympic rings, and I thought it had said MUNICH 1972. I couldn't be sure; it was no more than the afterimage of something glimpsed and only interpreted later.

25

Regardless of what the legal constraints are, you should not delude yourselves that a reduction of legal constraints or even a total elimination of them will relieve you of a considerable burden . . . the difficult burden of deciding for yourselves what the restrictions upon your actions should be if you don't want them imposed from outside.

—Antonin Scalia, "Discussion of Legal Constraints and Incentives"

Suma received the information of her brother's presence phlegmatically, according to Ian, who was delegated to phone her right away.

"She said, 'He isn't a bad person, he is doing the will of my father.'" The Al-Sayads agreed to keep her inside for a few days, or at least not send her on errands to visible public places. It would be up to Suma to decide whether to contact Amid. He had learned about the Cotters from Suma herself. "Of course I had to write to them," she said. "How else could I go back? I have to reassure them I am not bad, and they will let me alone. My school will be starting in two months." It was clear that in her mind, her Moroccan life was simply temporary, though in the mind of her rescuers it was meant as a permanent solution. The idea that she would make a new life here hadn't occurred to her for one minute.

The next morning, Posy and I walked over to the Al-Sayad compound, rather furtively, with a great sense of being followed, though it was bare, open desert between our two places, where anyone spying on us would be visible, and there was no sign of Amid. Of course my thoughts turned to the tableau of yesterday, Gazi's lunch with Ian— I had thought of nothing else, really, Amid notwithstanding, but by now I had rationalized my dismay into a belief that Gazi's familiar touch to her lips and Ian's palm meant something more like "my lips are sealed," over a banal secret, like a birthday surprise.

From the outside, Gazi's palace was like Ian's, with walls of the same color of ocher and the same waving bougainvillea, here an intense orange. A guard dozing—all guards seemed to doze here—leapt up and escorted us through the gates, without inquiring who we might be, though we explained profusely that we'd come to see Suma.

Inside the gates, we were amazed to see a large swimming pool. We'd thought, because Suma brought the Al-Sayad children to Ian's to swim, that there wasn't one at home. The house was sumptuous in the Mediterranean style of other Moroccan riads, all arched doorways and thick-walled passages. Gazi and Khaled were nowhere to be seen, but a maid went off to get Suma. We waited in the wide hall, open to the sky. Suma came from what appeared to be an office, and we told her in more detail about Amid.

"Someone is bound to tell him where you are," I said.

"My poor brother."

"Is he here to kill you?"

"*Je ne sais pas.* Maybe he still would," she decided.

"He has no idea where you are unless you give him the address. You are safe at the Al-Sayads', but Ian thinks you ought to go someplace like Essaouira for a while anyhow. Sir Neil will organize it." This was the message we had to deliver to persuade her to go. We didn't ask ourselves what the Al-Sayads' attitude to Suma's family drama would be. Obviously they wouldn't want her to be murdered, but in retrospect my hesitation about ascribing even that concern to them testified to my (and Posy's, for we talked about it) uncertainty and mistrust of Islam, or misunderstanding at least.

"You never know how they'll take things. Think of the Danish cartoons," Posy said.

Suma sat in one of the deep-cushioned white chairs, apparently ambivalent. We hovered over her like anxious carrion eaters.

"I think I am safe here. But I would like to see him. Maybe I could meet him somewhere, some public place. If I could talk to him, I think I could decide how his heart is now."

But we were all apprehensive. People working for Ian—Miryam and the other maids—knew full well where Suma was, if he thought of asking them. He certainly would ask the help at Neil and Marina's. He might bribe them or appeal to their religion. Did he know who we were or where we lived? How had he found the Cotters? We knew the answers to none of these questions except that Suma had written her parents.

"Should we tell our staff he might be asking after Suma?" I wondered.

"No reason he should, but it might be a good idea," Ian said, looking at Posy to do it, recognizing that her rapport with them was better than mine. Of course, he could have done it himself. Anyhow, the maids were instructed. We had the comfortably protected feeling of circling the wagons. A day passed.

Sometime overnight the next night, "Sheila" sent an e-mail, which I read in the morning, asking me to phone on a secure line as soon as possible, which meant going to the Mamounia for a public landline. It was probable that the Moroccan police monitored these public phones, but this was still safer than cells because they couldn't know who was calling. I asked Rashid to take me to the hotel at about ten a.m., unusually early, but the hour couldn't be helped. In the interests of appearing normal, I asked Posy to come along, but she refused, apologizing that she was a slow morning starter.

Walking to the car, I still found myself looking around for Suma's brother lurking somewhere, not that he'd have any idea where we lived, let alone where to find her, unless she had told him. Still, I couldn't lose the idea that he could have followed us, could be hiding behind a bush or giant cactus, or outside the walls. It even crossed my mind to wonder whether the brother, Amid, could actually be staying at the Mamounia. I didn't think it likely, but once, shortly after 9/11, I thought I saw Osama bin Laden at the Dorchester in London, tall, shaven, wearing a suit.

While Rashid was parking, I went into the hotel and directly to the phone corridor. What Taft had to say surprised me: He and two others would be coming to Marrakech later that day! I should get them three rooms at the Sheraton Hotel and rent a closed van. He'd tell me the rest when he got there, that afternoon. "It's an endgame of sorts," he said.

Hard to explain the complex rush of emotions—relief that suddenly here was something to do; simultaneous perception of the difficulties of, for instance, keeping from Ian, via Rashid, news of my renting a van. The hotel assignment was fairly easy, since the Sheraton was quite near the Mamounia. I could walk to it, had been there before for drinks. In a way, I liked it better than the Mamounia; it was more Moroccan-looking, with its mosaics and carved ceiling. Was it like Taft to have a refined and subtle set of hotel priorities?

I explained at the front desk about my visiting relatives, booked three rooms, gave them my credit card. In the lobby was an enormous Christmas tree. People were coming to Morocco for the holidays, there was nothing surprising about Santas and Christmas trees everywhere, and the crèches, Mary in her veil, the magi in their Moroccan robes and turbans—to them it must have looked a completely modern, normal tableau, Middle Eastern costume having changed very little from Jesus's time.

The rental car places were not far, so I sent Rashid home with instructions to come back for me at the end of the afternoon, and hailed a mini-taxi to take me to Avis, on Avenue Mohammed V. I was excited. This was the first truly clandestine action I had undertaken, though it was scarcely secret, standing in the Sheraton lobby with my credit card.

My fears that a woman couldn't rent a car in Morocco proved unfounded, though they reveal the depth to which I had internalized the Islamic strictures against women. At first there was some difficulty getting a closed van and some hesitation in my story about it, though I found that explanations came glibly after the first instant of blank panic. It had to be a closed van, I said, because that's what I'd been told to get; an employee, especially a female employee, doesn't ask for reasons. I wanted a closed van, not a pickup or an SUV, because those were my orders. Avis had pickups and station wagons, four-wheel SUVs—almost everything but a closed van. In the end, I got one from Europcar and drove it back to the Sheraton, crawling along carefully among the donkeys and people and ominously dented cars.

My supposition was that Taft and whomever he brought with him ("we") were going to smuggle something or someone in or out, possibly kidnap someone. I wondered if other people performing their first professional act in a new place might feel the same sense of fraudulence and imminent exposure. I was two people, the one calmly transacting a car rental, the other watching the first with wonderment and dismay to think she had put her hand (or foot) in an actual, possibly dangerous, activity with political and legal implications that could land her in a Moroccan jail. And moreover that this was my job.

All of it done, I had some time to consider what was actually happening. Can I truly say that I guessed there was a connection to Suma's brother? Perhaps the conjunction of his arrival and Taft's program suggested it, but with hindsight, I don't think I knew. It became clear soon enough. To be honest, my main thoughts were how to conceal the movements of my day from Ian, how to reappear at dinnertime with a plausible explanation for how I had spent the hours, although now that I was busy setting up the library, I was often out all day. I called Posy to say I was going over to the Tea Cosy, and did she want to join me? To my relief, she said no. Then I went to the Tea Cosy with a bag of books, my cell phone on silent vibration, to wait for Taft and to establish a presence for myself, drinking tea and pasting checkout registers inside the books for the library next door. At about four I went back to the hotel, got the room key, and went up to wait.

I remembered from training that the thing said to be one of the hardest among things you might have to do was waiting. There are mental techniques for getting through it—reviewing codes and ciphers, poetry, verb forms in other languages. Of course, as I waited, I thought about Ian, and other affairs I'd had. I admit that it crossed my mind that if I were married to Ian, I could either give up this job or at least reveal to him what I was up to, and that of those two choices, maybe giving up would be the better course, to enjoy freedom from secrecy. In other words, I daydreamed about getting married, like millions of other women.

At the same time I was really loving the idea that at last I was part of an action. A person doing a new job hopes to do it well, naturally enough, but I found myself excessively on edge, terribly anxious not to fail, anxious to please. I had always had a sense of my unimportance to Taft, and the whole organization, and the great scheme of things—truly I was hardly above a picket—but this was now intensely combined with a wish that it not be the case. What they had asked of me was simple enough—rent a room, rent a car; why on earth should I feel uncertain that I had done it right? But I kept reviewing every step of my recent actions, checking for mistakes. Taft's need for a van raised an infinitude of possibilities—contraband, smuggling, transporting things or people, escapes. I'd find out soon enough, but in some way I was hoping for the darkest of possibilities.

And I kept coming back to Ian and Gazi. One good thing about having a new identity is that it becomes real and allows you to forget, to a certain extent, the mistakes of your former life, your birth life, left behind like a shed skin, allowing you to become a wiser, calmer, more amusing you. I did think from time to time of the man I'd been in love with in Paris, but it was mostly to test my feelings for Ian, to see if they were as strong, and till now I would have said they were not quite as, or were tempered by wisdom, the way, people say, the second time under fire you aren't as scared as the first time someone shoots at you. The anguish of love had not been as strong, but now this new pang of jealousy made me as miserable as I had been before.

As I sat there, I also thought over the affair of Suma's brother, who seemed a forthright, rather French young man, and about what he had said about her having had, possibly, a sexual experience that had panicked her. I thought again about the abiding problems of belief. Did Suma believe, for example, that she was worth half of what a man is worth? I did see that she probably believed her value was intrinsically bound up with her virginity, and that if indeed something had happened, it could have been devastating to her interior composure, in whatever realm of cultural conflict she was obliged to live in, in Paris and here.

26

Secret Counsels are only inspired by Satan, /
In order that he may cause grief to the Believers.

—Koran 58:10

At four fourteen, Taft rang my cell phone. They had landed, were at the airport, and were on their way to the hotel. What name was the room under? (Mine.) In another twenty minutes, Taft and two other men knocked at the door. Taft shook my hand and briefly presented the other men: Walt Snyder and Tarik Dom, both American, Snyder black, Tarik some kind of Indonesian-looking person, both tall and well-tailored. They briefly acknowledged me, checked the room, and flung open the door to the balcony to let in the outside air, and of course to make sure that no one lurked on it. The room overlooked the garden and the drinks patio. A multicultural, harmonious murmur of talk rose up from the people below. All three of my visitors were taciturn and made no attempt to explain what we were up to—I soon saw that was because they were reluctant to talk in front of me, as if I were the secretary or the local hooker hired for the setup and not a colleague at all. I was always surprised to encounter some evidence of dismissive machism—at home growing up, my parents treated my brother just as they treated my sister and me. I persisted in my wish to know what we were doing.

"We have a subject. He's in town. When we find out where, we watch him for a few days while we settle whether the Moroccans are willing to interrogate him, and if not, the Egyptians will. We want to see who his contacts are."

"You don't know in advance whether the Moroccans will help you?" Us, I meant.

"Don't want to ask until we have the capability to pick him up right away, in case they tip him off. We aren't sure of them here." No discussing it with Colonel Barka, then.

"What should I do next?" I asked.

"The subject is a French Algerian who got into town yesterday, ostensibly looking for his sister. He'll have to contact an Englishman, Cotter. The sister is a young woman you know, initially placed with the Cotters. I gather she's moved. We'll find out where he's staying; it shouldn't be hard. We want to see who else he contacts, what the local scene is."

"Well, yes, we've met him already." I was stunned by this coincidence, if that's what it was. Though I had mentioned Suma from time to time as a kind of window dressing to my reports, I had thought of her as of no particular interest to Taft's inquiries, a separate subplot, nothing to do with his world. I didn't think to ask the questions that came to me soon after, such as: Did Suma know that her brother was mixed up in something illicit and was the object of surveillance? And, of course, I wondered what the "subject" was mixed up in—presumably terrorism and its related components of support: the money laundering, and arming and running its agents. Suma had figured into my reports, but I also couldn't remember if I had told Taft about her moving to the Al-Sayads'. I hadn't realized he was interested in her. Now he said, "Tell me more about Suma." He found her story interesting but didn't explain why. Of course, her story was interesting; anyone would think so. I told Taft I needed to know more, about everything.

"For instance, Amid. Is he a bad guy? Why do we want him? Did you know about the situation with his sister? Is it coincidence? I need more information here."

"You have the information you need. Knowing too much can compromise your role."

"Ian's involved, isn't he? Is that it?"

"I don't know. That's your role, finding out."

I could imagine a scenario in which everyone was into something. Ian and Gazi, even Habiba. How coincidental was it that I met her? That Tom and Strand knew her? And Tom and Strand? So well-placed to keep tabs on their foreign customers, fingers right on the pulse. Suma and the Cotters? Posy was the only one I couldn't invent a spy scenario for.

It had been made clear to me that a spy in my position was not to evaluate the reports of her pickets, only to pass them along for her betters to study, and from that position I had passed along some reports, especially—odd to say—from Habiba, but other things as well, that I had doubted. Of course I'd mentioned my doubts—let others decide—but to myself I did wonder about whether these were errors of understanding on Habiba's part, or deliberate disinformation, and if the latter, disinformation generated by whom? I remembered her years in Mecca and knew she was no longer married to her fellow American convert but to an actual Moroccan, though I'd never met him. I saw I should have found out more about him. Maybe he was a fanatic, one of them.

Many of the things she reported responded to my questions about charitable giving, and some concerned the situation in the Western Sahara, where Morocco and Spain both had interests now challenged by Algeria; it was home to half a million or more refugees and strays, in camps run by the U.N. This had struck me, because Ian was interested in the situation there, involved because of Rashid's family. He had mentioned it at dinners, in the general political talk. For all I knew, Habiba's husband was a Western Sahara activist or a member of the GSPC, who were a sort of North African Al-Qaida who were said to be growing. And Amid could belong to one of these groups. . . .

"I need to know," I told Taft.

"When you find out, tell me. You'd better go home, Lulu. Presumably, he won't cool his heels, he'll be trying to see the Cotters, we'll get on his tail over there."

"But he's already seen them!" I said, "His sister's not at the Cotters. They didn't tell him where she is." I explained about Suma's change of jobs. Taft looked skeptical, shrugged.

"You have my cell. Someone will be waiting here at all times if you have anything for us," Taft said, preoccupied. "Car keys?"

"Beige Renault panel, license 40719-40, keys with the hotel valet." I told them good-bye and left.

To tell the truth I wasn't amazed right then—I was in a state of excitement about everything, and especially at the idea that our "subject" was Suma's brother. Then, to add to a day crowded with events, leaving the room, I was amazed to see Gazi at the end of the hall, for the second time like this at the hotel, without Khaled in sight. She didn't see me but was getting in the elevator. This time she was veiled, but by now I could recognize her, the way, I suppose, Saudi children learn to recognize their mothers out of a group of veiled women, something about the shape, the height, the carriage, her way of holding the cloth around herself. Dark suspicions rushed in on me, that Ian was in one of the rooms and that they'd just been together.

On the stair, I called Rashid on his cell to see if he was anywhere nearby and could come get me. He said he could pick me up in a half hour. I walked quickly to the Mamounia and ordered a glass of white wine in the bar to drink outside on their terrace, insisting on the semblance of normality, mind racing about Gazi, what she could be doing alone on the upper floor of a hotel, though I could think of possible explanations, visiting a friend the most likely. I couldn't connect her to Amid, Suma's brother, unless Suma herself had told her about Amid, and anyway, who knew where Amid was? He could be here at the Sheraton.

Perhaps Taft knew, or soon would. I felt a certain institutional pride in our expertise, our functioning network, our virtual ears, to have spotted, surveilled, uncovered, exposed, tracked this dangerous person even into the heart of the English expatriate community of Marrakech, Morocco, even his connection to a modest French schoolgirl. So far was he from them, and yet they (we) found him.

I did feel some compunctions about what was likely to happen to him in some Egyptian or Romanian jail; I didn't like to think of myself as instrumental in getting him hurt, but I saw this wasn't an appropriate scruple. You have to be willing to be a person who changes things, even if you risk changing them for the worse. It seemed hard, though, to imagine consigning to torture someone whose sister you knew. I recognized this was a very Californian qualm, to hope that the evil you do won't count, like a video game.

When we got back to Ian's, he was just getting home himself, driving his jeep, so I knew he wouldn't have been wondering where I'd been all day, and Posy thought I'd been at the library. There would be no problem, no suspicions, no explanations—except mine about him.

It was rather late, almost seven. Colonel Barka had come for drinks and was sitting on the patio with the Crumleys and the new French painter, Pierre Andre Moment, whose name I had actually heard, maybe read of, in some art review, as a leading neo-Expressionist, an affiliation I was hoping he would define. Ian went up to change, but I sat down with the others. Colonel Barka's manner as usual gave no indication we had ever met. The day was still sunny and cool, and the shadows of the palms were long and dark against the glowing tiles of the walls, each with its tortuous ornament of tendrils entwined.

We had heard nothing more from Amid, but it was possible he had contacted the Cotters to say where he was. I had spoken with Suma that morning, and she had seemed strangely tranquil about her brother being in town, feeling herself safe behind the Al-Sayads' impregnable, anonymous walls and little knowing that we were going to round him up.

27

Some believe that intelligence work
will eventually become a science.

—Michael Handel,
    "Avoiding Surprise in the 1980s"

It actually proved more difficult to find Amid than Taft had
predicted. With the cooperation of the Moroccan secret service, the DST, we had a record of hotel registrations, and Taft had a
list of possible relatives and acquaintances, but this list was not as deep
as we'd hoped. It was the DST that located him, after two days, staying in a mosque annex near Guéliz. Taft wanted to watch him as long
as possible, to document his contacts and where he went. After his
sudden appearance, he had not called the Cotters as he had promised
to follow up on the whereabouts of his sister.

In the circumstances, I suggested to Taft that I accidentally encounter him and establish some sort of relationship, possibly by promising

to help find Suma. Taft congratulated me on this plan. Accordingly, Tarik Dom waited outside the mosque (in our van) till Amid came out, and Dom telephoned me at the library. It was child's play to walk toward him through the Jemaa el Fna and feign surprise.

"Oh, hello, *bonjour*," I said. "We met the other night."

"*Bonjour*, madame. I'm afraid I . . ." not connecting me to the Cotters.

"Did you manage to find your sister?"

"Ah, no, not yet."

"Perhaps I can be of help. I'm sure she is homesick and wishes all were smooth again between you."

"You know my sister." It was a statement, not a question. I admitted to knowing her.

"Yes, of course, when she was at the Cotters', I saw her often."

"And you know where she is." This seemed to be a statement too, so I said, "No, I have no idea." Outright lies were coming more easily to me by now. I have heard there are some of us who become so comfortable lying, they easily pass the lie detector tests we have to submit to periodically. I'm not nearly that practiced a liar yet, but I'm making progress. I think Amid believed me. "But someone might, at our house. We are friendly with the Cotters, the children played together."

"Do Madame and Monsieur Cotter know where she is? Why did she leave their household?"

"You must come to dinner one of these nights. Tonight, even, or tomorrow night."

He looked quite surprised, and I saw the look of thoughtful calculation come over him. After a second, he accepted for the following night. I gave him directions, and of course he saw that Suma would not be at our house or I wouldn't have invited him.

. . .

A semipublic performance was formally expected from the artists at Ian's artists' haven, and the following night was also the night Robin Crumley was going to read to us from his new work, poems written since he'd been in Morocco. A few neighbors had been invited in, though not the Al-Sayads. Mostly the guests were other Brits, but Madame Frank (and monsieur, a prosperous *pâtissier,* owner of a chain of fancy bakeries in France) had been invited to meet Moment, the painter, presumably so Pierre wouldn't feel so much the lone Francophone.

Inevitably, sitting with drinks on Ian's patio, before Amid got there, we discussed Amid and his sister, and those Muslim issues—suicide bombings, honor killings—which we are so unable to understand and find so crazy. "Which of us would die for Christianity?" asked Robin Crumley, and it was clear he meant this as a serious question. Of course, none of us would, "Onward, Christian Soldiers" notwithstanding.

"What about those monks in Algeria who were beheaded?" I said.

"That doesn't count," said Ian. "They didn't mean to die, they were just foolhardy to stay. Suicidal."

"A good Christian can't commit suicide for Christianity," Robin Crumley said. "Suicide being a sin."

"Les martyrs," said Madame Frank.

"What would we die for?" Ian wondered. "Britannia, I suppose? If she were attacked, as she has been over and over. People died for her in the two wars. . . ."

" 'Died for king and country,' " Robin sang.

"Our children," Posy said. "People defend their kids and homes. But not the monarch. I would think the queen should die for me, since I'm young and she's old."

"We've learned to mistrust abstractions, and they haven't learned that," Robin said. "Islam, I mean, hasn't learned. A feature of civilization is to mistrust the abstract."

"Mais non," protested Madame Frank, but, after all, the Franks were French, who love abstractions and are highly civilized, or like to think so. *"L'abstrait c'est l'idéal, la chose perfectionnée."*

The thing perfected. Keeping up a conversation was now a completely automatic, robotlike exercise for me, a disguise underneath which I could marshal the thoughts that kept pounding inside, about Taft, Amid, and Ian and Gazi. Now that I had thought about it more, it seemed unlikely that going to that distant lunch place to happen to see Gazi and Ian could have been coincidence. The colonel must have planned it, but what was the object? Was the intrusion of Suma's brother at this point coincidence too, or was there a complex interconnection I would eventually understand?

Of course I had told the others Amid was coming. We were all a little apprehensive. Ian's employees—Miryam, Rashid, the other maids—knew full well where Suma was. We had wondered whether he might try to bribe them or appeal to their Islamism. In the end, Posy, whose rapport with them was the best, reminded Miryam about the threat to Suma's safety and left it to her to persuade the others to say nothing if he asked.

Amid came at eight, neat and sweet-smelling with some sort of cologne, jeans, clean shirt, very much in the uniform of a young Frenchman coming to dinner. He didn't seem to know who, Posy or myself, was the official hostess, so he presented Ian with a gigantic sack of pistachios. In Paris, he was studying architecture at the École des Beaux-Arts. Very much the well-behaved young Frenchman, knowledgeable about the cinema and the coming French elections, willing to discuss the new

Werner Herzog film and redevelopment efforts in North Africa. Educated and employed was not the profile of a smoldering fanatic.

"Is there much honor killing in France?" said the resolute Posy. "In
Germany it's a tremendous problem, among the newcomers, naturally."

"I don't know," said Amid. "I have heard of it, but I don't know if
it is common." He didn't seem taken aback.

I remembered a conversation I had had with Rashid, about hypocrisy. *"Bien sûr,* we live in hypocrisy," he had said. "What else can a
poor Mussulman do? He cannot actually say 'Yes, I accept to work in
your country, but I cannot accept your absurd ideas that all religions
should be respected'; also, how can I tell you all your women look like
whores? No, I have to tell you I accept your right to your religion. Yes,
the Prophet, peace be on him, said we are not to lie, but lying is a lesser
evil, because I cannot tell you the truth, which is 'I am waiting to kill all
infidels.' That is the mind of the Mussulman; I know many like this."

We were having aperitifs—Amid accepted a *jus d'orange.* The discussion, mainly in French, generally concerned his attempts to find
Suma and how he was passing the time. Given that he knew—that we
or at least Ian and the Cotters knew—where she was, his manner was
equable and light. He seemed to accept our peculiar role, knowing
Suma's whereabouts but not trusting him enough to tell him; he
didn't seem to blame or accuse, but appeared to understand that our
position as protectors required us to conceal her.

He was not the picture of somebody in a murderous rage. But I
remembered having read that the family of a dishonored girl just del-
egates someone else to do the job, and that person isn't necessarily in
a rage. Deputized killings in cold blood seemed to me even worse
than rage, and I supposed they would seem worse to a court too. I remembered that if the intended murder is forestalled when authorities

intervene, sometimes this delegated person promises the authorities not to hurt the victim, but then after she trusts him, he kills her anyway, obligations to the Prophet's view of family honor taking precedence over mere criminal law or simple humanity.

We had learned various other things about Amid and Suma, from Suma. Their father had been a sergeant in the French army in the Second World War. Suma hadn't told me much about that; I'd assumed they were poor immigrants, but they were a military family—like my own. There was another brother, older, a teacher of geography in a lycée, married, with children, living near métro Picpus. The other two sisters were not mentioned now by Amid, but it was the profile of a poor but assimilated, upwardly mobile first-generation family, hard to reconcile with the normal profile of simple and status-deprived people who are involved in honor killings.

The others knew, of course, of his threats to Suma, but only I knew of the threat to Amid from Taft and from me, that we planned to drag him off to be tortured in an Egyptian jail, for that was what I was pretty sure we were doing.

"I won't deny that the issue of my sister's honor is troubling to my parents. Any plans for her marriage . . . it could be settled, for instance if she would go to a doctor."

We, Europeans, Americans, sat in an appalled silence for a moment before Ian defined what he meant.

"You mean get her virginity certified?" Ian asked, his tone ironical.

"Yes, a doctor can tell," Amid said. Again, no one thought of an immediate response. The gulf between our sensibilities and his yawned larger than we had imagined, probably impossible to cross. Finally, the always intemperate Posy leapt.

"It's disgusting. That is disgusting!"

"That is the paradox," Amid agreed. "Of course it's disgusting for a modest girl, it renders her immodest almost by definition, yet I'm told that an experienced woman doctor can conduct the whole examination with exceptional tact."

"This is the Stone Age!" cried Posy. Amid stared with a puzzled expression.

"Perhaps European girls have more to hide than modest Arab girls. But I assure you, Arab societies are not the only ones to value modesty. For instance, I happen to know that the American military demanded some such certification before a soldier could marry a French girl. This was during the Second World War."

"That's impossible," we all objected.

"Modesty is a moral virtue, it is not a physical state," said Robin Crumley. "A person can be modest and not a virgin; there is no contradiction. The same with honor."

"Excuse me, I use those words euphemistically. Modesty, honor—we are talking about virginity," Amid said.

"The Stone Age," cried Posy.

Amid shrugged. "Things change very slowly. I think my sister should take our parents' old-fashioned attitudes into account." His face had darkened—we had seen this irascible side of him before, and Ian intervened smoothly by assuring him that Posy and I would tactfully raise the issue with Suma: Would she consent to a virginity test? But despite my promises, I was by no means sure I could collaborate with such barbarity. I was with Posy there.

"Remember Ophelia's song," said Robin. Where she says—'Quoth she, before you tumbled me / you promised me to wed. / So would I a' done, by yonder sun, / An thou hadst not come to my bed.'"

"Shakespeare lived in the seventeenth century," Posy said in an icy tone. "Do you know Shakespeare, Mr. Bourad?"

"Why did she leave Mr. and Mrs. Cotter?" Amid persisted. "Was it Monsieur Cotter?"

"She found something that suited her better. Something secretarial, but I have no idea where," said Ian.

His expression was unreadable. I hoped mine was. Even in the midst of this confrontation with Amid, my thoughts would dart to Ian with Gazi, and the sight of him dissembling made me think of something that had happened twice: He and I were making love, and after my own pleasure, when it would normally be the gentlemanly Ian's turn, he had sighed and withdrawn, saying once that he was too preoccupied, the second time too tired to go on. This abrupt, disappointing ending had shown me that men may dissemble the way women are said to, and now I saw it that he could no longer conceal his thoughts of Gazi and had lost his desire for me.

My attention was drawn back to Amid again when I realized he had begun to sound off about Jews: "Oh, well, the 'chosen people'—we know who owns the banks and newspapers. And they make sure the educational system favors them, not the rest of us. It is this fact that makes us mistrustful of so-called democracy." I was not quite sure I'd heard this right. He went on.

"The issues are not between Left and Right or Arab and Christian, though we are made to think so. Really it's among various Israeli tribes, about ascendance. They decide among them what happens to the Palestinians. . . ."

"My dear fellow," said Ian mildly, "Israel, Palestine—you must know that all this seems very unimportant to us. These people will have to settle it among themselves." He was right not to try to argue, I thought. All at once, Amid seemed to realize where he was, or how intemperate he sounded, and fell silent. Robin Crumley had gotten to his feet and said he would be down in five minutes to begin his reading.

"Frankly, I wrote the Palestinians off after they killed the Israeli athletes." Posy can never resist that sort of remark, I assumed meant to irritate, but it suddenly seemed true. I had too—not the little children or poor beaten-down women, of course, but the men; what a bunch of defectives. It's hard to care about people who run around shooting each other. Posy and I had talked about this. "How are we supposed to think of them as men?" she had said. "All they do is throw bombs and run around screaming, and wave their bums in the air in prayer."

"Some cultures are just defective," she said now, as if intuiting my very word, and looking around to see who was going to make the politically correct objections to it.

"What did your fortune really say?" she then asked. My head was so full of other things, at first this allusion didn't register. "I was thinking about the man in the medina with our fortunes. I know yours said something ominous, and it was intended for me, and you changed it, I understood that and appreciated it, but ever since, I've been wondering."

Of course I'd had many afterthoughts about what I should have told her then: "It said 'You are beloved.'" I made up this lie under the calm eyes of Colonel Barka. I hoped he admired my facility. "So of course I wanted to keep it for myself."

It came to me later that it wasn't a lie, it was the truth I wished for, to be beloved.

"But you didn't keep it," Posy said, with a strange expression of mistrust. "You threw it away."

Robin Crumley retired for a few minutes while we prepared ourselves for his reading by shifting the chairs into rows as in a theater. He came slowly down the exterior steps that led from his lair, the writer's workroom Ian had equipped with computers and TV, no phones, according to his own notion of what writers should and shouldn't have. Robin spent many hours up there every day and, from his solemn, almost glassy expression, was evidently composing himself as he descended. I was impressed with the subtle change in his de- meanor, ordinarily rather weedy and blinking. Now, soberly dressed in a dark jacket, he radiated calm affability—the word "magisterial" even came to mind as he approached, carrying his papers and thin volumes, with becoming insouciance, with irreverent care, striking the right note between not taking them too seriously and taking his audience sufficiently seriously to do them the honor of approaching the question of their entertainment with appropriate gravity. He smiled, I thought stealing a glance at Posy that she responded to with a relieved settling in her chair. We sensed we were in an artist's power.

My heart had quailed a little when I saw the thickness of Robin's sheaf of papers as he stood up to read, but the time went quickly enough, as he told interesting stories between each poem, about what the inspiration was or how long it had taken him. It was wonderful to see the expression of pride and fascination that stole over Posy as she listened, and the polite attentiveness on Amid's face.

Robin's voice was not of the deep, booming, bardlike variety de- sireable for poets, but thinnish and even a bit quavery, so that we had to hush to catch every word, a technique for mesmerizing an audience that's just as effective.

"Of course I've fallen under the spell of the desert. So far from, so unlike, England—its alien and even repellent beauty explains so much about recent events. I think of T. E. Lawrence's writings. . . ."

His poems written in Morocco relied heavily, if I understood them, on the desert as a symbol of human abiding, futile and solitary but eternal, contrasting darkly with some lush, green, flower-filled English lanes, and made me wonder if he hated it here. I guess you'd categorize Robin as a nature poet, and nature is harsh in Morocco. I haven't been to too many poetry readings in my life, but I recognized my own ambivalent response, caught between admiration and the wish it would be over. It was easy for my mind to slide off, between poems, to Gazi and Ian's lunch.

As Robin read on—this was perhaps no more than twenty minutes in, but it did seem longer—I was aware that Posy was stealthily weeping. I could see in the lantern light that her cheek was wet—I hoped from happiness that her husband could compel us all, and above all her, with his art. Once, irked by her complaints, I had snapped, "Do you love Robin or not?"

"Yes," she'd said, with no hesitation. "I do, really, though it's not quite what I expected. Now I have sympathy for people I used to find irritating, like Nora Joyce. Or Frieda Lawrence; I used to just think she was a cow."

"You'll have a lovely baby."

"Oh, God," she cried, with sudden tears in her blue eyes, "I hope so. I think to myself, if I don't fall in love with this bloody baby, I'll kill myself." It was scary to hear her say things like that because of the quaver of seriousness in her voice.

"It takes a while to bond," I had said, as if I knew something about it. I'd heard that it does. "More than one look—a month, months."

"Well, metaphorically, one look," she said. "What if there's something wrong with it? If we were in England, they could tell in advance."

"They can tell here, I'm sure, if you'd go to the doctor."

"I wouldn't dream of it. Think how they treat women here. . . ." And so she didn't go to the doctor, which shocked me, and I had felt angry at Robin for not making her. However they had interviewed hospitals.

Ian, across from me, when he rose with expansive thanks to the "great Robin Crumley," seemed pleased as well, if only at having his generous hospitality so beautifully rewarded.

28

Most of the constitutional proscriptions we are operating under here are empty bottles. Phrases like "freedom of the press," "unreasonable search and seizure" have no precise content. What is "unreasonable"? It depends on what society thinks is unreasonable.

—Antonin Scalia, "Discussion of Legal Constraints and Incentives"

A book I've read three times, *The Good Soldier,* by Ford Madox Ford, begins with the narrator saying his was the saddest story he had ever heard. It strikes me now as kind of presumptuous of anyone to claim that distinction—who has a claim on sadness? But this is a sad story all the same, or if not for me personally, the story I have to tell is sad at least for some of us. Well, and for me.

Three days passed. Amid, watched by Taft and the others, seemed only to *flâner,* idly stroll, have coffees with other young men, and made no attempt to contact the Cotters again. On the third day, Ian's car turned in to the compound midmorning, which was unusual, in that he had left for his office only an hour before. I guess I heard his car subliminally; I was reading on the porch. Posy was out walking in the driveway, ever more slowly these days, her hands pressed against her lower back. Her back was hurting her more and more, and walking relieved it.

She saw Gazi Al-Sayad stumble out of Ian's car, and what was also unusual, Ian was bolting the large gates after them. They all came through the foyer into the courtyard of the house. I'd glanced up, then rushed over to help. Gazi had a large basket, and Ian carried a small suitcase. Gazi was somehow entangled in her abaya, flailing in it like a bear in a net.

She was crying. Without going into the house, she flung herself onto a metal garden chair and tightened her scarves around herself, muttering or sobbing something. Ian set down the case and touched her shoulder. Her expression was of fear, really of panic, and of relief. She leaned her head a moment against Ian's arm. Her speech had altered; she suddenly had a Middle Eastern wail, guttural and melodic, and tears filled her big, black eyes.

"I'm sorry, oh, I can't believe it, oh, God, be good to us."

Ian looked at me with a single glance of something indecipherable, perhaps apology or regret, something sorrowful on his face, and he held on to Gazi.

"Gazi's left Khaled," Ian said. Posy and I said nothing. What do you say? "That's great"? "Oh, I'm so sorry"? "What's it got to do with you, Ian?" Of course, that was what I wanted to know, and yet I probably knew already. If I'd seen them, so had someone else; Khaled had found them out.

There was almost no need to ask what for. It was easy to imagine, as obvious to Posy as to me; when she waddled up to Ian and Gazi, hands still clutching her back, she looked at me. It was clear we were seeing some drama of guilt and exposure being enacted in our own post-Shakespearean lives.

"He can't get in here," Ian said. "It's all right."

"May God be good to us," Gazi said again. Her Americanized accent had melted into the Arabic of the indignant, frightened women who shout tearfully into American television cameras over the rubble of their homes. It seemed to me she was trembling. "Oh, God," she said again and again. Thinking about it later, I'm sure she said "God" and not "Allah," and I wondered about that.

Ian took her into the house, carrying her basket and the suitcase, and came back without her to talk to Posy and me by the pool, where we'd remained more or less frozen in uncertainty about how to behave. Posy said, "Marital woes?" She was looking at me as if to take the lead from me in how to react. I wasn't sure myself. Were we sorry for Gazi, angry at her, indifferent to her plight? I wished Posy were not there. If she hadn't been, I might have spoken more forthrightly. It was clear that Ian did not mean to identify himself as Gazi's lover.

"Khaled is a jealous husband, and that's a deadly matter for a Saudi wife. Someone told him she's having an affair," Ian said. He was looking at me as if he thought I was the someone, the action of a jealous female scorned, and I couldn't bear that, nor did I deserve it.

"It wasn't me, Ian, I don't know anything about Gazi's life," I said, I suppose snappishly. I see now I shouldn't have imagined he was accusing me. At the time, the charge infuriated me. Would I have been in a more furious rage if there hadn't been a lie, a bunch of lies at the center of my life also?

Some fumbling explanations followed, oblique and shocked that things had come to such a pass. "Her life in Saudi Arabia, a woman like that, confined like that," and so on, his indignation making it as obvious to Posy, if she hadn't known, as it was to me that he was the lover, that it was his and Gazi's love that had been discovered. Still, he didn't say so.

The whole subject of adultery was apparently fascinating for Posy, a Brit after all, from a whole culture unusually obsessed with it (I had concluded from practically every British book I'd read), who pledged her support for the brave Gazi, defying the moronic mores of her Stone Age society, etc.

"We must protect her, obviously," Ian said.

"Of course," I agreed. "Having to wear those awful veils . . ." We rushed to condemn Gazi's entrapment in Saudi Arabia.

She had fled from her home at dawn, and called Ian's office from her cell phone. She hadn't been in any shape to say much. She'd been huddled at a bus stop for five hours till Ian got to his office and got her message. Why didn't Ian have his cell phone? She didn't know if Khaled was out looking for her. If they'd been in Riyadh, she'd be dead, but jealous husbands had to think twice in Morocco. On account of new protections for women, installed by the new king, it was no longer okay to kill your wife and her lover with absolute impunity; you went to jail for it, though maybe not if you were in a jealous rage, and anyway, when had laws stopped jealous husbands? It was a more primitive passion, territorial and irrational, some seemed to think forgivable. She believed someone had telephoned Khaled to hint that his wife was unfaithful. She didn't know what he meant to do. She didn't know whom Khaled thought her lover was.

I thought of the colonel. The caller must have been he. But why?

Later I wondered how she knew someone had told Khaled. Had there been a scene? Threats? Violence?

I think I behaved rather well at first, *sous le choc,* as the French say, about Gazi's escape and recent danger; but later, more hurtful aspects of it occurred to me. Maybe their affair had been going on awhile, a year or two, whenever the Al-Sayads were in Marrakech, with some poor girl always unknowingly playing the beard for Ian—Nancy Rutgers and then me, and maybe women before Nancy and me. It was pretty cold-blooded of Ian, like the cynicism of the husbands in nineteenth-century French novels who slept with their wives often enough to pass along their syphilis but never loved them.

When in an hour Gazi came down again she'd dried her tears and left off her veil, but she was obviously stunned and traumatized, and sat in the garden, staring into space. A maid brought tea for us all. Ian stood in the shrubbery, pointedly apart, as if it all had nothing to do with him or he feared making it worse.

29

If ye fear a breach / Between them twain / Appoint two arbiters /
One from his family, / And the other from hers. / If they seek to
set things right / Allah will cause their reconciliation.

—Koran 4:35

A few days passed with Gazi's presence hanging over us.
Like an unexorcised ghost, she was with us and not with us,
nearly invisible at first, then, little by little, among us. We all understood that she couldn't contact her husband, Khaled, and there was
no sign from him. The two villas of Ian and Khaled were like two me-
dieval fortresses on adjacent peaks, menacing and blind toward each
other, Gazi like Helen of Troy, captured in the enemy's camp.

"I am the crying camel," said Gazi. "The Prophet, peace be with
him, found a camel cruelly tied up to a post; the poor beast was starving and exhausted, and the Prophet said to its owner, 'Do you not fear
Allah because of the way you've treated this camel? I gave him into

your care.' Well, the owner of the camel was sorry and said, 'I have done wrong.' Fine, in the Koran, but I know Khaled never will."

We were half afraid Khaled would come bursting into the compound brandishing a curved scimitar, so we had marshaled security—being careful to bar the gates, for example. Though Ian, the Crumleys, Pierre, and I went about our business, there was a sense that we were as entrapped as she, also imprisoned and oppressed by, in part, the torpor of a strange Indian summer of hot days and nights returning after some days in which the weather had been cooling. It was now December, with nights in the forties, rains beginning most afternoons, though as yet not heavily, and people were commenting that it was a drought.

With Christmas approaching, it was strange and even sort of upsetting to get letters from my parents and sister, at various times, copied out in the unfamiliar handwriting of the mail-drop person, yet sounding so familiar in phraseology and message, especially in their concern for my morale. From my sister:

"Hope you're liking Morocco and things are working out on all fronts (!!). Is it funny to be away at Christmas yet again? You must be getting used to it. We miss you especially during the holidays. . . . Don't get gloomy. Your present is on its way. I know it's boring—I won't say what it is because you'll get this before it (coming by long sea). But useful . . ." I never did get the parcel, though.

I thought quite a lot about what to get Ian for Christmas. It should be intimate but not embarrassing; it shouldn't presume on the unspoken, but I wanted him to know it was a love present, now complicated by Gazi's being here. By the twenty-first, I still hadn't bought anything. I consulted everyone—Tom and Strand, Posy, and finally even Taft. This was before Gazi, of course.

"What are you hoping to get for Christmas, Sefton?"

"I *will* get the usual—socks and ties," Taft said bleakly.

Christmas would be in three days. It had been possible, amid the cactus, to forget the scenes of snowy beauty and cottage coziness with which Americans, even Californians, are imprinted—the decorated tree, the trail of smoke from the chimney, the yule logs, the growing mound of packages. Every person of right sensibility feels the gloom of it—the distant loved ones, the gap between the ideal and the real. You are not going to get what you want for Christmas. Especially if you want peace on Earth.

Posy and I scrounged up two artificial Christmas trees, relatively realistic-looking, each about four feet high, one for the library and one for Ian's, where it stood on the hall table opposite the front door. It didn't occur to any of us that the religious significance of this holiday might be sensitive, because it didn't seem to be. The kitchen staff and maids were well aware they were working in a Christian household, it was no big deal, and Gazi had certainly spent Christmases in America during her college years and had confronted the iconography then. Also, Marrakech was flooded anew with French people—the Mamounia bar was crowded and merry, and garlands of bougainvillea were draped around the mirror behind it. Tom and Strand brought an armload of poinsettias dug up somewhere in the Atlas foothills. Santa was everywhere in Morocco, in cardboard life-size versions in shops, in supermarkets, even on a street corner, where a skinny young Santa in sheepskin with a red hat and cotton beard posed with polyester-spangled children in their best clothes. Did they even know St. Nicholas was a Christian saint?

I bought a cute dark green velvet dress for Amelie, Tom and

Strand's little girl, and a Moroccan ceramic bowl for Posy and Robin, but was still stuck on Ian's present. It was also possible we weren't going to celebrate Christmas, out of tact at Gazi's plight.

Mostly, Gazi stayed in her room. We still didn't know if Khaled, or anyone, knew where she was, so when visitors came, she ran upstairs. She bewailed the absence of her children, so close by and yet forbidden. "I'll never see them again, I just know. I know, I'll steal them away—Fatima especially must come with me to a new life. . . ." Sometimes her voice, in complaint, took on a note of that ululating cry of grief of Arab women. She imagined a solitary life in some place like Kuwait, still Islamic, but where women were freer than in Saudi Arabia. At first, I was tempted to pass a word to Suma to let the children know that their mother was safe, but this raised too many problems. Who knew if Suma could really be trusted? We had no choice but to trust Ian's servants and warned them that no one must know Gazi was there, but we were rather pessimistic that this injunction could be followed.

Anyway, Gazi, suddenly passive, seemed content to sit around. She had an amazing ability to do nothing. She would sit in the garden or sometimes swim. She was a good swimmer. She braided her long, black hair in a pigtail that lashed behind her as she did furious laps, then undid it to dry as she sat by the side of the pool.

There was no sign of special intimacy between her and Ian beyond the affectionate concern that everybody felt (professed to feel). It was explicitly understood that Gazi had burned a bridge and could never go back to Saudi Arabia to be divorced, publicly charged with adultery, or more likely, just disappear, or drown in her swimming pool, or tragically electrocute herself—these were the fates of women she had known or heard of. Just being suspected of adultery was all it took to doom you. We should not assume she was an adulteress, it was that all women were adulteresses or potentially so in the Saudi mind, not to be trusted for a second out of the gaze of a trusted servant or male relative, unable to master themselves, with the primitive urges of stoats.

"Two princesses of the royal family have electrocuted themselves. People make jokes about their amazing obtuseness around electricity." She laughed.

Whether she was or wasn't an adulteress—how odd and stern that old-fashioned word sounded, so seldom used nowadays—was never discussed. Without ever alluding to a lover, or to a grand passion, the convention adopted in our talks about Gazi's plight was that Khaled was under the delusion that she was unfaithful but this wasn't the case. When she was present, this morphed into an analysis of Saudi attitudes and realities instead of seeming to allude to her particular case.

"It's a question of his honor. It doesn't matter what really happens. Women who are raped are accused of adultery," Gazi herself said. Sometimes, though, she was more positive about Saudis. "No one is really executed for unfaithfulness in Saudi Arabia. Well, not for a long time. They are in Iran, though." She spoke with an odd mixture of defensiveness and pride when her religion or her country, or Khaled, came up. "Mostly they disappear, they aren't put on trial or executed. They used to be, though. Families deal with their own questions of honor."

"Someone should talk to your husband." It was Robin Crumley who believed this most firmly and offered to do it. Her plight seemed to have stirred his poet's soul, and it was an unusual departure from his normal detachment.

"No, no," Gazi would say. "I cannot go back. He will never believe the truth." None of us felt able to demand the truth, though, and she never explained.

If Ian crept into her room at night, I had no way of knowing it. He would come in to say good night to me, much as usual, but never stayed. His light good-night kiss was brotherly, or maybe merely businesslike. My whole body yearned for him. Sometimes I lay awake listening, trying to hear someone stealing down the hall or his door closing. I never heard him, but the little cat we had adopted, Stuart, had taken to coming into my room to sleep on my bed, whereas he usually slept with Ian.

I couldn't help but wonder what Ian's plan was vis-à-vis Gazi's future. Maybe he was just chivalrously rescuing her, with no commitment beyond that. Or did they have dreamy plans to go live in a cottage in Surrey together, or do African social work? Can you have love without a plan for it? I had unconsciously planned to spend my life with Ian, and now I saw that was not going to happen.

30

Perhaps the greatest impetus for the establishment of a peacetime U.S. intelligence service was the argument that enough information had been available to predict the attack on Pearl Harbor—if all of it had been laid on a single desk.

—Angelo Codevilla, "Comparative Doctrine and Organization"

What Taft and the two others were doing for these several days wasn't clear. I knew they were still keeping Amid Bourad under surveillance. Presumably, he'd lead them to his contacts, people he was in touch with; evidence or money might change hands. It was apparently Taft's belief that I should be ignorant as far as possible. I no longer chafed at being in the dark; I agreed that innocence is a good defensive position. As he said, an agent needs to know some things, but real ignorance makes you less vulnerable in case of interrogation: It was enough that I knew that we wanted Amid, and I knew the general activities that got you wanted and watched.

But it isn't surprising that I felt closer to Colonel Barka than to Taft, if only because the colonel's refusal to share certain information was expected from a DST (I assumed) agent, while Taft's mystifications I found insulting and uncollegial. Was I not a foreign intelligence case officer? To him I was a beginner and a girl.

The colonel was my tutor in many things, though it didn't always help me understand Morocco. Once Posy said in front of him, "It doesn't appear to me that honesty is particularly admired here." The other English people present (the Cotters and a couple named Wyatt) gasped their dismay at this rude political incorrectness, which pleased her of course. She defended her position by mentioning bargaining, and also the Moroccan tendency to tell you what you want to hear, and I had to agree that these practices were founded on untruth, but the colonel pointed out that she didn't understand the underlying assumptions, things the locals understood perfectly going in, and I could see that he was talking to me.

"They might be telling you, for instance, in saying 'It's over there,' and pointing in the wrong direction, that it isn't done for women to go there, and a Moroccan would understand that message," he said. Posy sniffed resentfully, but I took it to heart.

I knew I ought to be more open than I am to Islam, like Madame Frank, like all those who rejoice in the color, music, revelry, and charm of its souks and squares, with the snake charmers, and photo-op camels, and rugs spread out, the donkeys and horses, the poor goats. Why could I only think of the cruelties that people poor as this inflict on each other and on animals, and not of, say, the kindness of Moroccans to their children and the systems of trust among the old men in the medina that enable their businesses to work. Instead, I always think of Mohammed Atta and wonder if he had told the others they were going to die or whether he had told them something else, some lie about going to Cuba.

Since I had rented the rooms for Taft and his party at the Sheraton, and he was publicly a guest there, he and I met more or less openly there—Taft might be my cousin, my brother-in-law—the DST probably knew who he was anyway, and via the colonel, it certainly knew about me. The other two agents, Dom and Snyder, were never to be seen. Taft and I would have a drink, and he'd ask questions.

"How're you doing, Lulu? It's not hardship duty here, I trust?"

"In what way?"

"I always think of Ingrid Bergman in that Hitchcock film, where she was married to Claude Raines so she could spy on him but she'd rather be sleeping with Cary Grant."

"No, it's not a hardship. I don't feel that useful, though." I wasn't going to discuss my feelings for Ian.

"You'll be useful soon. The Thursday after Christmas, no symbolism intended. That's when we'll pick up the kid. I'd as soon wind this up. We've got a lot of information already, and I'm starting to feel nervous about something going wrong."

"What'll I be doing?"

"Driving. I brought you something." He put a plastic sack on the table, and from the clunk it made, heavy and metallic, I could tell it was a gun.

"You should have this," he said. "Do you have a safe place to hide it?"

"Sure," I said. "I'd just like to know why we're picking him up."

"Believe me, Lulu, I'd tell you, but every bit of info you carry around is eventually going to show. It shows in the eyes, it shows in the set of the shoulders." This is what Taft always said. Once, I had asked him directly what our interest in Ian was and what we were going to do with Amid Bourad, and he had shaken his head. Evidently I was supposed to admire his opaque eyes and the resolute set of his shoulders against the weight of hidden knowledge. A man just past his prime (and in my view a man's prime comes a little later than some believe); a trifle overweight and a smoker. To give him credit, he had mastered every detail of the literacy program reports I'd been filing for months, and every name involved, and was familiar with all the locations in my photographs. But now he gave me the feeling my immediate utility was over, except for one last service, coming on Thursday.

Taft was interested in Gazi's story as he would be in a soap opera, and of course he already knew from me that his quarry had actually dined with us in connection with Suma. "How strange to find yourself in this embattled bastion of beleaguered Muslim females," Taft said. "'Embattled bastion of beleaguereds,' haha."

I saw what he meant about knowledge affecting your posture. I had so much guilty knowledge by this time—Suma's whereabouts, Gazi's whereabouts—I was almost afraid to speak out loud to anyone about anything. Were the situations of Gazi and Suma similar? I couldn't tell. Both were in fear of their lives, but to be fair, it was hard to remember that when, if you talked to them, both preserved natural, even contented facades. This suggested that being in fear of your life was not so different from other constraints they had internalized since infancy and hence didn't react violently to. It was only a little bit worse, so where I would have been in a hysterical panic, each seemed serene in her way.

Maybe that's what's meant by lives of quiet desperation, or else neither one believed that the retributions decreed by the Koran or by their respective societies would really be exacted. And, again to be fair, as they made sure to tell me, the Koran didn't dictate death for adultery or premarital sex. In Suma's case, she had an inner sense of innocence anyhow. I didn't believe in Gazi's innocence, but she did stonewall and never admitted that our general discussions about the conservative precepts of Islam had any relevance to her particular case.

"It's all a ghastly mistake" was her frequent remark.

Gazi was nice to everyone, but especially to me. I figured this meant either that like everyone else, she knew about Ian's relationship with me but accepted it to keep me in place as a cover, hence needed to reassure and deceive me, or she didn't know, just liked me or just liked Americans, thinking fondly of her college days. Or she wanted to make use of me: "Darling Lulu, if you went over to my house to see Suma, you could check whether my children are all right." Of course I understood how hard it must be not to see her children, but in just a corner of my hard, hard heart I heard generations of WASPy ancestors saying, "Well, you should have thought of that."

Nor could I seem to talk about Gazi with Ian. I didn't know the source of my compunctions about confronting him with what I knew or thought I knew. Was it that since I myself was living a lie, in the phrase, I had no right to call someone else's lies to account? More likely I just really didn't want to know, didn't want to hear him say, that he loved Gazi.

Posy and I both looked at Gazi with interest from the point of view of her habits, attitudes, life rhythm. We felt its difference from our Western ways, as different as our red, razor-bumped skin from her satin, depilated chamois-colored skin. Her long black hair was braided in the morning by one of the maids, who did it cheerfully as they sat in the patio. The black lines of kohl around her eyes went on in the evening, but even without it, her eyes were huge, and Posy and I despised our pallid blue ones, squinting ineffectually against the Maghrebian sun or hidden behind our shades. I didn't let myself dwell on the scene that always came to my mind, Gazi's body, hairless as a statue, pressed against Ian's muscled torso, enjoying his cock.

Every day, she seemed more and more at ease, friendly and admiring of all household details—Miryam's cooking, the menus, the candlelit evenings, the chats at breakfast before we moved into our respective days. When I commented to Posy on how happy she seemed, Posy said, "She was probably raised in a harem. She was brought up within a female group. Group life probably feels normal to her." We eventually asked if her father had more than one wife, and she said, "Yes, two. I am the daughter of the younger."

Of course we were fascinated. Her mother had been married at fifteen and was still only forty-nine years old!

"She is beautiful. I have a picture of her but, very stupidly, left it at home. I mean, with Khaled, for now I have no home." Of course we burned to know if Khaled had more than one wife, but assumed not, for where were they?

"Oh, well, most Englishmen have more than one wife, eventually," said Posy. "How long have you been married?"

"Fifteen years. I was married when I was seventeen. My mother thought I was an old maid."

"I thought you went to university in America."

"Yes, but I was already married. Khaled and I went together. How else do you think I could be permitted? Saudi women—in those days even more than today—we couldn't study abroad unmarried. Oh, the princesses do."

"Do they ever marry Americans?" I wondered. "Or Englishmen?"

"No. The government needs to give permission to marry foreigners. Saudi men can, though, they can marry English women, even Christians."

"Do they?"

"The occasional blonde airline stewardess. Rarely college girls."

One morning, at the library, Posy said, "You seem so good-natured about the Gazi situation." I was a little shocked, because though everyone knew me to be Ian's mistress, no one had acknowledged any special connection between Ian and Gazi. Or, for that matter, between Ian and me; a sort of tactful discretion hung over everybody's treatment of everybody, and I had never asserted any rights as mistress *in titulo*—didn't step into the role of hostess, for example, even though, having heard Posy's conversation with Marina about Nancy Rutgers, I knew people understood my relation to Ian; it was no mystery. Still, in the general atmosphere of British good manners, it was easy for everyone to pretend my connection to Ian was simply as houseguest. Now Posy was saying I ought to defend my rights.

Of course I wanted to ask—to confront—Ian and get an explanation of his ties to Gazi, but a new straw had floated by for me to clutch at: the idea that Ian and Gazi, at the Sidi-Ali Restaurant, had been plotting her escape from Khaled and Saudi Arabia. They were friends and neighbors—to whom else could she turn? As Suma had turned to the shelter in Paris, so the desperate young Saudi woman had turned to the solvent and managerial Ian—what could be more natural? That they were only plotting her escape would explain the absence of any simmering looks and tiptoeing in the hallways now that she was here.

And it would mean that the colonel hadn't betrayed them, important for my own view of his trustworthiness.

These thoughts, along with an inner reluctance to know more, silenced me. I also felt that this personal problem was a sort of an imposition on Company time; I shouldn't be thinking about it so much.

Now, I must have looked rueful, and Posy plunged on: "You haven't said anything to him, have you? I know you haven't, you're so reserved. Maybe 'inhibited' is a better word. Americans are supposed to be so voluble, but you're a sphinx. How do you expect him to know how you feel?"

"He hasn't said anything to me about her," I said. "She's just there. I see, I can see . . ." And at this I was taken by surprise with a sudden big sob and tears that flooded in, though I wiped them away. Posy gave me a hug—I could feel the baby in her distended, slightly churning belly as it pressed against me. But our embrace, and my tears, lasted only a second. Posy seemed pleased at the accuracy of her perceptions, and I must say, I envied the faculty of accurate thinking, wished mine were accurate.

"I thought I was imagining it," I said. "He's in love with her." The truth is, I hadn't imagined I could talk to Posy about intimate things, because it would seem like gloating. She seemed slightly disappointed in her own erotic life, as if what had been revealed to her was no big deal after all. It was a turned-off quality I'd seen before in married women.

"Oh, yes, it's very plain. He's infatuated," Posy said.

"I am going to bring it up and say something," I said, and it was a firm resolution, but what would I say? I had weighed bugging Gazi's room, which I could have done easily, but resisted this frivolous and self-indulgent course, partly because it seemed to lower my profession to the sleazy level of divorce detectives, partly because I was afraid of what I'd find out.

To my shame, one night soon after this, the anguish cost me an entire *nuit blanche,* shedding tears of chagrin to be so sleepless, chagrined to be so obsessed and wracked with jealous egotism. We had all come up to our rooms at midnight—we'd been to the house of a former American ambassador to Tunisia, at a riad in the medina near the Cotters. I'd been uneasy the whole evening. We didn't see that many Americans, and I found it slightly disconcerting to meet this one, as if, in the spirit of "It takes one to know one," the ambassador would spot me as a spy and *poseuse.*

Back home, in my bedroom, I was still keyed up and found myself sitting at my desk fooling around with my computer, listening out for any noise or tiptoeing from Ian's room, even from time to time going into the bathroom to be closer to Ian's door. Then, at two, faced with going to bed or owning up to myself what I was doing—staying up to spy—I couldn't avoid understanding that I was in the grip of personal misery I couldn't really master. I sat at my desk for endless moments more, then lay down on my bed, sleeplessly, ears straining and hearing nothing but night noises and, at four thirty, in the silent desert, from afar somewhere, the call to prayer. Then, despite my intention to sit listening the whole night through, I must have dropped off, because it was seven thirty, and I did hear footsteps in the hall, but it would be maids or Ian getting up.

Then I knew Posy was right that I should confront Ian and ask for an explanation of what was going on. Can you be sleeping with someone in the happiest way—happy at least till recently—and not sense insincerity or reservation? Apparently, yes. The history of spy literature, for one thing, is full of Mata Haris and Christine Keelers and their abashed victims—seduced, susceptible males who didn't notice even a hint of treachery. Can it work the other way? Of course—there's the whole history of prince consorts and gigolos. But there I was, clinging to the idea of the beauty and sincerity of the sexual act and thinking I couldn't be mistaken that Ian loved me. I longed to confront him, yet I was afraid of what he might say.

31

To what extent was the past, the history of the phenomenon under examination, understood? Were past trends identified and their origins and significance perceived?

—David S. Sullivan,
"Evaluating U.S. Intelligence Estimates"

We kept closed the big wooden gates leading into the compound. These were ordinarily barred at night, but since Gazi came, they were barred in the daytime too, and the watch-boy who was always sleeping on the doorstep of the little shelter at the entrance began to wear an alert, pleased air of rendering an important service. When Ian left for his office or Posy and I went somewhere, it was with a great clatter of unlatching and the scraping of the doors along the gravel of the drive. Shut behind these gates, we were a nuclear facility, a radiation zone.

This state of things lasted several days, until we inevitably relaxed our guard. We had braced for the arrival of an infuriated Khaled

Al-Sayad, but he didn't appear. Either he wasn't coming, or he hadn't put two and two together yet, or he was content to let Gazi go. Ian and I, in my room at night, discussed the possibilities: Maybe he didn't really care that Gazi had gone, maybe he was glad to be rid of her. It seemed unlikely that he didn't know where Gazi was—she'd been at Ian's nearly two weeks, apparently reassured by the thick walls and the care we took to bolt the gates, but surely a kitchen girl or a gardener would eventually tell someone despite Ian's instructions. Other than closing the gates, we didn't any longer go to unusual lengths to hide her.

Ian, by his perfectly bland manner, still gave no sign of his relationship with her and facetiously expressed sympathy for Khaled. "What a handful," he agreed. We were not having a private talk; this was before dinner, and the Crumleys were there. Ian avoided being alone with me even during the day, it seemed to me, though there was still the nightly perfunctory visit to my room. "However, when he gets back to Riyadh, how does he explain why she hasn't come home with him? 'Oh, I just lost track of her when we were in Morocco'?"

"They're used to that, in Riyadh," was Posy's comment. "Gazi told us, wives disappear all the time."

At dinner we often discussed Gazi's passport. Without it, she was trapped in Morocco forever. The problem seemed insurmountable. She'd left without it, and it was locked in a safe at home, in Khaled's office. Moreover, Khaled worked in his office all day long. I knew, of course, that I could get a passport for Gazi. We did it all the time. But how could I admit to having this power? And could I justify it to Taft? Now, looking back, I suppose I didn't want to help her—yet I did want to get rid of Gazi, I wanted her to go away, wanted Ian to be as I had thought him, wanted love to reign.

"Suma is the obvious person to get it," Ian said. "Or one of your kids could get it, Gazi. Khaled must trust Suma. Maybe she knows the combination."

"No, how could she?" Gazi said. "Anyway, it's a key."

These were terrible times for me, inopportune times for me, with Taft in town, and we were about to kidnap someone, and my thoughts kept veering to Ian when I ought to have been thinking about work. There were other things I had to do. Ian was applying for grants to rebuild the burnt factory and build some more. Since I had some experience with grant proposals, I was able to help him with writing these. His plans were ambitious and idealistic; I felt he should take an administrative fee—my suggestion and the usual practice—but he wouldn't hear of it. I didn't know the details of Ian's apparently adequate finances: Where did his money come from and how much did he have? Again, I felt funny looking into it, even though it was germane to my mission—it was even my duty to look into it. I could certainly confirm in my reports to Taft about the general flow of development money and charitable donations in Marrakech that sending some of it to Islamic extremists would be easy and probable, innocent donors not knowing where their money went.

Working on his grant proposals, thus did I morph from a mistress into a secretary.

It had occurred to me before this that we had made love maybe only once a week for some time now, with me initiating it, and sometimes my provocative moves were ignored, leaving me with disagreeable feelings of longing and resentment, a frustrated need that was worse than forgetting about love altogether. I thought desperately of the occult, charms or potions, or beauty measures, or sexual arts—maybe of *The Perfumed Garden*: "If a woman intends to contract her vagina, she has only to dissolve alum in water, and wash her sexual parts with the solution, which may be made still more efficacious by the addition of a little bark of the walnut tree, the latter substance being very astringent. . . ."

But I knew there was no way I could demand that somebody make love to me, or find a walnut tree either. I did remember a scene in Anthony Powell, where Jean, Nick's mistress, greets him at the door in the nude, and how it turns him on, and I tried that. When Ian came in for his evening talk, I arranged, at his knock, to be naked.

"Oh, sorry," he said, and began to back out.

"No, come in," I said. In fact, this worked very well. Men are such uncomplicated creatures, basically, I guess; I didn't know how reliable this stratagem would turn out to be in the long run, though.

My double life was also threatening to become more complicated when Taft thought of this or that for me to do at hours when I'd usually be at the library or having lunch with Posy. For instance, since he had assigned me to drive the van on the day we picked up our subject, he sent me several times on a practice route into the outskirts on a side road leading to the highway to Rabat, urging me to unsafe speeds along the dirt track where small children from the mud shelters on each side threatened to toddle into our path. "You must be the only woman your age in the world who can drive a stick shift," he said, a tiny trace of approval in his voice at last.

Most mornings, Posy and I left as usual with Rashid, Miss Pring came for Ian, and Robin Crumley and Pierre Moment went off to work at their respective arts. Gazi might be in the garden gathering the blossoms of the saffron or tangerines, or sleeping late. I found myself spending at lot of time at the Mamounia or working at the library, avoiding her. Pierre Moment, however, spent less and less time in his studio and more and more time with her. We all noticed that.

"Quelle femme adorable," he said. *"Imaginez sa vie en Arabie Saoudite."*

The night he came to dinner, Suma's brother Amid had said, "My mother is not well. It's important my sister knows this. Please, if it happens that you see her, tell her this."

"I'm so sorry to hear it. Maybe she'll happen to call Madame Cotter," Ian had said. "We'll suggest that Marina pass that news along." Whether Marina had or hadn't, we now had four reasons for getting hold of Suma, to tell her about her mother, to get her to submit to a virginity test, to find out about Gazi's kids, and now to get Gazi's passport. Talking to Suma was of course made trickier since Gazi was with us, and so we'd procrastinated. Suma knew about Gazi's flight, obviously, but for her to know where Gazi was could put her in a difficult position. What if Khaled asked her, or blamed her, or thought she was involved? When I did call Suma with news about Amid, we decided I was to pretend we hadn't even heard that Gazi was gone. How would we, after all?

It turned out that Suma didn't know it either, had the idea Gazi was just traveling. Things seemed to her normal at the Al-Sayads'. The children were fine. I had to decide then and there how to ask her to cooperate, and concocted the following story: Gazi was traveling in Morocco, but had decided to go to France and thus needed her passport. Could Suma get it out of the safe? As soon as I outlined this plan, I saw its flaw—why wouldn't Gazi just call Khaled and ask him for it?

And now, if Suma asked Khaled for the passport and said she'd been asked for it by me, all the dots would be connected in his mind—he would realize she was at Ian's, and Suma would know that Gazi had fled instead of being away on a trip. I told her not to mention it after all.

Gazi called Suma herself, in the morning, and in a wheedling tone asked about the kids and whether Suma knew where the safe key was. I couldn't guess what Suma was saying, but evidently a lot, because Gazi did more listening than talking, and eventually she said, "If you knew, you would not blame me." We heard her say this several times, "If you knew what my life was like . . . ," leaving us, as we hung on this conversation, to imagine that Suma was reproaching Gazi, which didn't sound like the meek Suma we were used to. Gazi was starting to speak sharply, then modulated her tone and said, abruptly, "Good-bye, Suma."

Gazi turned to the rest of us and began to cry again, as she had the first day, sobbing bitterly into a thin shawl she had worn against the chilly morning and now pressed against her eyes. I think Ian wanted to take her in his arms to comfort her, but he didn't. How could he, in front of me?

On Christmas Eve, Gazi danced. As the weather was now cool, we'd eaten inside in the dining room and had gone into the salon for mint tisane (I always asked for coffee, though). But outside, tonight the night was strangely warm for this crisp time of year, and the candles were lit on the paths. Tom and Strand had been by earlier, but now it was only the Crumleys, Pierre Moment, Ian, Gazi, and me there. No one had been invited since Gazi's arrival, though I had argued for keeping to our normal pattern of dinner parties and people visiting, which would seem more natural and not draw attention to us. I had had tea with Colonel Barka at least once during this time but didn't tell him about Gazi. I had told Taft, of course, about Colonel Barka; he knew about it anyway, and he had told me to keep that relation intact.

In the salon we had been listening to Handel's *Messiah,* but now, maybe in the spirit of ecumenicalism, we had CDs of Moroccan music, soft, wailing dinner music that added ambiance without compelling attention, and then somehow the music had intensified; maybe someone turned it up. It developed a sort of bump-and-grind beat that couldn't be ignored. Ian, joined by Robin, Pierre, and Tom and Strand, urged Gazi to show us a Saudi Arabian dance. Eventually, after the de rigueur disclaimers, she got up, laughing self-consciously, and rolled up on the balls of her feet, first one, then the other, and flipped one hip up and down.

"There wouldn't usually be men present," she said, looking at the men. "All right, just for one minute." The music, the ouds and whatnot, was dominated by the sonorous, insistent beat of the drums. She wiggled to get the time and pushed up her sleeves. Throb, thrum, thump—she measured the drums and the sound of sticks clacking against each other, then she began a strange progress across the room, arms extended, hips rising and falling, at half-time at first, then she caught the full beat and doubled her pulsations. She added a little shimmy of her shoulders, her breasts moving softly beneath her shirt, stopped it, tried it again, all the while pendulum hips in motion. The music seemed to speed up. Her eyes narrowed and lengthened, and she did this dance all around the room, and might have stopped but didn't, into it now, another turn around the room. I couldn't look at Ian, couldn't watch him seeing her doing this sexy bump, grind, pelvic thrusts, exotic in her velvet pants, which were low-cut and showed her navel, so, belly dance. She was paying no attention to Ian or to any of us. I think she was dancing her freedom, another and another turn around the room before she stopped, laughing. We all clapped and cheered.

"We can all do it, every Saudi girl," she said. "I'm not very good."

I took this to mean she knew she was good. Women danced for each other at women's parties, she said. Some perhaps for their husbands eventually. I wondered if she'd done this dance for Khaled. I could imagine his gaze, smoldering with desire, now turned to murderous rage, like Othello's.

Ian then surprised me. He'd been watching, like the rest of us, and now said, " 'You are the music 'til the music stops.' Did you write that, Robin?"

"T. S. Eliot. 'You are the music while the music lasts.' It's a little different point." He recited a few lines more:

> These are only hints and guesses,
> Hints followed by guesses; and the rest
> Is prayer, observance, discipline, thought and action.

Prayer, observance, discipline, thought, and action—this was a good mantra, I thought, for anyone in my line of work, or for anyone: prayer, observance, discipline, thought, and action.

32

On Christmas Day, Suma appeared at the gate at lunchtime. We had planned a Christmassy lunch of turkey and yams, and plum pudding imported by Tom and Strand from England, and were about to sit down, a little subdued by the friendly indifference of Ian's servants, which strangely intensified the religious significance of the holiday, as if we were Christians huddled in a cave, hiding from the Romans, with Gazi for a hostage. I had spoken to my parents, and my sister in Paris, lying to them as usual, and that made me sad too.

The gate boy let Suma into the compound, and she rang at the door of the villa. Gazi, by agreement, was not in sight. I was in the dining room, but I could hear Suma come in, talking to Ian in her rather sweet, Frenchified voice.

"Oh, monsieur, I came directly."

"*Merci,* Suma, I'm sure you want to help."

"If I can, monsieur. I'm not sure that I can."

It emerged that Ian had telephoned her too, to ask for her help in getting Gazi's passport. I was surprised at that and asked myself if he would have discussed the wisdom of this with me before Gazi. Before Gazi, I think he and I would have talked over whether Suma was likely to help, wondering whether she instead would tell Khaled; we would have relished all the nuances of this question.

"I'm sure you can help. Come in. You know it is a difficult situation, I hope not too difficult for you in any way."

"I am sorry, I mean, I just cannot help," she said in a rush. "I've thought about it. It would not be right." She spoke rapidly, and her cheeks were flushed. "I wish you would talk to Mr. Al-Sayad. He is very upset, and so are the children. I am so sorry for them." She explained in a torrent that she couldn't steal the key to Khaled's safe, it would be stealing, forbidden by the Koran, and she couldn't help Gazi without stealing. Also, she could not condone a woman leaving her husband.

"I cannot help Madame Gazi, peace be with her. I am so sorry."

This was so off the wall I could think of no reply or remonstrance. Docile Suma, French-educated, a modern girl. Had she never seen a Feydeau play or read *Les Liaisons Dangereuses?* I went to join in the discussion.

"Sit down, Suma," Ian was saying. "You know we've seen your brother? He was here the other night." Suma followed us into the salon, seeming unsurprised. "Of course we didn't tell him where you are. He says your mother isn't well."

"No, I telephone her often, she is a bit better."

"I was hoping you've thought again about helping Madame Al-Sayad." We sat in the salon, and Miryam, as if acknowledging that Suma's status was above that of a servant, if not quite equal to ours, brought glasses of tea and served Suma along with the rest of us.

"I would like to, absolutely, she is so nice, but it would be to put myself in a false position, with my religion, and with my employer too." She looked at me as if I would explain this obvious moral choice.

"I don't know the details, Suma," I said. "I think Madame Al-Sayad was very unhappy." And I said a bit more about unhappiness in marriage. It seemed hard that I should be urging her to help save my rival, Gazi, but I did, which must at least have allayed Ian's suspicions that I knew about him and Gazi, if he cared. "A very abusive relationship."

"That's not true. Mr. Al-Sayad is a gentlemanly, mild person, very nice to his wife and children," she said. It crossed my mind she could have fallen in love with Khaled herself, or some complication like that.

No amount of persuasion weighed with her. We thought of getting Miryam to talk to her, or Rashid, since they were Muslims, but how could they avoid betraying to Suma that Gazi was here? It seemed to me that Suma was combining some of the worse traits of both cultures she belonged to—Islam's lack of humanity and respect for women, its excessive reverence for men, and an absence of sisterly feelings that can be very French.

As we talked, all at once, Gazi herself, evidently listening to the whole conversation, rushed in and seized Suma as if to shake her. "Do you want me to die?" Rattled and surprised, Suma pushed her away. Gazi's hair flowed over her shoulders, she wore some sort of little sleeveless shift and thong sandals. Suma seemed aghast. Maybe she had never seen her so undressed.

"What have I done to you?" Gazi was demanding.

"Do you want me to go to hell?" Suma said.

This chilled me even more. I had not guessed that Suma was religious enough to believe in hell. Why hadn't I seen her piety? What clues had I had? Could she really believe she'd go to hell for telling a lie? I hadn't even known they had a hell.

"Just a little key. It's on his key chain. Take it when he takes his bath or goes swimming."

"No, I'm sorry. I'm afraid as well."

"You agree he's dangerous, cruel," insisted Gazi.

"No, no, no."

"He has his bath at six, every day before dinner."

"I will not steal, or open his safe."

"He puts his keys on the dresser. I've seen them a million times. The bathroom door will be shut."

"No."

"I'll get them myself then," Ian said.

"Won't he miss them?" Posy asked. We stared at each other. Naturally he would miss them.

Of course I knew how to take an impression of a key. It's simple, using paraffin, or sealing wax, or even cold butter—my wax pencils are designed for such uses. My mind foraged for an explanation of how I might have come to have an esoteric skill like that, and I couldn't think of any to give them.

"How long is his bath?" Ian asked.

"Twenty minutes or so," Gazi said, hardly enough time to run the key over to the locksmith.

"You have to make an impression," I said. "In wax or something. I've seen it in movies." Ian gave me a "We'll talk about this later" look.

"Suma, at least agree that you won't tell Mr. Al-Sayad that you've seen his wife," he said.

"I don't know. *Je ne sais rien.* I need to think, I need to ask," she said, opening her arms dramatically, as if to invite divine intervention. Ian, exasperated, stomped out of the room, followed by Gazi, leaving it to Posy and me to drink our tea with Suma and utter mollifying sentences about poor Gazi and her terrible life. Suma seemed ruffled, even distraught, though having refused to help us, she was presumably spiritually clean and soon relapsed into a mood of surly serenity, if such can exist. I wish I had realized how actually distraught she felt, with her murderous brother in town, her mother sick, being pressured to filch things from Khaled's safe. I knew nothing of her life really.

We switched the subject to the medical examination her brother had proposed. Here she was more tractable. She sighed.

"Maybe I should agree. I refused before. Why should Muslim girls have to endure these things?" But it seemed she meant, more or less, that non-Muslim girls should be as prepared to prove their virginity as Muslim girls were; it still hadn't occurred to her that virginity was not an ideal, universally prized quality. It hardly seemed the time to reex-amine that old subject.

"You know what's involved?"

"Of course I know what's involved. Has my mother ever spoken of anything else? 'Sumaya will not take the gym class. Sumaya, never jump over anything, you might break your precious *puce,* then your life will be over!' If I lose it, her friends will despise *her,* people will laugh at the family; I am the sole bearer of the family reputation, it's all up to me. Your father and I want the best for you. No nice boy—no nice Algerian boy—French boys out of the question—no one will marry a girl who's been spoiled." I couldn't help but think how horrible the men must be, brought up to think this way. No wonder they had produced the ugly writings in Arabic—"Know, O Vizir (God be good to you!)"—about those bad exhalations and cures for a wide vagina and so on.

"How awful," said Posy, as if reading my mind. "I'd have given mine away tout de suite just to end the matter." I supposed she was fishing, to find out what the doctor would likely find in Suma's case.

"It's not simple," said Suma. "You can't just live for yourself. I do care about my family. Luckily we had the sorceress in." Suma smiled. "That calmed my mother. The sorceress puts a sort of spell on you that keeps you intact." Sometimes Suma's moral certitudes were more French than the French, but sometimes she seemed to be speaking ironically, and I never knew which.

"We can call someone if you like. Is there a special doctor? You'll have to see about this yourself," said Ian, who was back but was clearly uncomfortable with this female subject.

It was a strange conversation for Christmas, and of course Christmas brings back all Christmases, all incidences of family love, all memories of infantile credulity, the better to throw in relief the bleak present reality of a furtive Christian holiday in an Islamic country, a tenuous relationship with an Englishman of uncertain loyalty, and a clandestine job of indistinct utility and considerable improbability—all this a metaphor for real life, maybe, but not conducive to a mood of happiness.

33

Brabantio: Are they married, think you?

Roderigo: Truly, I think they are.

Brabantio: Oh Heaven! How got she out?

—William Shakespeare,
Othello, act 1, scene 1

Of course we knew it was only a matter of time before Khaled learned where Gazi was; there was no real possibility of hiding her, only of protecting her behind our fortress walls. We lived with the constant expectation of a furious Khaled Al-Sayad arriving on our doorstep, so that it was almost a relief when it happened, a few days after Suma's visit. He drove up, parked outside the outer gate, and confronted the gate boy, a fourteen-year-old, who stuck to his instructions about not opening up.

So Khaled just came in through the smaller door at the side and walked into the compound and up to the house in plain view of any-one in the garden, which included me, waiting for Rashid, who was bringing the car around. Khaled was wearing jeans and a sport coat, and he seemed calm. Turning away from the door while he waited for someone to answer it, he saw me standing by the drive and waved. The door opened behind him, one of the maids, who said something, shook her head, spread her hands, saying whatever she'd been told to say. The door closed, and Khaled began to walk toward me.

Of course I'd planned to lie when this happened. But when he came up, he seemed so completely informed, there was no point. Just as I was trying to think of how to circumvent the "I know you know my wife is here" part of the conversation inevitably to come, he said directly, "What do you think I should do?" With his beard, longish hair, and anguished, duped expression, he looked a little like the Jesus of Italian painting. It was a look of almost sweet resignation, as if to say "What a fool I've been, with my fancy American-formed ideas of female liberation. My friends are always telling me I should beat the shit out of her."

He didn't look like he was going to kill her, though, and everyone knows that it's often these nice guys and long-suffering spouses who somehow most invite the indifference and infidelity of their mates.

"I have no idea," I said. "These things—"

"I can't call the police, I can't break down the door. Maybe I can call the police, I could say kidnapping."

"Everyone would just say—"

"Well, God curse her, just tell her to go to hell," he said, his voice breaking like a teenager's. This seemed like a lame curse to me. He didn't look frightening or murderous, he looked like a man in pain.

"I'm sorry," I said stupidly, and of course I was sorry, he didn't know the half of it. Had he known the half of it, maybe he would have commiserated with me; we could have had at least a misery-loves-company kind of conversation. He looked at me rather wildly for a second more, then walked off down the path, and just then Rashid drove up anyhow.

In the car, I said to Rashid, "Do you know who that was?"

"The husband of the new lady?"

"Yes."

"He who can't control his women is a fool," said Rashid. " 'Leave her ye in the sleeping-place and beat her.' "

I had begun to think of how nice it would be for me if Gazi got her passport and could fly off somewhere out of my life; the idea of Khaled's key began to torment me. It would be easy to creep in and get it, if all was as Gazi had described it, and easy to make a wax impression, and get another key made, and open the safe and get the passport. Ian had only been speaking with bravado when he said he'd go get it, but I thought about it in earnest. As a clandestine action, it should not have been beyond me. Not only for reasons of love did I think about it, either; it was a sort of professional challenge, though I also knew it was absolute folly to take chances for merely personal reasons like getting rid of Gazi.

I was obliged to confide in Posy to a certain extent, and she agreed it would be exciting to steal Gazi's passport for her. We would go visit Suma, to discuss her virginity test or her brother, and Posy would distract her. It had to be during Khaled's bath, and he would never know we were there anyhow. The keys would be on the dresser; it was the work of a minute. It wasn't clear how we'd keep Suma from knowing, though.

"You could ask to use the loo," Posy said. "She and I'll be talking."

"What about the other maids and people in the house? And the kids?" There were things to be worked out, certainly. We talked about this a few times, then let it drop, but I got Gazi to draw me a floor plan, and she was enthusiastically behind the idea.

"An easy thing. Khaled is a predictable man. After afternoon prayers, he goes with his telephone into the bath, and there talks to Saudis and does various deals and talks to his office while soaking in the bath. How long he takes depends on what he has to do, but it is never less than one half-hour."

"What do the maids wear at your house?" I asked.

From her stare, she thought this was an odd question. "Why doesn't Suma help me?" she cried. "What have I done to make her angry? Nothing! She has to write a few letters in French for Khaled, type a little, she has her dinner with us, not the children, she has some time off every day."

"If I dressed up like a maid . . . ," I said. I could imagine the safety of the black robe, the veil, my hair covered.

"The maids would not go into Khaled's room during his bath," she said. "Never when he was in there."

This was two days after Christmas. Taft had told me to be ready on Thursday to drive the van to Rabat: I should set up my excuses for being gone all day. He wouldn't say why we were going to Rabat, though I knew we intended to pick up our "subject" then. I wondered if Taft didn't altogether trust me and thought I would tell the colonel our plans. Or maybe he didn't trust the colonel. If the colonel knew what we were up to, he would have time to warn Amid, and then if Amid wasn't where Taft had determined he would be, we would know he'd been warned. The leak would point to me having told the colonel and would also mean that the colonel was in touch with Amid.

But I did tell the colonel, and I will always wonder whether I was right. At the time, though, I had no paranoid suspicions and appreciated Taft giving me warning to allow for me to set up a cover story about going to visit a literacy program near Rabat.

34

One paradox of intelligence . . . is a further inherent problem in intelligence calculations. Certain military operations seem too risky to be taken seriously; yet precisely because of the tendency to discount extraordinarily high-risk operations as impossible, the risk involved is actually minimal.

—Michael Handel, "Avoiding Surprise in the 1980s"

On Monday afternoon, Posy and I walked over to the Al-Sayad compound to tell Suma about our success in organizing the virginity test. Ian's maid Miryam, who was in Posy's confidence, had found a special doctor. "Miryam says, 'Guaranteed results,'" Posy said. "Meaning, presumably, he finds what you hope he'll find." We wondered if it would be expensive and whether we should offer to pay.

"The brother should pay if it's so important to him," Posy said, "but of course we'll pay. I wonder if she is a virgin?"

"Growing up in France? I can't guess. Amid obviously thinks not."

We had discussed virginity tests with Gazi. "Girls are mortally afraid of them. They faint and scream with pain," she said.

"Why pain?" Posy had asked. "Are Muslim girls anatomically different from us?" Gazi had peered at her, as if unsure whether she was being made fun of.

"Not at all," she said.

"Way more hung up about it," I said.

Gazi said, "I'm not sure I understand that expression."

"It's so disgusting," said Posy again now as she lumbered along. "I just couldn't wait to not be a virgin, just to put it behind me, could you?" Not really. It had never been a focus of my thoughts, and not being one had not changed the essential me. But for girls like Suma, their lives were shadowed before and after the big event by the irrevocable, desperate step they were taking, and God knew what psychological damage was foisted on them by all these layers of rather dirty beliefs, shared by their mothers, brothers, fathers, friends. How could they ever shake this dirtiness off? All the smug disciples of cheerful, positive sexuality smirked with us from our corner, from D. H. Lawrence to the manuals we were given in seventh grade sex-education class, preaching its beauty and naturalness, while scraggly imams thundered at the poor Muslim girls about its forbidden nature and their mothers examined their underwear.

"Have you ever noticed, in the Koran, if you substitute the word 'cow' for the word 'woman,' it still makes perfect sense? 'Beat them, and then if they mind you, leave them alone,' things like that," Posy said.

I was having trouble walking as slowly as Posy these days. My steps would run ahead; I would have to slow and wait for her. She was aware of this and cannot have been unaware of herself as an example of the pitfalls of nonvirginity. "I'm sorry," she said. "I'm just as big as a cow. I can hardly put on my shoes."

When we drew nigh the Al-Sayads', their gatekeeper, seeing us, vanished inside, then came back out and opened the driveway gate, although we were on foot and could have gone through the door at the side. We had come at Khaled's bath time, but I wasn't committed in my heart to trying to get the key; I just planned to see how it went.

Suma was waiting in the hall; perhaps she had risen to the post of official hostess in Gazi's absence. She asked us in, not into the living room, or wherever the center of the household was, but into a room off the hall we had seen before. I tried to review the floor plan Gazi had drawn me, but it was turned around, and I had to reorient it in my mind. Either Gazi had drawn it wrong on purpose or had misremembered; it was just backward. If we'd come in the main entrance, then the kitchens were off to the left of this office, not the right, the bedrooms behind the court to the right, not the left, and so on. I didn't think Gazi would mislead me, it was too important to her, but it was hard to reverse the plan in my mind.

Posy began telling Suma about Miryam's efforts and the doctor and so on. "You don't seem thrilled," she said, her French less fluent than mine but not bad. "Thrilled . . ."

"*Bouleversée,*" Suma said. "*Non. Oui,* I'm insulted my family would think I'm so dumb that I would have a romance and throw away everything. I would not. I have my plans. But I do think it's unfair that Muslim girls are held to standards other girls aren't. *Mais c'est comme ça.* We are the winners too, to have our ideals and our faith." She went on in this vein, the great unfairness of it, but it was clear that Suma thought there was something to virginity all the same, some idea of its sanctity that to us was just an excuse to put conditions on womens' lives and control them.

"Men are privileged in all religions and women inferior, it is the same in all," Suma said. "They have twisted the Koran to mean things it doesn't really say."

"One thing," said Posy. "Supposing—even allowing that you aren't worried about what the doctor will say . . ." I could see she was searching for a tactful way of saying this. "How do you know that you have a, well, an intact membrane? Anything can pop it, horseback riding, bikes, Tampax. Some people don't have them in the first place?"

" 'Sumaya, don't lose your *trésor,*' " Suma said in her mother's voice.

"It's nothing to regret. There's a first time for every single thing in life," I said, "and usually each new thing improves you." I was thinking of the first time I drove a car or shot a gun.

"My first brain surgery," said Posy. "My first case of botulism."

"But you know what I mean."

"Well, when do I do it?" Suma asked. "I'm perfectly aware of what's involved, it's only a matter of a piece of paper acceptable to my parents, if that's what it will take. Before, I said no, but . . ."

"I don't think you should do it," said Posy suddenly. "Sod them, it's so demeaning."

"May I use the *toilette?*" I asked, jumping up. She would probably send me to the powder room along the hall to the left. That would be near the living room, and it would be necessary to go out into the courtyard and across it to the first set of French doors, which we could actually see from the room where we were sitting, but Suma not from where she sat with her back to it. She rose and led me to the door.

"The second door right there."

This caper seemed immensely foolhardy and risky, though nothing was really at stake, nothing fatal anyway. I was wearing a dark dress and in my bag had a black headscarf, in case anyone glancing out saw me. I put it on in the bathroom and tucked in my bright hair. I have the theory that women are somewhat invisible, especially in a household where there are lots of maids and visitors.

Also in my bag was a pat of dental wax, melted down from the wax pencils in my kit of stuff. On the dresser would be a bunch of keys; Allah was going to help me know which one was the key to the safe, I was going to take an impression of it, and it would only take a few seconds. Posy met my eyes, so I knew she would keep talking, discussing Suma's fate with her and organizing how we'd have to send a car from our house so no one at the Al-Sayads' would know where she was going.

I scuttled across the courtyard, a distance of maybe forty feet, and opened the French door I thought would lead to Khaled's room and did lead into a small foyer with an easy chair and magazines, like a shrink's waiting room, with a door at either end. If the floor plan was truly reversed, the left-hand one would be the bedroom. I hesitated before opening that door, listening, and heard nothing. I prayed the door wouldn't squeak. If someone was inside I'd say "sorry" boldly and walk away.

No one was inside. It was dim, dark, the shutters closed, in the desert way I can't get used to. The bed, grandiose headboard, neatly made with a leopard-printed velvet spread; two doors, behind one of which, presumably, was Khaled in his bath. I thought I dimly heard splashing. The dresser sat between the two doors, so that I'd have to steal across the room and not rattle the keys, if they were there.

I was afraid, though I saw that my physical manifestations of fear—pounding heart and damp hands—were out of proportion to the actual danger. Khaled was not a killer, presumably, and I had plausible explanations at the ready. It was more that I saw that I wasn't going to be good at this kind of illegal, risky activity in my chosen profession. It was too late for me, I lacked the anarchic core, some fuck-it mentality that Taft had; I was too goody-two-shoes. But maybe you improved, got used to crime the way I'd gotten used to being Lulu Sawyer.

The keys lay with coins and a watch on the dresser. I got out my patty of wax and studied the keys without touching them, trying to decide which one went with the safe. There was one obvious choice, thin and oddly shaped, among normal-looking car and house key shapes. Next, how to pick up this bunch of keys without jingling them? The stillness was suffocating, and now there wasn't even splashing from the bathroom, though at one moment someone might have hummed. In the manner of playing pickup sticks I moved the keys one by one around their ring to isolate the right one, then immobilized the others with one hand and lifted the bunch. It was necessary to take the target key off the ring; it couldn't lie flat enough on the mold because of the ring itself.

I had to decide whether it would be better to risk the noise or to take the whole bunch outside. I risked the noise, because I couldn't have stood to come back in. It was the wrong choice, as it turned out, but in the event, I could almost silently fiddle the key ring open. Then it was only the work of a few seconds to get a pretty good impression—as nearly as I could tell in the dim light—put the key back, and get out of there, not breathing for so long I thought I might pass out. Just as my fingers were releasing the keys, there was a noise, and Khaled was standing before me, towelless, naked as the moon.

We both screamed in unison; I remember only his look of horror.

I'm sure mine was the same. I fled out the door and across the court-yard; the image of his pale body in the dark room was etched on my retina. He would have to put his clothes on to pursue me, which gave me time to rejoin Posy and Suma, saying, "Oh my God, I went in the wrong room." Maybe that's what he thought too. Maybe he didn't recognize me in the black scarf. Why would he imagine it was me? We could hear him bellowing something in the courtyard.

Posy was already standing, ready to leave. I wondered how long I'd been gone; it had been like being underwater, seemingly forever, but was perhaps only a couple of minutes. My chest hurt now. "Let's go," she said.

"Tomorrow we'll come for you in the car at ten," I said to Suma, tense, waiting for Khaled to burst in wearing some provisional clothes, damp and furious.

"It's against my principles," Suma grumbled, "but I can't stay in Morocco, *c'est certain,* so, whatever it takes." Her sigh expressed the fatigue perhaps felt by all people torn between two cultures; for her, it was exhausting and bewildering to be Muslim and French—I would have thought to be anything and French—having to uphold some standard of civilization all the time.

Khaled didn't come out of his room.

I didn't think I could ask Taft to help with making the key; I couldn't see where he would get it done quickly. I knew of no company re-sources in town, so he would have to drive it to Rabat, and it would probably be me appointed to do the drive. Anyway I thought I could trust the colonel, who most obligingly took the envelope containing the mold, no questions asked except one, which I was prepared for.

So when the colonel said, "I hear you have some visiting relatives,"

I didn't panic. Since Taft had left such decisions to me, and I thought it highly likely the colonel knew Taft was in town anyway, I decided I could tell him, both to prove my good faith and to answer the question in my own mind about what game the colonel was playing. I thought we were unlikely to lose Amid now, as Taft and the others had him in constant view and the pickup—extraction, rendition, whatever we were calling it—was so soon. I couldn't help but think about Amid, being delivered by us into a limbo of torture and confinement. But now was no time for compunctions, and I didn't have any really—I believe in what we're doing and that people shouldn't blow each other up or murder their sisters. I pitied him all the same; a thin person, with dark eyes I could imagine staring hollowly from a cell, his ribs sticking out, like a starvation victim in a Goya.

"Or so I'm told," the colonel said cheerfully. "What will they be doing during their visit?"

I decided to be truthful. "It has to do with Suma Bourad's brother. I was hoping you could tell me why he's of interest."

"*Moi*, no, I was hoping you'd have some idea." He shrugged. "All we can say is that there appears to be no connection to the Casablanca bombings. That's what would interest us. He has a French passport, he's here as an ordinary French tourist. We welcome French tourists here."

That's as much as I learned: Amid had no connection to the bombings in Casablanca. Still, it was revealing that, of all arriving French tourists, Colonel Barka knew about Suma's brother, which meant either that he was visible in some connection other than his connection to Suma or that the colonel was aware of all French tourists, which seemed less likely. I was glad I'd been candid with him, augmenting my credentials as an ally and friend.

35

As to those women
On whose part ye fear
Disloyalty and ill-conduct,
Admonish them first,
Next refuse to share their beds.
And last beat them (lightly).

—Koran 4:37

The next morning when Posy and I picked Suma up in the car with Rashid, she had a younger girl with her, who seemed thirteen or fourteen, both their heads demurely covered. The pudgy, sweet-faced little girl kept her eyes resolutely down and said nothing.

"You remember Desi," Suma said, only that, with a nod of her head toward Rashid to indicate she couldn't say more in front of him.

Rashid had trouble with the address, and we had to back out of a little wrong street and were a few minutes late for the appointment in Guéliz. The clinic was a stucco, one-story structure with a respectable, clean appearance and a classy brass nameplate on the door, DR. MOHAM-MEDINE AZIZ, GYNÉCOLOGUE. The little waiting room was filled by one nurse behind a desk, three chairs, and the inevitable dwarf palm in a pot. I had expected a woman doctor, I had heard that only women doctors examined Muslim women, but, alarmingly, a man in a white coat crossed the room behind the nurse's desk and vanished into his office.

The nurse greeted us and went to tell the doctor that Mademoiselle Suma Bourad was here. Beyond the open door, we saw the examining table—more like a chair—slightly reclined, like a dentist's chair, with stirrups that would hold the knees widely splayed apart to afford the doctor an up-close view of the vulva of the victim, who was obliged to lie like a split pomegranate, her lower legs flopping unsupported from the knee brace. A wicked array of specula and spoon-looking devices lay on a tray nearby. The poor little girl Desi seemed to pale when seeing all this, and I thought she uttered a little sob in her throat. Suma pushed her toward the man, who beckoned, without a welcome, as if in his mind he already knew she had committed the transgression she'd been accused of. There was a strange odor of clinic and female that emanated from the doctor's examining room. I thought of terrible recipes in *The Perfumed Garden.* "Boil well in water, locusts," said the book. "This immersion is to be repeated several times. The same result may be obtained by fumigating the vulva with cow-dung. . . ."

Then a new doctor, a woman after all, appeared and closed the door on our anxious gazes. The nurse stared balefully at us. Almost immediately we heard poor little Desi scream. I wondered who was doing what. The woman doctor would examine her, and then the man doctor would sign the certificate, the nurse explained.

"She is frightened, *elle a peur,*" Suma said. "She believes she is hurt forever."

"They are often frightened," the nurse said in French to Posy and me. "The doctor is very careful, she is very gentle."

They were gone no more than ten minutes. The nurse was already preparing a document of some kind, and the woman doctor came out after Desi, waving a drying Polaroid photo. Desi gave Suma's name and birthday, as she had been told to do, and the nurse looked at her sharply.

"*Bien sûr*, I'm paying her mother," Suma said to us as we walked outside and waved to Rashid, who was parked. Suma had her arm around Desi's shoulder, and Desi's relief at still being alive and, apparently, undamaged had shown in smiles now. Suma spoke to her in Arabic.

"Or you could say Monsieur Khaled is paying," she said to us. "Of course the doctor was careful not to damage . . . anything." We all looked inside the envelope containing the certificate, at the photo that showed a viscous pink anatomical something, like a tonsil or the underside of your tongue. Desi stared at it, as fascinated as we.

"I was afraid he'd insist on taking a picture of Desi's face, too," Suma said. "That is, of the person who has sat for the photo. They do that, to make sure it is really *vous-même*. I hope this is good enough for Amid." Of course we had questions, Posy and I, but we didn't ask them. For instance, what had she meant, Khaled was paying?

I suggested we should go get it copied now, and I would see that Amid got a copy, and we'd get one for her parents.

"Thank you, madame," said Suma. "Please tell me what Amid says and what you think he feels."

36

Music hath charms to soothe the savage breast,
to soften rocks or bend a knotted oak.

> —William Congreve,
> *The Mourning Bride*, act 1, scene 1

The next night, the eve of our planned rendition of Amid, *le tout Marrakech* would attend a well-publicized concert at the French Cultural Center to benefit the Hassan II hospital and associated charities. The Paris Baroque Ensemble, chorus, and soloists would perform Moroccan and French sacred music, and the French consul would host drinks beforehand and a reception at the entr'acte in the courtyard. My status as Ian's official companion, as opposed to mere houseguest, was confirmed in public for the first time by my being there on his arm. This should have pleased and reassured me, but I saw only its utility for him in deterring speculation about Gazi being at his house, if any such existed. I knew it was my role as the beard.

Half of the invited guests were Moroccan, the other half French, with a few Brits and Americans thrown into the mix. Strand was there, but not Tom. The Moroccans were mostly wearing European clothes, with important jewelry, but some wore splendid embroidered djellabas and caftans. I half wished Americans had a native costume for ceremonial occasions, though I suppose it would be jeans. One of the king's sisters was to look in, at least for the first part of the concert, which would feature works by Messiaen, Telemann, and Verdi, and the Moroccan composer Mohammed Abdel Wahab, and extracts from the *nouba* Ochaq, whatever that would turn out to be, all to be performed on the piano, violin, oud, qanoun, and ney.

"The princess'll sensibly miss the works of Olivier Messiaen, Trois Petites Liturgies of the Divine Presence," said Ian, reading from the program. "The most deeply horrible music imaginable, I should think, Messiaen." I was impressed that he was so musically literate but apparently of conservative tastes. I wasn't familiar with the music of O. Messiaen.

But I must have been more aware than others of the presence of the DST, the Moroccan secret service, stout men in suits hovering near windows and exits, obvious to me by their burly size and expressions of alertness dissembled by nonchalance. That wasn't surprising, given the royal attendance, but I was totally dumbfounded to see Taft, elegantly dressed in a dark suit. To see him, moreover, moving toward us, accompanied by a well-dressed CIA-wife type (gray-blonde, slim, and fiftysomething, in a cocktail suit). He wore a hearing aid, or so it was meant to seem.

"Lulu! How nice to see you!" He kissed me on one cheek and waited to be introduced to my companions. The woman was called Peggy Whitworth. I introduced Ian, Posy, and Robin with elaborate correctness, unsure, though, whether to present them to Robin first, as the famous and oldest one, or to Peggy, the female, finally choosing the famous poet.

"Peggy drove down from Rabat just for this. Her husband, Dick Whitworth, and I were together in Korea. Honored." Taft nodded at Robin and shook all the hands.

"Dick's not much of a music lover," Peggy said, to explain her solo presence. No attempt was made to explain how they and I were acquainted, though I tried to think of one for later.

"Ian was just saying he wasn't a great Messiaen fan," I said.

"It's bloody hell, I'm sure," Posy said brightly. "French. The whole program is designed to goad me into blurting my most philistine thoughts. I know Robin hates it when I do utter them. Perhaps he sincerely doesn't have them!"

"Messiaen you have to have heard a few times," Robin conceded. "I heard his Mass for Double Choir at the Madeleine in Paris, and it was overwhelming," he said, not contradicting her on the cultural correctness of his inner life. Or maybe he didn't hear her. It wasn't the first time I'd had the suspicion that Robin was slightly deaf; he had that way of declaiming to forestall conversation. "Is it great music? Just possibly. It's hard to know. Or is it 'an empty, high-spirited trip through a complicated score,' where nothing happens, as, I think it was Adorno, said. And what we can expect from the Parisian Baroque—is it?—Ensemble cannot be guessed. . . ." He went on with his monologue in this incomprehensible way.

What was Taft doing here? Was this his way of telling the DST he was here on the up and up, with nothing to hide? Looking around the room as best I could, I didn't see Colonel Barka, but I knew he'd been worried about Taft being in town, a circumstance puzzling in itself, since it was our people who had put me in touch with him.

"Don't worry, we all want to roll these people up," Taft had said, meaning, I took it, Amid et al. Now he said, "Peggy is a talented pianist herself."

We found seats, which were not reserved, and somehow I was sitting next to Colonel and Madame Barka and the Crumleys, with Ian and Pierre Moment behind us. I was acutely aware of Madame Barka, whom I had never met; I had never been sure there was a Madame Barka.

Some efforts of beautification had conferred an air of musical seriousness to the basic auditorium style of the French Cultural Center. The small stage raised the musicians a little higher than the audience. Behind them two vases of flowers stood in niches against the back wall, which was decorated with framed photocopies of music manuscripts, perhaps Debussy or Satie. The soloists sat in folding chairs to one side, and a quintet of instrumentalists sat in the center, while the chorus crowded in and out as they were required.

The music started, beginning with "Nouba Raml al Maya," with the Chorale Josseur, for "violin, oud, qanoun, and ney," followed by "Va Piensero" from *Nabucco*—perhaps this work is obligatory wherever French people gather—and a short choral extract from Telemann. To this piece, the oud, qanoun, and ney contributed their sounds with a peculiarly discordant effect so metaphorically appropriate to the idea of East and West attempting harmony. Next we stood at our places during a short break in the program while the royal lady departed, a youngish woman in brocade with a dozen people in attendance.

The works after this pause were politely received. I was relieved that I was now able to hear Arabic music with more pleasure than when I first came, but I wasn't sure how much pleasure the locals were going to take in this French work. Perhaps it could pass as ecumenical;

though it did mention Jesus quite a lot, the words spoke more generally of love, and it seemed quite possible that it was supposed to be
taken as referring in religious terms to profane love as internationally
understood, the opposite of the Song of Solomon: *"Mon arc-en-ciel
d'amour / Désert d'amour chantez, lancez l'auréole d'amour . . ."* All of
which made me think only of profane love, of Ian, of Ian and Gazi, of
other passages in my life, though the music itself tended to blight any
reveries with its intrusive cacophony of atonal sounds and peculiar in-
strumentation.

You are the music while the music lasts. When the music was over,
we all stood up for the real interval, with dreamy smiles of approval
masking relief, and drifted toward the area where the drinks would be
served. I couldn't see Ian, who had been sitting behind me.

"Heavy duty," said Strand.

"Mademoiselle Sawyer, let me present my wife, Aisha," said Colonel Barka. I inhaled her perfume; she was a stoutish lady in European
dress, with a beaming, pretty face and the dyed black-red hair one
sees so often on brunettes of a certain age. Apparently she spoke no
English, so she did not attempt to speak to me at all but smiled in a
welcoming fashion, understanding that I was an acquaintance of her
worldly, estimable husband, he who went out every night. This took a
few minutes of chat as we shuffled along in the slow-moving aisles toward the foyer.

How are strange, upsetting things gradually borne upon you? It
didn't strike me in a flash, but just with a dawning sensation of dread,
that Ian was no longer there. Wasn't in the crowd, wasn't looking for
me, wasn't to be found. At the same time I was aware that Taft, with
a significant look at me, was moving rapidly toward the foyer and that
some DST guys, who had seemed to leave at the interval with the

princess, now moved in front of the windows of the lobby. The colonel, however, and Madame Barka shuffled along with the rest of us, unconcerned, talking of music.

"Drinks" were fruit punch and a slightly rum-spiked version, signified by different glasses, passed by waiters with trays of them. When, after ten minutes, Ian didn't come back, I felt afraid and flew to the side of Robin Crumley. Imagine a world in which Robin Crumley seemed a haven! I clung to him, and to Posy's enormous bulky presence, hoping the three of us would make a target big enough for Ian to find us.

"'E probably went to the gents'," said Robin in a strange, faux-cockney accent. But when we had stood there another ten minutes, Ian hadn't appeared.

"I think I'm not perfect," Posy was saying.

"My dear, to what do we owe this disarming admission?" said Robin.

"I mean, it might have to do with the baby. Or I'm just hungry. My stomach could be upset."

"Good God," said Robin.

"Maybe I'm wrong," Posy said. "There for a minute . . ."

I wasn't paying that much attention to Posy—she'd been saying things like this for a few days. I was thinking about Ian: Maybe he he'd gone to the men's room; but other possibilities flooded across my mind, suggested by Taft's presence and by the vague questions that surrounded Ian, even if I didn't articulate them. "We're going to roll up these people," Taft had said.

Peggy Whitworth in her brilliant yellow cocktail jacket came up to us, radiant, and said, "We get so little music in Rabat." Now I didn't see Taft, either. Maybe I was just having an attack of paranoia. Strand was next to me. "Do you know Strand Carter? This is Mrs. Whitworth," I introduced them automatically, and it seemed to me they exchanged a look, the tiniest glint, that said they did know each other. Was I imagining this? "Have you seen Ian?" I began to say to each person I knew, keeping Robin in sight. I went outside, where people smoked. Rashid, waiting with other drivers at the curb, had no notion where Ian was, had not seen him, or so he said. I went back inside.

Now there was Taft again, grim, and he said in a low voice, "Shit, Lulu, something's off here." It seemed to me then that everyone else was in on some plan, and knew what was happening, and were conspiring together to keep something from me. My head swam. Like a bride waiting at the altar, I insisted on standing in that lobby until everyone got impatient and made me come back to sit down.

I went back in. The second half of the program was about to begin, and it was about seven thirty. Afterward, the Moroccans would be going to restaurants to have their dinner, and we were expected at Madame Frank's. It struck me that maybe Ian would turn up there.

As I sat down, I was occupying myself with these observations, trying to train myself to notice, notice, when, in a way I've gone over and over trying to account for, in my peripheral vision, something jarred. It was a small note of discord in an otherwise calm atmosphere, in which I was apparently the only distraught person; I assumed my agitation at not finding Ian was peculiar to me.

I had been thinking of explanations of why Ian wasn't there, and about Posy's intermittent labor pains, and about how I was failing her by my insufficient interest in the drama of birth. I'm interested in it, of course, but just then almost everything else was more absorbing: my Amid journey; Ian's whereabouts; Gazi; when I should go back to Khaled's with the key, which the colonel was to slip to me tonight but hadn't, to get her passport. Who was Peggy Whitworth? Still, I did feel for Posy and resolved to be more of a sister or mom to her at her hour of need.

Nor can I account for my own actions next—they seemed automatic, and in retrospect I can see that if I'd thought through what to do, I'd have hesitated or fled. This wasn't something I'd been trained for, wasn't the automatic action of a well-trained person, and was not anything I'd ever faced; it was an impulse. But it was that I saw Desi, little Desi the certified virgin, kitchen maid at the Al-Sayads', sitting at the end of the row ahead, where no one had been sitting before.

Her clothes startled me. They seemed wrong. She wore a bulky, padded coat in an Indian print, but in retrospect, it wasn't even that so much, it was the fact that she was there at all, this child, a maid at the rich Saudi house—what on earth was she doing here? She was sitting in front of me and a little to the side. Without thinking, I moved over a couple of chairs to be directly behind her and leaned forward to make sure it was she. Strange: When I moved places, I took my purse with me. From behind her, I could inspect even more closely; the bulky, long garment she wore was not a garment she would wear, and the curve of her thin little shoulders and—for I leaned around to see her profile—her look of glazed despair, tears dried on her cheek, told me I was right to be scared.

The person whose chair I'd taken appeared and was tapping me on the shoulder. *"Madame, je pense que vous avez pris ma place . . ."*

"Oh, *désolée*," I said without looking, intent on what I was going to do—speak to her calmly, and at the same time trap her arms without letting her hands or arms touch her sides.

"*Bonjour,* Desi," I said in a low voice, smiling. *"T'aimes la musique? Tiens . . . sortons."* I imprisoned her arms and hands with all my force and hissed at her to be quiet. She jerked, gasped, froze.

This is not what I should have done. In such situations, the rule, or police policy, may actually be to shoot someone who appears to be loaded with explosive, before the suicide bomber can detonate his load; but I was not police, and she was just a small girl. Also, I might not have been right. She might have been a music lover, guest of her oud teacher, anything. I only thought later of good musical reasons she might have been there.

The danger was of setting her off in any struggle, blowing her and all of us up. I also should have shouted for people to move back, but my throat was sealed up; I had barely been able to whisper to her to stand up and walk outside with me. "Please move away," I said to the couple who were trying to reclaim their seats, but they were backing away anyway, mystified and alarmed.

Desi didn't cry out, she had frozen between my hands, but she stood at my direction and let me frog-march her to the foyer, where the waiters were clearing up the drinks. To the eyes of spectators, she might have been taken ill, was being helped outside by a friendly female companion. Perhaps all this took a minute, not more.

Taft, to my relief—I would be impressed with this later when I thought about it—was at my side, wherever he'd been, and said to Desi, "Slip off the coat," in a hoarse, scared voice, in English. Now Desi had begun to cry and protest in Arabic. Once the coat was off—it was guiltily heavy—Taft took it out of the building. The DST men moved toward Taft, waving their arms.

"Doucement, doucement," I said to Desi. She recovered her French. "Oh, madame, madame!" she wailed.

"Who brought you here, Desi? Are they here?" I feel I would have found out, but the DST converged, guns pointed at her, and took her away almost instantly, trembling and sobbing, under the eyes of astonished ushers and whoever happened to have been standing in the lobby. Did she know she had escaped death? From inside, music rose, choral voices, singing from a Haydn oratorio (I had read in the program) the words: "The great work is achieved." I couldn't tell if she knew what had been averted, or even if anything had, for I hadn't really seen inside the coat. Was she crying because she had welcomed death or feared it? Because I had scared her? Did she even know what might have happened?

This had all taken place in perhaps another minute, without causing any alarm among the audience within, much in the way someone fainting or having a coughing fit is dealt with at the other side of a concert hall without disrupting too much your enjoyment of the music. The music continued, discordant, atonal, played on strange instruments, and flowed out into the foyer like a soundtrack to our actions.

"Close one, maybe," Taft said. "How did you spot that?" I was shivering by now and could only shrug.

Even among professionals like Taft, there's an impulse to indulge the wish to hash things over, a sort of debriefing. "Let's have a drink," he said. "We can come back before it's over. Tell me what you know."

We sat in the café across the street, where we could see people when they began to come out. Mostly I was exhilarated. My heart still raced. I heard myself talking too loudly. I was expecting his praises. But then he said, "She wasn't going to detonate herself. I don't think so. No. She probably didn't know what she was wearing. Someone else was going to detonate her, or it was set to go off; I'd bet on that. Anyway, you saved her ass, Lulu. They might have shot her. Or I would have. You can't take chances like that, don't ever do it. Just get out of the way."

It was only then I realized, like a cold stab at my heart, that Taft and the others had seen Desi too, maybe all along, and might have shot her, but I had got in the way. And it was only then that I began to feel sick, really woozy, nauseated, though I knew it was just a reaction. The thing averted is worse afterward than during it.

We spoke of the horror of people who would send a young teenager to blow herself up. Taft's ire was also directed at the DST, at the promptness with which they had whisked Desi away, out of our clutches and those of her handlers.

Suma? Lots of things pointed to Suma, especially her influence over Desi, but didn't clarify her role. Maybe her whole presence in Morocco had been orchestrated, which, as I was telling Taft about Desi, came to seem especially likely, especially her move to the Al-Sayads' from the Cotters. Orchestrated by whom? Maybe Suma herself, maybe Amid, maybe others. It was hard to grapple with all the possibilities and the complete absence of any explanations. Say there was a bomb—to what end plant a bomb in the French Cultural Center? Obviously, to attack Western interests in Morocco, for that seemed to explain this venue, this night, and implied a master plan by any of the many possible evil forces—Al-Qaida; the North African subgroup, Al-Qaida of the Maghreb; other North African organizations; plots out of Pakistan; maybe the Al-Sayads themselves. Everybody wanted to get rid of Europeans and Americans, frighten them off.

So was Suma a dupe or a willing participant? And could Gazi be a plant, sent to spy on us? What was the role of Amid? God only knew; but I liked the idea that it wasn't love but policy that brought Gazi into our midst, that she was some sort of spy. I would have liked to talk to Colonel Barka about these things but he was nowhere to be found. He had disappeared, like Ian, after the entr'acte. Had they expected an explosion?

I told Taft how I had recognized Desi and that I didn't think she was a fanatic, just a clueless thirteen-year-old.

"Ah, what swine," Taft said over and over, "that little young girl! These people are unutterable." It was the first emotion I'd seen in him.

"What will the Moroccans do to her?"

Taft shrugged. The waiter brought us a demi-pitcher of *rouge* and said, "Bomb, did you hear? They got the Avis agency." He had no details. It almost didn't register with me.

After twenty minutes, the first people began to come out of the Cultural Center. I saw Ian's car start up, with Rashid at the wheel, and get in line among the other cars, come to take the Crumleys and me to the Franks'. Ian wasn't in it. Taft and I got up and crossed to mingle in the foyer as if we'd been there all along.

"Dom or Snyder will leave the van outside your place, outside the gate, along the road, keys under the front right tire. See you tomorrow," Taft said as we parted. It was so casual, we might have been arranging to have coffee, and no more was said about averted bombings; but his relief was as obvious as mine, a kind of palpable joy, even glee, that made us soar. Taft put his hand to his ear, his hearing-aid ear, and made an astonished grimace.

"They blew up Avis, some library, and an English tearoom tonight, must have all happened at the same time," he said.

37

If a man will begin with certainties, he shall end in doubts.

—Francis Bacon

In the car, I explained to Posy and Robin my missing the last part of the concert by saying I had been hunting for Ian. Everybody pitched in to devise explanations as to where he'd gone. Taken ill, kidnapped by terrorists, received a telephone call, and Posy's contribution and half my secret fear: eloped with Gazi. The other half of my secret fear was that it had something to do with Taft being at the concert; Ian was incriminated in something, and he'd taken fright.

"I'm sure he'll turn up at the Franks'," Robin said. "He knows where we'll be." Then, to Rashid, he said, "I think Posy's time may have come." I remember this odd locution, not immediately comprehensible;

it was a second or two before I saw it was the biblical expression meaning Posy's labor pains were increasing. Meantime, Rashid slowed the car at the Franks' gate. "If you could stay outside," Robin said to Rashid. To Posy he said, "Are you sure?"

I got the sense that Robin wanted me, or some other female, to interrogate her about the details of what she was feeling. Of course I had no idea beyond what anyone knows from a lifetime of moviegoing, that you have to time the contractions, and something about deep breathing. Posy had been such an unreconstructed pregnant person, however, so resolute about not talking or thinking about it, that I had no idea what she knew.

"I'm not sure . . . perhaps . . . false alarm . . . you hear . . . ," she said, relaxing with a reassured smile. "That's better. I think it's a false alarm. Just some twinges during the Haydn, and just then another."

"Shall we go home? Shall we go to the hospital?" Robin asked, with a tiny note of impatience, as if Posy was always doing this, intruding her personal condition on happy social occasions.

"I don't think so," said Posy. "I'd rather be at a party. I'm better now.

"Oh, no, it's not really anything," Posy said presently, in a piteous voice, as another spasm hit her. And so it went the rest of the evening. Every half hour or so, she would suddenly stop talking, with a look of concentration and concern, then smile and shrug as the twinge passed.

The Frank riad was in the medina, like the Cotters', and was superior to it, I could see, now that I had learned the criteria: size, antiquity, the care and taste of the restoration, and, to a certain extent, the panache of the decor. I suppose Madame Frank, with her real estate connections, had had an inside line on this superb example, which, as she explained, they had done up from a complete ruin, with passionate attention to authenticity, using craftsmen now irreplaceable to do the mosaics; and even the shutters were carved *à l'ancienne* with wooden tendrils and hand-hewn slats.

Madame Frank was alerted in confidence that we might have to leave her dinner party abruptly, and she reacted with bright understanding. "Ooh la la. How splendid. *N'attendez pas trop longtemps!*"

"No, I think I'll know," Posy said. "I don't think this is really it."

"Where is Ian?" Madame Frank asked. "We have certain things to discuss, you know—not that we would have a business conversation tonight, no, no, but I wanted to set up a real business appointment, to discuss the matter he mentioned."

I didn't even have to guess. He was selling her his developable tract of land in the Palmeraie.

"I'm so happy about this, the area is too lovely for his factories, that's the problem for him. Luckily for me, he could not get the planning permission for an ugly factory. I'll build something beautiful, and of course he'll be able to buy in at cost if he would like one of the units for himself. I hope you encourage that." She smiled trustfully at me.

"I don't know where he is," I said. "He had to leave the concert. I expect he'll be along."

Dinner was served rather promptly, with no aperitifs beforehand, maybe out of concern for Posy, maybe because it was latish, now after ten. There were puff pastries stuffed with sesame and chickpea, there was a delicate cucumber soup, a *tagine* of lamb. I watched Posy. Her face was slightly puffy, making her eyes smaller. She was still pretty, but I wondered what she looked like not pregnant.

As expected, the talk concerned the bombings. Madame Frank had been watching television and had more information than we. There had been bombs at the library and the Avis agency. A Moroccan employee of Avis had been killed, and at the library, an Englishwoman, the volunteer on duty, had been killed—an Elsie Pring. We expressed our shock and dismay, truly felt. Miss Pring was Ian's secretary. Our library, a few books, the life of a mild English spinster. It seemed so pointless.

"It's beginning, it was bound to," said Posy.

"Oh, they will control these people," said Madame Frank. "It was to be expected, there is so much unrest elsewhere. But the Moroccans know it is in their economic interest to have peaceful development and European investment. They'll round up the fanatics soon enough."

"The Algerians probably thought that too," Robin said. "And look at Lebanon."

"Yes, but here the natives are culturally very French," Madame Frank repeated—her favorite delusion. Then she brought the talk back to center on the property market in Marrakech, and the errors to be found in this or that restoration, and the criminal tendencies of Moroccan contractors, who had to be watched like eggs boiling. There was a slight tension over Posy's condition, and conversation would slow if she made the slightest stir. She skipped the cucumber soup, I saw, a first for Posy, who has the appetite of a drover. I could only keep thinking of little Desi, now in the clutches of the DST, and wondered what had really happened and whether Suma was connected to it. And of course, of Ian.

"I've noticed that here, Yvette, and at other French occasions, the food is better than at Ian's, where the cook is plain Moroccan. Do you French ladies teach your cooks a thing or two?" remarked Robin gallantly.

"Bien sûr," said Madame Frank, showing all her dimples. "The village cooks only know a few dishes—*tagine,* couscous—and tend to overcook those. I fancy I've made some impression on them."

We left before midnight. Posy's pains were still intermittent, or even seemed to have vanished—she couldn't say precisely—and they had not really impeded her enjoyment of the evening. "It's more of a backache," she said. I supposed they would worsen in the night, and that's what happened.

When we got to Ian's, it was just after midnight; as we pulled inside the gate, I could see the dark shape of Taft's van already parked outside on the main road across from the entrance. Inside, the maids were all in bed, Pierre too, evidently, and a pall of oppressed silence lay over the house. In the dark, the odor of the jasmine was almost like ether or chloroform.

There were no lights on in Ian's room. I went into the bathroom and listened, then knocked on the door to Ian's room. When no one answered, I peeked in. Undisturbed bed, no signs of anything moved or out of place. There was total silence except for insect noises from the garden, heard through the open window, but small and desiccated sounds; there were no robust crickets or frogs here. I looked in his closet, but since I'd never looked in it before, I couldn't tell if things were different. There were no papers, records, incriminating notes; things were almost hotel-like in their austere neatness. Ian was simply not there and his stuff was.

I went back to my room and changed out of my concert-going clothes into the pants and shirt I'd wear in the morning. Then I sat on the edge of my bed and just reexperienced the anticlimaxes of the evening—Ian vanished, bombs that didn't go off, babies that didn't arrive. I tried to relive the high of the moment when I'd grabbed Desi, but the feeling was gone; it was an action that now seemed banal in its simplicity and questionable wisdom—perhaps, after all, her coat hadn't been loaded with bombs.

I eventually fell asleep, thinking about Suma and about the moments the night before when Ian had come into my room. He was trying to make it seem like one of his regular visits, including the possibility of making love (signaled, usually, by his unconscious gesture of loosening his collar), maybe just to hash over the day; but we both knew it had been weeks since he'd slept with me and that some unnamed condition had intervened—I had a name for her, of course. It had been awkward, but I could see he was trying to make his visit seem friendly, normal. Nonetheless it also seemed valedictory, so that when he said, apropos of some local gossip, "Lulu, it's wonderful having you here, it's remarkable what a Moroccan you've become—I think you really belong here . . . ," his tone of deanlike congratulation, hearty and impersonal, was the same to me as saying good-bye.

Now I tried to sleep a little, dozing off and on, and was waking when Robin tapped on my door, at about four, and asked me to come help Posy. "This is surely it, I think," he whispered. I came fully awake; I had to start out in the van at five thirty. I wasn't sure what I could do for Posy except offer moral support, but I went up to their room with Robin.

Tiptoeing up the stair, we met a boy tiptoeing down—a Moroccan boy, dressed in a white shirt, jeans, little slippers, and a little hat, which meant he must have been about thirteen or fourteen, very pretty, with large, dark eyes. Above on the landing, the door to Pierre's room was hastily shutting. I had no time to absorb this or ask what it meant. Pierre and the local boy hustlers, why should I even be surprised? The boy was startled but, looking away, slid past us, buttoning the shirt, and went out into the court.

Posy was dressed, putting things in her bag, or rather taking them out and putting other things in. She'd been packed for a while. "I knew this would happen," she cried. Whereas before she'd been calm, now, evidently in pain, panic had taken her. She appeared to feel that maybe Robin wouldn't be the most reassuring companion, not likely to know what to ask in her behalf, and that a woman friend should be with her.

But of course I couldn't go with them—I don't know quite what I said, how I put it. "I'll be there as soon as I can," and so on, though it must have puzzled them to think I had an appointment at five in the morning. I connected it to Ian, thought I should stay by the phone, vague things like that. It was unsisterly, almost a betrayal, not to go with them. My concern was to get them gone, so that they wouldn't see me driving off in the van. Even panicked, Posy, going off to face childbirth, was calmer than I, but I hoped my fears didn't show.

Rashid was up—I didn't actually know where he slept. He was standing alertly by the car, clearly eager for a wild ride, an urgency, a drama of some kind. I knew he didn't have children of his own—Ian had told me, when I had mentioned Rashid's brother the taxi driver, "The brother has six children, Rashid sends them almost all his money." He also had said, "The Saharawi are like the Palestinians, and it's going to finish the same way, I'm sure, only those poor bastards are stuck out in the desert besides. The Palestinians have water at least. . . ."

I walked to the car with them.

Robin looked at me, shaking his head, and said, "Really, I never thought I would have fantasies of fatherhood, but really, I was just now imagining the child—a great playwright. Not even born and his father is planning his life! These truisms I never imagined of paternal excitement . . ." He looked absolutely thrilled.

Posy said, "Lulu, please, please come with us," and stretched out her arms like a drowning person, tears in her eyes, frightened to be condemned to go off and give birth in the presence of sinister, swarthy, woman-despising North African strangers. I said again that I couldn't. Of course she accepted this, but I saw she hadn't expected such a rejection, a blow, even a shock that she had so misunderstood our friendship, to see I wouldn't trouble to go with her now. I embraced her, and felt her shrink a little, and saw them safely driven off, out of sight. Then I went back upstairs to get the gun and a bag of necessaries I'd packed—just like Posy. The difference in our aims didn't escape me.

38

Shall the prey be taken from the mighty,
or the lawful captive delivered?

—Isaiah 49:24

At the appointed hour, a few minutes before five, I crept out through the main gate, aware that I was seen by the gate boy, who'd been wakened by Posy and Robin's leaving. Though we were far from the mosques of Marrakech, sometimes the call to prayer drifted across the sands, maybe from the radios of the village nearest us or wafted by some crusading current of air, especially before dawn, as today. It was beautiful, and it was possible to feel it as a kind of blessing for this venture.

The key was under the tire. I got in the van. I wasn't prepared for the paralysis of my mind when it came to making the smallest decisions, things I hadn't thought through or learned: Was it better to idle the engine or wait to start it up when I saw them coming? It's prudent to examine each action, but this need for deliberate thoughtfulness was unnatural; normally I would just plunge on.

I tried to think the problem through and decided it was quieter and used less gas to wait with it off, but then I was too anxious to do that, afraid that it wouldn't start, had to know if it would, so I started the motor and then turned it off. The tank was full, and I put the firearm under the seat. I noted two ten-liter cans behind the rear passenger seat, either gas or water or one of each. The light before dawn made the landscape the deep color of violets, the square stucco buildings and walls like cubist paintings from someone's blue period. Though the first call to prayer had sounded, no one had heeded it that I could see. Not even a rooster had crowed, but then I heard the first one, and in a few minutes, three figures appeared at the end of the street. I started the engine again. I put on a head scarf, a black one left by Gazi, and I had her big abaya in my bag, though I wasn't sure why.

As they came nearer, I was reassured to see they were Dom and Snyder. They were . . . not pushing, but sort of bearing between them an unwilling man whose face was covered by a cloth bag, his hands behind him, probably taped, his mouth too, probably, judging by the silence, the absence of protest or cries. The only noise was the dragging and stumbling of his feet, the crisp strides of Dom and Snyder.

Dom came around to the driver's side to look at me—to make sure it was I, I guess—and said, "Good girl," then helped Snyder push the man, presumably Amid, against the side of the van. They began to undress him. With impressive teamwork, they peeled off a slipover sweater, then his shirt, then they unbuckled his jeans and pulled them down. As I watched, they pulled down his jockeys, knocking him down in the effort to get him to lift his feet, Amid resisting. Then they yanked him to his feet again. His poor little prick was shriveled with the morning chill, and with fear. I thought they would put something else on him, but they didn't, just pushed him naked backward into the cargo space and then pulled him out and to his feet again. "Say something to him," Dom said to me, I guessed so he'd know a female was there. That's supposed to be especially humiliating.

"Okay," I said. "What shall I say?" I hoped he didn't recognize my voice. I was afraid they might ask me to help with the interrogation later. I had no training for that, and a vivid memory of that dimwitted girl soldier at Abu Ghraib holding the guy on the leash. Now, if Amid was finding this humiliating, he gave no reaction except to thrash against his bonds. Dom next put a loose shirtlike thing over his head; Snyder put a belt around his waist and then began to unwind the tape from his wrists and chain them to the belt. Dom put on a rubber glove—a particularly creepy action—and now, suddenly, punched him in the belly; and when Amid doubled over, Dom turned him around, parted his bare buttocks, and appeared to stab him with something between his cheeks.

Despite my qualms about all this, I was impressed with their efficiency and air of calm. They didn't seem hurried or to fear being seen or interrupted. Maybe others—maybe Moroccan DST—were keeping watch for us around the corners. I knew I'd rather be on our side than Amid's. Later, I saw how peculiar it was even to think of taking sides; of course I was on "our" side. But I'd also begun to see that ambivalence is built into life in the shadows; even as you hope for unshakable convictions, you feel them drain away. Part of me would rather have gone to the hospital with Robin and Posy, out of friendship and curiosity, and the special excitement of a new baby coming, and in the name of female solidarity. But only a part; why did the other part feel glad to be getting behind the wheel?

"Okay," Dom said, and nodded at me to get back in the driver's seat. Snyder drew out his gun and walked around to sit next to me. Dom, evidently not coming, waved us off. I knew the way.

Snyder wasn't talkative. From time to time, he reassured himself that Amid was still inert, hence docile—there was no metal divider between us and him. There wasn't much traffic, trucks mostly, and the occasional cart, horse or mule-drawn, lumbering along, going where?

"This isn't so bad," Snyder said. "We used to have to get them to Salé, or even Damascus."

I'd calculated it would take us about seven hours, at worst, depending on the roads and traffic. The van handled well in the windless morning: The day might be unseasonably warm. With luck we'd be there and back by dinnertime. That's if we just dropped Amid off and didn't stay around. That's what I hoped.

I was glad I didn't have to meet his eyes. I tried to think about him as a fanatic, a danger, a cruel brother, master of murderous intrigues; but I had little preparation for this way of thinking, as I had never met a murderer or dangerous person that I could think of. But of course, in my line of work, at some point I would meet one, would interact with one—I remembered Desi but somehow couldn't count her. So far, no dangerous people except maybe my own experienced colleagues Dom, Taft, and Snyder. Maybe they'd killed people. Anyway, they knew when to duck, had a wariness that came from experience. I would be like that eventually, though people assured me most of us go a whole career with perfectly clean hands. Why shouldn't I?

These were my thoughts as we sped along. I was happy to be going fast on an open road—it made me homesick. Amid kept my mind off the subjects that really made my heart pound: Ian, Gazi, and Posy. I imagined Posy groaning and writhing, suffering in her labor, chewing

on a rag, Robin mopping her sweaty brow—a scene from *Gone
with the Wind,* maybe, or any Western in which a baby is to be
born.

Snyder seemed so glum, I had to battle a hostesslike urge to draw
him out, as we drove along, with questions about nothing, banalities
that wouldn't reveal us to Amid, if he woke up and was listening.

Me: "So, did you get a chance to see the mosque?"

Snyder: "Yeah, I walked around the garden. Very nice."

Me: "Lovely mosaics."

Snyder: "They can't depict the human figure. Why is that?"

Me: "I don't know."

Snyder: "Some edict of the Prophet. His whims."

I agreed with Snyder there, except that the Prophet seemed not so
much whimsical as just a man limited by his era and desert background. It was the fault of his followers that they couldn't tell the difference between a durable general injunction like "be good" and some
specific tribal management issue like "only four wives to a man" or "a
camel is worth four cows."

I tried to imagine what Amid was feeling or thinking, but I
couldn't. My own self-consciousness too painfully intruded: What was
I doing here, how had I come to this, barreling along a road in an Islamic country with a naked victim and a gun? Other imponderables:
What about Ian, and where was he? Was Pierre a sexual tourist? The
true nature of Khaled? Posy's baby? Would she ever forgive my seeming indifference to her one real-life adventure? Probably Amid wasn't
feeling anything; he still hadn't moved. I was vaguely angry with him
for cheating me of a conversation in which I would have probed the
subject I cared most about—whether he had planned to kill Suma.
The interrogators at Ain Aouda weren't going to ask about that.

I began to think Amid should stir. He was still lying with a disconcerting limp inertness that made me want to poke him, just to see.

"What was that we used on him?" I asked Snyder.

"Shot of pentathol," Snyder said. "Practically instantaneous, but the downside's the time, it's short-acting, so, the oxycodone suppository."

Seven hours ahead of us. With the light, storks gathered by the side of the road, so correct for Posy's enterprise. The goats were already up the trees. Maybe they slept in the trees—I didn't know, and neither did Snyder. In the months I'd been here, I'd gotten used to the strange sight. Eventually we turned on the radio—Moroccan music. Our map took us 280 kilometers, almost to Rabat, then we were to turn off south on a road to Ain Aouda, a small city off of an even smaller road, then go by unmarked road to the prison facility the Moroccans were building with our help.

It was a "black site," a place we didn't acknowledge existed, a heavily fenced cement-block building, cars and vans within, guards at the gate. We had passwords and IDs, which were carefully checked by two teams of people, Moroccan, with somewhat startled looks at me. While they were conferring, I put the scarf over my hair again. I'd pulled it off in the hot car.

"We have cargo," Snyder said at the inner gate, nodding at the lump under the blanket. "Client," I said, pronouncing it the French way, "cleeyant," in case the guard didn't speak English. He leaned in to look for himself, nodded, and we drove into the compound. Men with guns ringed the van. Snyder got out, opened the cargo door, and pulled the blanket off Amid. He hesitated, as if he saw something strange, then pulled on the inert Amid's arm, which flopped. Two guards helped Snyder pull him out and lay him on the cement. There wasn't going to be a quick turnaround here, so I killed the engine and got out too. Snyder said, "I think he's dead, the son of a bitch."

We all stared in dumbfounded silence. I had that numb feeling you get when your first fears are confirmed. We should have stopped to check him. Snyder dropped to his knees and pulled the tape off Amid's mouth. The boy was a funny color, and he looked pale, limp, and waxy. Then his mouth opened and vomit oozed out, cupfuls, foul and foamy, in a torrent of reeking bits. Someone began running.

Snyder pushed uncertainly on Amid's chest, then tried to rearrange his limbs in a better position for resuscitation. I could see him hesitate and think of mouth-to-mouth resuscitation. But almost immediately, a big, red-haired man, maybe a doctor, apparently American, took over and wiped Amid's mouth, then felt around inside it.

"Aspiration tube," he said to someone. "Probably too late." I was impressed there was medical assistance here at such a level, for tubes came flying from somewhere, feet, shouts, an IV bottle on a stand was rattled over from another building. Snyder and I backed away so the doctor could work. Minutes went by.

"Dead on arrival," said Snyder, looking at me. "Son of a bitch. Shit, that's tragic. He took a hard blow to the gut."

"Allergic to the drug?" I said, but mostly I was thinking, This is my fault. If only I'd said something when I'd had the feeling something was wrong, when he'd lain so still. Still, how could he just die like that, without a twitch or objection? But he was dead, apparently had vomited and choked on his vomit. I thought of the blow to his belly and of how silently he'd lain there, tranquilized, so we'd thought. At some point choked but had given no signal, no resistance or protest, perhaps was unconscious and hadn't even known.

Snyder was as shocked as I. We waited, as at the scene of an accident, for someone to take some action, interrogate us, make a report, but no one did, Snyder cursing at Amid as if to curse him back to life. Eventually the doctor sat back on his heels, shaking his head. The men glanced at him and away, hiding the reproach in their glances. Stupid, arrogant American bastards.

All at once, two men standing nearest us turned to me and began angrily shooing me away with flaps of their arms, as if I were a goose; go, go, shoo, just go, I took them to be saying. I backed away and went around to the other side of the van where they couldn't see me, but I could see them through the windows. Snyder came to stand by my side a minute. "Probably one of their prohibitions. No blondes," he joked. Then he went back to talk to them. To my surprise, Snyder, whose conversation was monosyllabic and profane, spoke fairly voluble French and Arabic when he had to, learned at Georgetown.

"No women," he came back to explain. " 'A woman may not gaze upon a dead man.'" He stood with me awhile longer, almost protectively. We watched through the car windows while the men loaded Amid's body onto a stretcher and covered his face. Then they took him into the hospital building. I began to think about Suma and whether I could hint to her that her worries were over. I tried to tell myself the world was better off without a terrorist collaborator who'd kill his own sister, but would he really have?

When the peculiar cortege was out of sight, I came out from purdah and insisted on going inside with Snyder. For one thing, I didn't want to sit there by myself in the bleak prison courtyard. Also, I needed to pee. Snyder was looking at me as if he were seeing for the first time that I was more than merely his driver—I was a liability. At that moment, I tended to agree with him.

As we went in, the Moroccan governor of the prison came out and issued orders to the smattering of men still there, but he seemed to have nothing to say to us. Was there reproach in his glances too? Stupid arrogant American bastards can't drive a man two hundred kilometers without going to this extreme.

We had no one to say sorry to. We were sorry, though. I, at least, was anguished—you can't just go along killing people. I hadn't planned on that. In our training, the suggestion was out there that target practice and elementary pharmacology were all "just in case" and that such things were almost never needed.

We were in trouble, surely? Should Suma be told? His family? Or would he just disappear, never to be heard from again, they would assume vanished into Iraq or Pakistan? "I don't know, Maman, he said he was going to Rabat," she'd tell the poor mother, they would never know.

Sometimes your life is just in a wreck. For the first time, I felt like I was in the wrong life. I could have done lots of other things—studied orangutans in Sumatra, gone to the Cordon Bleu. I was feeling this discontent, though, not for the first time, because in other lives I'd felt it too. I'd examine the question of my basic adjustment further at some more convenient time, for of course this wasn't a time to think of myself, I knew, even though my thoughts kept sliding in an undisciplined way into a preoccupation with my own skin. Only unpleasantness lay in the future: an interview with Taft, an interview with Ian—for he must eventually come back to his large establishment, mustn't he? An interview with Suma, necessarily mixed with lies.

"Will they do an autopsy?"

Snyder looked unsurprised, as if he hadn't realized how dumb I was, to imagine he'd know. "I don't know what kind of records the

Moroccans keep. Probably have a category for tragic accidents. Who knows? I know the Koranic burial rules—they hustle them into the grave pretty quick."

As it worked out, we had an afternoon of reports and hanging around, in an atmosphere of Kafkaesque bureaucratic business, and didn't get on the road back until after five. Snyder offered to drive, and, feeling sick, I would have been glad of it, but I didn't want to shirk, so I drove in the growing darkness, on the lookout for un-lighted carts, and had a couple of near misses. My feeling kept grow-ing, of culpability, of having crossed over some impediment of dismay and reticence, and now I was a dangerous person myself.

I had never before done anything really bad, not really, and now I had.

Mostly, I kept thinking of the nice young man in the clean shirt who'd come to dinner and given no sign he was a fanatic, and maybe wasn't. Had they—had we—snatched him from his prayers that morning? Another reminder of the scary unpredictability of life. What is the argument? That you should live as if dying daily. Montaigne? St. Augustine? Or that it's dangerous to believe anything? He was killed for his beliefs. I wasn't having any coherent thoughts at all, I was just in a turmoil of pointless agitation, of unfocused and unproductive sorrow.

If only I had spoken up more insistently when it seemed to me he was lying too still. Instead of saying that, I'd asked what the drug was, the elliptical form of the question. Hadn't wanted to seem to criticize—hadn't meant to, was simply uneasy. Maybe that's what Taft will say, that I should have spoken up; maybe this will officially be my fault, my responsibility as driver of the car.

And, over and over, what were we going to tell Suma? I kept com-ing back to that. I knew we wouldn't tell her anything. He will just disappear. She'll never know what happened to him. She'll always imagine he's still stalking her; her life will be ruined. The parents will never hear from him, will wait forever, will assume he fell in distant Baghdad or Kabul, or Pakistan, or perished on some mountain pass.

On the road, we telephoned Taft, who was angry but didn't seem to blame us, just circumstance, cursing the loss of somebody who was going to be the key to us knowing a whole lot of things about North African terrorists. But he was also philosophical: At least there was one less bad guy in the world. He was surer of that than I was. It seemed on the drive back that Snyder felt as bad as I did. This came out in the way he would blurt out from his silence, from time to time, "Just one of those things," or "These things happen."

"What will happen now?"

"Many reports," he said. "Many, many reports."

Taft was waiting at the Sheraton, up in the room, with a bottle of bourbon, and poured stiff portions for Snyder and me. He handed me half a glassful. He and Dom were already drinking. They had a sympathetic air, but Dom's was slightly patronizing to the screwups, or, at least, to me, to the point that, once, I blurted out that it was he who'd calibrated and administered the dose, not me. Like a whiny child, a tattletale, blaming others.

"We're not playing the blame game here," Taft said. "There'll be plenty of shit to go around."

We hashed it over and over. The recitation was a form of torture in itself.

"When did you notice he wasn't moving?"

"We were almost to Ain Aouda."

"We weren't looking for him to move," Snyder said. And much

more in this vein. Taft asked questions and Dom wrote down what we said. I was desperate to go back to Ian's and somehow wash it off. But I knew I couldn't, any more than Lady Macbeth could.

It was almost two a.m. before I got home to Ian's. As we had planned, Snyder drove me in the van as far as the road that led past the little shanty village where, I guess, the maids live, near the villas of their employers. He still had to wipe the van and leave it at the airport; I would walk from the village—the villagers asleep, no one on this road. I had brought one of Gazi's abayas to wear for invisibility, and in the black night I did feel invisible as I slid past the small houses with their tin roofs and blue doorways. Somewhere a radio played a wailing voice, like a lament for Amid. Posy and I had walked this road before, only about fifteen minutes from Ian's, yet now it felt menacing and long. My heart was frozen in an absence of thought, except about how dark it was.

"I'll be fine, Walt," I'd said, getting out of the van, but now I was scared.

At one point, a few houses had sprung up at a bend in the road across from the others, so that the road ran between the old and newer habitations, making it necessary to go for a few hundred feet through the village itself. I had thought that at this hour that stealing through unseen would not be a problem, but coming around the corner, I was stupefied to find a scene of life, men and boys in a ring around something I couldn't see, maybe a cock or dog fight, though I hadn't heard of those in Morocco. I was shocked; I had so banked on finding everyone asleep.

I was in a fragile state of mind, unable to decide what to do, unfamiliar with whether a woman would be out alone and what would be concluded about her, unsure of the safest course. Did I walk confidently along the road? Run? Sneak around the periphery of the houses, off of the road, like a prowler or thief? But I hesitated too long and was seen—the group turned to stare, it moved together as if it had been swayed by wind, not hostile, necessarily, but awakened, shocked in its turn to see a black-robed woman crouched there. A figure darted out and toward me, a boy. My impulse was to run, but I was mesmerized. He took me by the hand.

"Mademoiselle Lulu, I will see you home."

Who could this be? I had no idea. I thought I was hallucinating or dreaming. This boy took me by the hand and led me down the road another hundred yards, me like a little donkey trotting at his side, my abaya sliding foolishly off my shoulders, a little woozy from Taft's whiskey now. No one came after us. This boy must be someone we knew. It came to me eventually that it was the gate boy. I hadn't recognized him—I had never really seen him, though he was always there, and now he had come to my rescue, if it was rescue I needed.

"It is so dark," he said. "Did you have problem with the car?"

He left me at the gate and headed off toward his village again. It was lucky I had a key to the door next to the gate, for the place was locked down. There were still lights on in the kitchen, and the lights in the courtyard had been on, as if for me, but clicked off as I came in. Pierre Moment was sitting alone in the inner patio, though it was cold out. Maybe he'd just been saying good night to some little catamite. I looked to see if there was anything on the table, but it had been cleared except for two glasses and a bottle of red wine. I was starving, though it seemed paradoxical to be both hungry and sick at heart.

"Is there any news of Posy?" I asked.

"*Oui! C'est très bien, une petite fille!*" Robin had just telephoned but was not yet back, he said. Pierre was waiting up for him. "He ees *complètement* berserk."

"Posy's okay?"

"*Très bien. Fatiguée. Tout s'est bien passé.*"

39

And now you've aired all your smug Western views, probably even having a few laughs deep down at our expense . . . but by inflicting your own naive ideas on us, by rhapsodizing about the Western pursuit of happiness and justice, you've clouded our thinking.

—Orhan Pamuk, *Snow*

My restless dreams were not of Amid or death but of strange childhood things. My fears for my parents. Bandits stopping our car. Someone saying, "Take their skin," and when I cry in fear, the bandits say, "Not you, little girl," not understanding my terror is for my parents.

My first thoughts in the morning weren't of Amid either. These rushed in only moments later, with a sickening swell of despair at what had happened and couldn't be undone. Where I had thought him a terrorist, now he seemed a handsome, promising young man taken (by me) before his time. I tried to tell myself some of the things Taft had told me—"Death doesn't scare them; they're transfixed by hate"—but I couldn't see him otherwise than as a person with his life ahead.

My very first conscious thoughts had been of Posy and were of a lightness and happiness I'd have liked to prolong. But then the events of yesterday came to me, and the earlier problems—Taft, Ian gone, Desi, the little boy on the stairs, the gate boy—all the ugliness and complication gave me the feeling I was caught in meshes of illegality and danger I would never escape from, but was only doomed to struggle against, and with struggle would tighten my bonds. For, looked at realistically, such was the case—my state was one I couldn't get free of; I must forever thrash within the category of killer.

I lay there a few minutes, dreaming backward into sleep, of being a young woman again, before college, hanging out and necking in cars, with no thought of the future. Then back to the present: contractual obligations, love, rage, guilt. I reviewed what I should do next: I should try to find out where Ian was—check his room more carefully, talk to Suma about her situation, find out more about the library bomb, and talk to Colonel Barka, not necessarily in that order. There was nothing to do about Amid.

But I couldn't seem to move. Gradually, I came to realize I was ill, probably had a fever. I got up and opened the shutters, but I swayed dizzily, and the light streaming in hurt my eyes, and the air seemed to me suffused with the same ammonia smell that had overcome me at Ian's factory. I tottered back to bed and lay there longer, thinking I had a hangover from Taft's whiskey or something monthly like cramps. Thoughts of illness had the power for a few moments to crowd out memories, but these soon enough came whirling back: Amid, vomit, the silent efficiency of the men at Ain Aouda and their haste to banish me from the sight of what they were doing, their conviction I didn't belong there. Above all, what to tell Suma.

A maid came in about noon, believing I'd gone out, and gasped a little when she saw me still in bed, then asked if I was all right and went to bring me some tea and hard bread, which must be what is prescribed for the Moroccan sick. I asked if she had heard about Posy's baby.

"*Oui,* madame. Allah bestows female children on whomever He wills," she said.

I spent the rest of the day in bed but tried to get up for dinner, only to fall back, not without a certain sense of satisfaction, believing this to be a psychological illness. I was satisfied to think I had moral compunctions that had made me sick. Perhaps it was the case. Robin Crumley tapped at the door and asked if I could be helped; later Pierre, and the maid—Aisha—again, asking if I wanted the doctor and food.

"Suma was here asking for you," Pierre Moment told me, standing delicately in the doorway. "The young woman from Paris." Maybe I'd gotten sick to avoid Suma. I relished the Victorian suitability of falling ill in response to life. Yet I was ill, and could not get up, through the second night.

On Saturday morning, I thought I was better, reluctantly, seeing that I'd have to go back to real life, beginning with a better look in Ian's room. A guilty conscience is just a luxury in my line of work, and a self-indulgence; and mine, I now like to tell myself, was not so much a moral qualm—for I do believe in our side of things—as chagrin at having screwed up.

Of course, there was nothing in Ian's room, just the socks and shirts and cuff links of an orderly life. He had an office, he would naturally keep important things there; only women were obliged to tuck their flash drives among their pantyhose and business letters under their pillows. I knew I should go to the office, ostensibly because of Miss Pring's death, and look through Ian's business records.

I telephoned Posy, apologizing for not coming to see her yet; I listlessly read my mail—communications from MEPI, the grants organization I was compiling my literacy reports for; a letter from my parents, them grumbling as usual that it was archaic to be putting pen to paper, what was the matter with my e-mail; a strange letter from Ian's father, in a heavy cream-colored envelope with the initials GPLD, which meant nothing to me. I opened it and turned right to the signature: Geoffrey Drumm. It was short, saying only:

Dear Miss Sawyer,

It was a great pleasure to meet you during my visit to Marrakech a few weeks ago, and I find I have often had you in my thoughts since then, and so have indulged myself with this note to say how pleased I would be to see you again, should you find yourself in London. I may be in a position, perhaps, to help you in some way if you thought, for instance, of relocating here. (Morocco not being much to my taste, I can imagine others coming to the same conclusion.) This is my private telephone, the best way to reach me: 207 392 2013.

I send my best regards, and the hope of meeting again in the near future.

Geoffrey Drumm

How typical, I couldn't but think, of successful and domineering men, to horn in on their sons' friends and lives. Poor Ian; probably this had gone on always. I noted the phone number and threw the letter away, then retrieved it, in case. In case of what?

I went down to the patio to sit in the chilly sun. Miryam herself brought me tea. Pierre, with his easel set up, was painting a boy of thirteen or fourteen, who sat on a chair shivering, in a light white burnoose and picturesque blue headdress, in the manner of the nineteenth century—though Pierre was an abstract expressionist of some evolved postmodern kind.

"It's a kind of an homage to Delacroix," he said.

Pierre painting, I lying on the chaise longue—and into this tableau came Suma, wearing jeans but also the *abaya,* and a worried look.

Me, the languid invalid: "Hi, Suma."

Suma: "*Bonjour,* mademoiselle. I hope you are better. They told me you were *malade.*"

Me: "Yes, thank you."

Suma: "I came because I am most worried about my little friend Desi. She hasn't come home for two days. Her mother is frantic. We have called the police. Little Desi the virgin?" She smiled at our secret, but then stopped smiling. "You were at the musical soiree—I was hoping—did you see her there?"

This was really a hard question to know how to answer. If everyone (Suma) knew she was going to the concert, had she really been going to blow herself up? If I said "Yes, I saw her," was I obliged to comment on her bulky coat?

If I said no? "No," I said. "Was she there? That seems—she seems young for a serious evening event."

"I had the ticket of Madame Al-Sayad, and I gave it to Desi and organized with her mother. In the end, Monsieur Khaled didn't go, and I could have gone with her instead; I should have.

"She's so young," Suma said. "This is all my fault. She's thirteen, and she didn't understand about . . . the test, and she came away thinking something was seriously wrong with her, or that the test had damaged her. She was so upset. I explained and explained, but she is only a Moroccan village girl—they are way more simple than in France; she can read, though. There was a school there. Apparently lots of them can't read. She was the only girl who went to the school. She has a good memory. I was amazed at her memory, she can recite the Koran and anything else she's ever heard. She thinks she's so fortunate to have a job in Marrakech in a household. Her mother found the Al-Sayads, found her a job there."

Yet there was something insincere about Suma's expression. What could she know? She knew only that nothing had blown up at the concert and that Desi had not come home.

"I don't know," I said. "I didn't see her." Even this small effort of mendacity made my head rage, and I prayed she wouldn't mention her brother. What could she read in my expression?

Miryam came in with a plate of tea cakes and with her most diffident manner asked Suma if she would like some tea. "And monsieur?" She said to Pierre Moment.

He refused. *"Je n'aime pas la menthe,"* he said to me. *"Mohammed, tu veux du thé?"*

"Merci, non, monsieur," said the boy, shifting and squirming. Probably he didn't want to prolong the sitting.

"Suma, you should not be over there in Mr. Al-Sayad's household when Madame Gazi isn't there, your brother will freak out. The way it looks, I mean," I said.

"There are a dozen women there; someone has to supervise the children. Anyway, we 'servants' don't count."

Miryam passed the plate of little cakes to Mohammed, and he hungrily took several.

"My dear Lulu," said Robin Crumley, walking down the stairway from his study. "Are you better?" His tone suggested that maybe I shouldn't be down here infecting everyone, something I hadn't thought of.

"I think I am," I said, though I wasn't sure.

"I must go," Suma said. "But what should I do? I must do something. She is only thirteen."

"What do the police say?"

"Only that they are far too busy to notice the wanderings of wayward adolescent girls."

I wondered how she had come to look to me for opinion and advice. Did her dependence imply that she knew I had some responsibility? Some competence? Did it involve Amid? I must be careful not to seem competent. I remember my aunt saying to me when I was little, "Never tell anyone you can type."

"Her mother should go talk to the police," I said. "I'm surprised she hasn't. Or else ask Monsieur Al-Sayad to do it."

I couldn't decide, I couldn't raise my thoughts enough to decide, whether to tell her about Desi.

"Was she interested in religion, that sort of thing?" I asked.

"Was? What's happened to her?" cried Suma.

"Is she religious? I'm sure she's fine, I just wondered . . ."

"Yes, she's a good girl, very pious."

"But jihad? That sort of thing?" I was remembering the coat; maybe it was just an adult coat, too big for her. I had to talk to the colonel. "Suma, I might have seen something. There was an incident at the concert, a young woman was taken outside. We'll try to find out."

This was the worst thing to have said, for Suma now began to cry, wailing that it was all her fault, and I could see how close under her taciturn surface were her fears.

"*Depuis son enfance*—since she was only three years old, she has had to mind chickens and goats, only a little child, but she was so smart and she wanted to learn, and she loves music. I should have gone with her, but I was afraid to, because of Amid. Things are much worse here, mademoiselle, for girls."

"What have you done with the *attestation* about you?"

"Mailed the original to my parents. I believe they will call him off. But only if they can find him, and they wouldn't have had time to do that."

We agreed this was all she could do, for now, and that I would try to find out about the incident at the concert. But she was still in tears as she left, not reassured.

When Suma had gone, without knowing any more about Desi's fate—and indeed what had been her fate?—I foundered with dismay (again) at the poignance of the catastrophe: a poor little girl at her first concert—and probably no one but Suma had ever noticed her brilliance—now thrown into some terrorist holding tank. I tried to imagine what the Moroccan police would do with a girl of thirteen. My imaginings led to horrors of rape and torture, though reason suggested that unless she had been involved in bombs, they would send her back to her mother. So where was she? My sense of how long it had actually been since the concert was weak—four days? Three days? Only two!

The Cotters had been invited to Saturday lunch, maybe by Robin. The others had a kir in the salon, and I struggled along with them to the dining room. They were aglow with gleeful gossip, and if I looked ill and strange, the visitors seemed not to notice.

"Ian still not back! No wonder!" Neil Cotter began, delegated to carve the roast of lamb in Ian's absence. "I had the most extraordinary visit from George Ward, the British consul. This is jolly good, you will laugh, if you didn't know already."

"It's as we thought—you've probably known all along," said Marina, with a note of reproach that we'd been holding out on them.

"George had a visit from the Saudi ambassador," said Neil. "My word, intervention at the ambassadorial level! Complaining about Ian on behalf of Khaled Al-Sayad. About Ian having gone off with his wife. It seems he's jolly ticked off. Ian eloped with Gazi Al-Sayad! You must have known all along!"

We were silent a few seconds, people I suppose wondering what to say in front of me.

"Yes, he seems to be involved in rescuing Gazi," Robin said. "She took asylum here. We were locked down in an atmosphere of utter secrecy." The Cotters continued to look at us reproachfully.

"George had been looking everywhere for Ian—trying his office and such, wondered if I knew anything. I said, 'not a thing.'" Again, the faint note of reproach for having kept him and Marina in the dark in this cruel way.

"In Saudi Arabia, it seems these things are managed with—if not death by stoning, then a payment of goats at least. Sheep? Camels? Reparations of some kind. In Khaled's case, he apparently would accept money. He's trying to do the modern, Western thing. This is what George told me."

"It's delicious, in a way, but—" Marina stopped, probably thinking of me. "Does it really help them, their women being educated in England and America? I think it just confuses them."

"I'm not sure it's cultural confusion—it's old-fashioned lust. Gazi is very beautiful," Neil said.

"In a Semitic, overblown way, I suppose," Marina conceded.

Robin said, as if to change the subject from their tactless allusions to Gazi's beauty in front of me, "If Ian doesn't turn up soon, I suppose we should ask Lord Drumm what we should do about things around here." It was the first I realized that Robin might like me, to be so caring of my feelings. Usually I felt myself as invisible to him as Posy was.

"Ian isn't dead, Robin," I said.

"Still, it would be useful to know what the time frame is."

"The long and short of it is," said Neil, "a British subject has robbed a Saudi of his wife—that is the nature of it: a diplomatic incident! Well, we know what we know."

"What did you say to Sir George?"

"I said I didn't know anything about it. True enough, as far as that goes, though a half truth, since we knew Ian had vanished." They went on hashing this over. News of it had spread everywhere in the English community and probably among the French: Ian had run off with a Saudi wife.

"Some say we shouldn't interfere in Muslim marital affairs, but I defend Ian," Marina said. "She was obviously desperate to get away. He had no choice but to help her. We saw them socially, after all. We sent them Suma. I wonder if it was a question of a second wife."

Eventually I pleaded my illness, excused myself, and went upstairs, followed by their sympathetic glances.

40

How is the gold become dim! How is the most
fine gold changed! The stones of the sanctuary
are poured out in the top of every street.

—Lamentations 4:1

How repetitious these protestations of dismay of mine! Yet
it seemed there would be no end to new demonstrations of
my misjudgment and culpability.

"Lulu, do you think Ian would object if we had a few people in tonight?" Pierre had said as I left the lunch table. "I've asked a few
people over."

I said I was sure it would be fine and went up again to my room,
feeling sicker than ever and sure it was all in my head. In my room, I
e-mailed "Sheila" and telephoned the colonel: Somehow we would
have to find that little girl. Really, I had no confidence we could. At
one point during the evening, I dressed and tottered downstairs to

look at the party I could hear going on. There was Pierre handing around a plate of something—hash brownies, judging from the expressions of the people helping themselves.

The atmosphere of frivolous sin did reinforce my impression that everyone I had met at the boozy but otherwise staid occasions (European and Moroccan both) in Marrakech was here in the thrall of some unacknowledged vice or taste practiced outside of my view. For that matter, this had been my whole life experience, to radiate some inadvertent primness, to be sheltered from what everyone else knew, me only noticing belatedly, if ever, the hanky-panky to which everyone else was drawn as horses to water. Alas, this credulity was not a good profile for someone in my profession, and, for that matter, may explain why I was drawn to it, in compensation, seeking the feeling of being for once in the know. Here were the clank of ice cubes; animated music in the French-Moroccan idiom; strong smells of grass and whiskey, patchouli, sandalwood; light young voices speaking Arabic; a steady underlying drumbeat accelerating the pulse; couples, mostly male, draped in corners and on sofas; a few rather hard-looking European women; servants I'd never seen before passing drinks. Here was Robin Crumley, alone, his wife and new baby still in the hospital, standing pale and slightly boiled-looking, goofily waving his glass amid a crowd of dark young men, declaiming, I believed it was Yeats.

There's something almost enjoyable about a scene of depravity, for the feeling it gives of being in the know, even though the real depravity is happening somewhere else offstage. Hypocrisy is another matter. That seems omnipresent. It also came to me again what doubtless other people have always known, that Islam like other religions has its share of the worst people masquerading as the best. Muslims took the same amount of dope as others and sold children into prostitution the same as in Thailand or Bucharest.

An odd moment: Into the party came George Ward, the British consul, wearing a white suit, though we were in winter, and an astonished expression as he beheld this transformation of Ian's tranquil living room. People lounged, smoking; two boys stood up to dance in a jitterbug fashion I associated with 1950s films, people pushing and catching each other and twirling around to "Jailhouse Rock" played rather fast. The drums became deafening.

He made a beeline for Robin Crumley, they spoke a minute, and he left, obviously not there for the revelry.

Next, just as I was thinking, What if Ian came home now, Ian did come home—walked into the hall carrying a small suitcase. I wondered if he had met Sir George in the courtyard.

"Ah," he said, fascinated, peering into the salon at the festive guests. He soon seemed more or less pleased that people like Pierre felt enough at home here to invite others—not disturbed, anyhow—and wore a bemused, welcoming expression, like someone returned from the dead to watch mortals frolic. I hurried over to welcome him; I wanted him to know I was forgiving him for his leaving me at the concert—and whatever else he had been up to in the ensuing days.

"We've missed you," I said, striving for a light tone.

"Hello there. I was in Spain." He didn't kiss me.

"Where's Gazi?"

"In Marbella. I'll tell you about it, but I'll take my stuff up." He nodded at Pierre, whose eye he caught, and went off upstairs with his suitcase. I went up in a minute, not especially to be following him, just wanting to lie back down, still feverish, and unprepared for how happy

I was to see him and for the swell of dependence, the feeling of wanting to dump everything in his lap, a feeling I couldn't indulge. I felt again what a burden it is to have the poisonous and omnipresent weight of a seriously guilty secret. Maybe it was truly Amid who was making me ill after all.

41

The Stream of Consciousness is the river of hell.

—Elémire Zolla, *Archetypes*

When I'd flopped down on my bed, still woozy and confused about how to behave to Ian, he tapped on my door and came in, beginning with the time-honored way of heading off recriminations: "Lulu, before you say anything—"

"I wasn't going to say anything." I wasn't; I could barely raise my head.

He sat on his usual chair across the room, not tugging at his collar. He launched into a speech: "I know I haven't been candid with you, but I didn't intend not being candid, I intended, I sincerely tried to . . . you don't want to hear this right now, do you? . . . Lu, are you all right? You look sick."

"Yes, no, I have the flu," I said. "I just need to sleep. I'm sorry, I think I have a fever."

He put his hand on my forehead. "You feel hot."

"I think so."

"I'll just talk—you don't need to say anything. No, I'm sorry. Do you need the doctor?"

"I think it's just flu," I said.

I couldn't raise my head, but I could think. As I lay there, I couldn't stop thinking, in fact, thoughts whirling around and pulsing in my ears, not very coherently. Of Ian, of Gazi, but mostly of Amid. How sorry I was that I didn't believe in being forgiven. I didn't know how that worked. Amid would just sit with me forever, not, eventually, a wracking guilt, probably, but an uneasiness forever. Maybe I would do even worse things, next to which Amid's fate would sit lightly. That was certainly one way out.

I was aware that Ian stood there a long time. He touched my face, tenderly, almost amorously, it seemed. I heard him tiptoe out.

Would I have let him stay? No! Fresh from Gazi's bed—he wouldn't have dared. Anyway, I was probably communicable, and I wouldn't have allowed him to stay, if I had had the strength to prevent it.

42

Oh what a tangled web we weave, when first we practice to deceive.

—Sir Walter Scott, *Marmion* C.VI, stanza 17

By Sunday morning, I couldn't ignore that I was truly better and had to get up and set about doing things, beginning with a visit to Posy. Posy was still in a posh little clinic, a complex of low buildings in Guéliz where, I gather, most Europeans and well-off Moroccans gave birth. She lay against her pillows, looking exactly the same size as before around the middle, but flushed and feverish. I kept my distance because of my recent illness and could only peek in from the doorway. The baby was not in the room, but a nurse brought her past me as I stood there. She was the smallest of creatures and, despite the great bulk Posy had attained at the end, weighed only six pounds, with a furze of marigold-colored hair on her pink scalp. Her wide, bright eyes, already seeming to track and focus, were a tentative blue. Maybe it was too early for them to reveal their ultimate color. She was called Marigold.

"Robin insisted on that," she said. "It's a nice name, but a bit silly with Posy. Posy and Marigold."

"He's envisioning a Rose, a Daisy—a whole bouquet to come," I said.

"I thought you'd never come; you were sick, I heard," she said.

I hoped she would think that my illness explained my not coming with her the night she went into labor. "Yes, I'm sorry, I don't know what it was. I was afraid to come when I felt it coming on. I have a sort of fear of hospitals besides."

"Sod this place, I want to come home," she said. Marigold was already three days old, she was eating, and Posy felt fine, but Morocco viewed European women as fragile and obliged them to stay in childbed for days, resting and eating.

The room had the milky baby smell. Maybe I wasn't immune to babies, for I fell under the charm of this smell. But Posy was stiff and frightened when she took her baby up and seemed unsure of how to hold her to the breast. The hospital women found this funny, and good-naturedly mimed comfortable nursing positions and piled pillows on Posy's lap to prop the baby on. The clinic seemed chilly to me, and they had wrapped a shawl around her shoulders and around Marigold.

She told me Ian had come to visit her already this morning. "He was going on as if he hadn't been away," Posy said, "but I came right out and asked him about Gazi. She's in Spain, that's all he'd say." She was trying to suckle, but the baby kept breaking loose and whimpering. "I don't know what it is; I have plenty of milk, that's what they say—the woman, the nurse," she complained desperately.

"Do you think the Cotters would take Suma back, if she left the Al-Sayads, even just for a few weeks?" This question seemed to divert her from her anguished struggle with little Marigold.

"Probably. What, does she want to leave?"

"I haven't actually talked to her about that," I admitted. "But it must be awkward for her there, and her terrible brother will assume the worst has happened, her having been alone with Khaled like that. I think she should get out right away."

"The downside is the brother could find her more easily at the Cotters'." Thus we discussed the pros and cons of Suma's situation and her options, without hitting on anything just right for her. I said she'd be perfectly safe in France. If the family accepted the virginity test, they'd call off her punishment.

"Sod it all, I want to come home."

When the nurse had taken Marigold, I ventured close enough to kiss Posy before taking my leave, and could see the deep panic in her eyes.

The same afternoon, I had a rendezvous with Taft, who had responded to my anxious e-mail with the suggestion we meet at the Mamounia. Rashid took me there after lunch. Ian had not been seen for lunch or breakfast.

Taft startled me. We were in the Mamounia bar, and he was wearing a djellaba and the white cap the local men wore. I almost didn't recognize him sitting at a table near the door, he looked so natural. Most non-Moroccans look too pale for this comfortable costume. Now, for the first time, I noticed Taft's eyes and hair were as dark as those of most of the men there. I wondered if he was going to carry this disguise to the point of refraining from alcohol, but he ordered a vodka tonic, and a glass of white wine for me.

I plunged into my worries about Desi, maybe not emphasizing the real extent of my fears and feeling of responsibility, trying to be cooler than that.

"We should be able to find out what they found on her," he told me, seeming surprised that I should be worried about this. "They haven't gotten back to us, but they've had a lot to occupy them, with bombs going off all over town." This led to the subject that interested him more.

"At least we have the satisfaction of being right, telling them things were heating up here," he added of the bombings. "All directed at driving away tourism, driving away foreigners. Aimed at the French, I would think, as much as Americans."

"Nothing has happened in France lately," I said.

"Nothing since Toulouse. But it looks like something is coming down already on the subject of our late friend. It could be serious shit, Lulu, in Washington and in Paris."

I wasn't surprised. Here was the official reproach, the finger of blame, coming closer. "Already?"

"The disappearance of a French national in American custody. They heard about it right away, and the French are vindictive, like the Italians were. Encouraged by the Italians, probably—they'll pursue it in the courts, they can make a serious international fuss. They don't like us to begin with, and they really don't like our cooperation with the Moroccans, whatever they say."

"Please, Taft, what are you talking about?" My stomach did a slow crawl. I didn't see how France could know what happened to Amid, or anything that would connect me to it. I had thought about this pretty thoroughly; it was obviously someone from Ain Aouda—someone there, in our own facility, had reported the event to the French. It could be anybody who saw us at Ain Aouda, even Snyder.

How did they find out? I asked. My dismay at this was less about my personal safety than at being let down by someone I had come to trust, had liked—say if the rat were Snyder. But I had no reason to think it was. Quite soon I would become concerned for my personal safety too, when it sank in that I could go to prison, even that they might have capital punishment in Morocco.

"I don't believe it," I said.

"It's not impossible Amid was working for the French, NOC, infiltrating radical groups. We hadn't heard that, though."

"And planning to kill his sister as a cover? That seems extreme."

"Separate issues. A side issue or part of his cover to help him infiltrate the local scene. This is speculation on my part. I haven't heard this."

Could Suma be complicit? I thought about her right away. Could she and Amid both be some kind of French agents? Details of Suma's behavior, including her move to the Al-Sayads', made sense both if she was spying on them, or helping Amid, and also if you assumed the opposite, that she was being protected from Amid by the Al-Sayads, which would also imply that they knew something. Or maybe she was spying on them because they were the money launderers? But would they want to have anything to do with library bombs and Desi's attempt at the concert? I couldn't believe that.

"They know you were there, in Ain Aouda. You're noticeable, Lulu, especially in the context of a black site. Not a lot of girls around. My fault, I should have thought of that. Told you to wear a hat and shades."

"Shades, I did."

"Cover the hair."

"I did. Anyway, there are lots of blonde European women with driver's licenses," I said. "How could they identify me?"

He sniffed. "Be on the lookout," he said. "It seems clear someone outed you—us—to the French. I'm thinking about it. We'll take care of it, somehow. We aren't going to hang you out." When Taft said this was when I knew he might. Though our agency had a reputation for sticking by its own, it often didn't, when the convenient fall person was an alien of some kind, like the Iraqis after the first Gulf War or now, or the South Koreans, and I was an alien of some kind.

Working bare. The significance came back to me now. Under some circumstances, we can't know you. They'd warned me about that. It was hard for me to feel a sense of personal jeopardy—protected American law-abider I thought of myself as—but reason reminded me that working bare meant that if France pursued me, I'd be given up to them.

"Why are you wearing those clothes?" I asked Taft, to conceal the panic that began to rise.

"Comfortable. I like 'em. Less restrictive in the genital area, better for male all-round health. I'm taking some of these robe things back to Spain. I have some news: Peggy is getting a divorce, and she's coming back to Spain with me."

For a moment I drew a complete blank. Peggy?

"Dick Whitworth is a son of a bitch; it's about time. She and Tarik and I'll probably leave tomorrow. Walt Snyder has already gone. Best to get him out of here, he doesn't have the handy . . . skill set you have to save his skin with. Have you decided what you're going to do about the girl? The Arab girl?"

I knew he meant Suma, not Desi. I'd about decided what to tell Suma: that Amid had gone back to France. She'd presume I'd given him news of the virginity certificate. Then she'd assume her parents were reassured and would call to find out more, and they'd tell her they hadn't seen him. Meantime, we were on record as believing he'd left Morocco. I couldn't see a hole in this, and it had the advantage of giving Suma less need to feel afraid that he was lurking around every corner.

I also wanted to know from her about the state of mind, or the actual whereabouts, of Khaled Al-Sayad. I had a moment's fantasy that Gazi had gone back to him. We went over a few such matters, and then I left for my next appointment, hardly feeling up to it, now obliged to include in my worries the menacing scenario laid out by Taft, in which I'd take the blame for Amid's death, whatever horrors that involved of punishment or prison.

Snyder called me soon after this, from Cádiz.

"*Ciao*, Lulu."

"*Ciao*, Walt."

"You've heard?"

"Yes."

"I've decided not to worry. Fuck it, we've got plenty of recourse."

"I'm happy to hear that. I wish I knew what."

"Something will turn up. This is a message of solidarity."

"Thanks, Walt."

"OK, *ciao*, Lulu, we'll be in touch."

"Walt, do you ever have second thoughts?"

A pause. "Yes. But it's a job."

"I guess. *Ciao*, Walt."

43

The label "surprise" . . . can be affixed properly to
the unpleasant results of deliberate gambles.

—Dr. Klaus Knorr,
"Avoiding Surprise in the 1980s"

The eerie sameness of the three days that followed seemed
to efface the unreality of our situations. Pierre, Robin, Ian,
and I shared game little meals without the company of poor Posy, still
kept in the clinic. Apart from that we saw little of each other except in
the evenings, when, the first night, Robin again read a few poems, pae-
ons to fatherhood, and the next night when we kept a dinner invitation
to the former American ambassador's, now retired here. When invited,
we had explained that Ian was away, and he had heartily urged us to
come anyway; now we warned him that Ian was coming after all.
Rashid asked no questions of any of us but ferried us hither and yon, to
our visits to Posy and to see the wreckage of the library—which had
been bombed rather ineptly, so that the front was blown off, and the

table where poor Miss Pring had been reading while many shelves were intact at the back. I salvaged from the wreckage a few books, belatedly, that others had felt beyond reclaim. Those book corpses brought home the horror of explosions, indiscriminate fragmenting of reality, a vicious contempt for the material world I hadn't understood before.

Despite a strange lethargy that slowed my steps and made me feel sleepy all the time, I went each day to visit Posy, and so did Robin and Ian, at different hours. For the rest, Robin was working in his study. Pierre set up his easel in the courtyard to do some watercolor sketches of the maids and gardeners, picturesque in their turbans and wrappings. Madame Frank came once to call and, I thought, to look around covertly. Maybe Ian was planning to sell her his villa too? The expat community telephoned one another to expostulate about the bombings, and Khaled's lawsuit, and whether it was safe to go to the medina and the public gardens. Ian and I didn't continue our conversation. Nothing more from Taft, Khaled, or the colonel; it was as if the past week had not happened.

"I have a bit of news," Habiba told me on the way to visit a village to the south. "Assan and I, after much soul-searching, are going back. For me, it's forty years. I've got such mixed feelings." I thought she meant going back to Mecca, where they used to live.

"Isn't it dangerous now?"

"Probably. That's why we feel we have a role, an important mission, actually, to further understanding of the Muslim religion. People like us—like me, anyhow, a mainstream Californian—can make ourselves heard, and Assan is a moderate imam who can be a force for good. We've hashed it over endlessly, and it's the right thing to do."

I objected. "I'd think especially an American would be suspected. . . ." It took a while for me to grasp that she was talking about going to America, not Mecca. They were going to Connecticut, to a small town, where they would be visible good citizens. I remembered Habiba's family money.

With Ian's return, I felt the dismay come back that had slowly been abating after Amid's death day, for now I saw that nothing was solved or soluble and that maybe the answer to personal misery was to have no personal life or feelings at all. A solution a lot of people had arrived at before me, no doubt, maybe including Habiba.

Ian and I didn't have any more talks about our future. He was mostly at his office or somewhere, dealing with the death of Miss Pring. At night he would come in to embrace me tenderly, stirring my desire; but we didn't make love. He never mentioned Gazi.

At the end of the week, I went with him to visit, with a view to investing in, an experimental garden project in the foothills of the Atlases. The Moroccan farmer and his children greeted us, smiling and brown, a boy and two girls, barefoot, who ran out of a garden shed where they were stacking shrubby branches. The air was delicious, heavy with lavender and herbal scents of other kinds, mysterious and redolent of aromatherapy salons. With his planting, the farmer had made some effort to construct a pleasant garden, or maybe North Africans always think of gardens in this fashion, as needing to be delightful to meander in, formal in design, full of surprises of hedges and tiny ponds. In a little office, he showed us bottles of oils from the various herbal shrubs he had planted.

"We sell these to a shop in Covent Garden, in England," he said, "and we have many orders. We are exploring a soap made from this blend of herbal oil, and other products, perhaps perfumes. We are also replanting the argan tree. The precious oil of the argan tree . . ."

"I'm glad to hear that. I've been interested in the argan projects," Ian said. "The women's cooperative in Tidzi, for instance . . ."

Ian knew a lot about it and was impressed, he said later, with the farmer's ambitions. What promising developments lay in store for Morocco, what energy and intelligence among its people, what resources the country possessed. . . . And his hopefulness did give me a momentary glimpse of promise and peace lying within reach.

All the more reason for our literacy work; I could look at it that way. I asked the farmer if his daughters went to school. His expression didn't convince me, but he said, "*Bien sûr,* madame, they are good students."

All the more reason for Taft's and my work too, I suppose. To protect the women's cooperative, the schools, the optimism.

Perhaps it was in the context of this hopeful expedition, with its promise of a productive future, that led Ian, as we drove back, to bring up the subject he had begun the night he came back. "I know when you came here, you didn't expect any more than I did. That is, we were both hoping, I think, that what we had in Kosovo would continue to grow," he said. "We like each other so much, we get along so well—we hoped for more. And I do feel more for you even than I did then—I love you very much."

And he went on longer in this vein. As you might at the doctor's, getting a complicated diagnosis, I tried to concentrate but felt my thoughts exploding. This wasn't what I expected, nor what I believed, and I was silenced by this tack, in what must have seemed an ominous silence, for he went on, almost more words flowing from Ian than I'd ever heard from him, about love, about compatibility. Finally he said, "I know I have to speak about Gazi."

"Well, yes," I said.

"We were in love for a long time, six years, only possible to meet when they were here in Morocco, of course, and only possible under the most ridiculous and clandestine conditions—her very life depended on me, if we were ever found out. Her life in Riyadh was impossible. Of course the very clandestinity made it exciting beyond all—"

"Oh, Ian," I found myself saying, "you don't have to explain. I'm sorry you didn't tell me sooner though. It might have saved me some tears."

"I hoped it was over. We both did. It was an impossible affair, with no future and the probability of ending in the worst way, we both always knew it. But Gazi was—is—reckless. Desperate."

"Why no future? She's escaped. Where is she?"

"In Marbella. She hopes to fade into the Spanish landscape. We'll get her some papers somehow."

"How did you get her into Spain without papers?"

"Through Algeciras. She hid in my car. The Spanish aren't uptight— a respectable Englishman in a rental car, crossing to do some shopping, no problem at all."

I could think of all kinds of reasons it could have been a problem, but it was true there wasn't a lot of trafficking in women out of Morocco, nor were middle-age, upper-class Englishmen big people-traffickers. There was nothing about him to excite official vigilance.

"What's to stop the two of you, then?" I asked.

Ian shrugged. "It's hard to explain. What I'm trying to say is that my hopes for the future involve you, Lulu, and I regret what I know must have disappointed you and put you off, but I had to see it through with Gazi, and I just hope you and I can get through this and go on together."

Though this was what I had hoped myself, it was the last thing I expected from him now, and I had no idea how to respond. Something must have gone wrong with Gazi. He leaned over and kissed me in a somewhat brotherly way, and I didn't object. I felt my body respond, but I told him I needed to do some thinking, and I did.

"Gazi needs to understand freedom for a while. She's been a captive her whole life," Ian added.

"Anyway, thanks for sparing me any hypocritical remorse," I said.

I lay awake well into the night, tormented by thoughts and lingering fever, wondering about what to do, especially about Desi, a frightened little girl in some cell or worse, but now also about Ian—about everything. Did Ian have any contacts among the Moroccan police that could give us information about Desi? I worried about losing my job, as a matter of course, having screwed up, Snyder and I. I mourned Amid, and if he had had to die, I was sorry to have looked at his penis.

Probably Ian was thinking of marriage. We would be happy; I was sure of that, and he apparently thought so too. He'd had his fling with Gazi, and judging from his reticence now, something hadn't worked out. It was the kind of issue in his life I couldn't ask about if I didn't want questions myself, though Ian didn't seem curious or emotionally possessive the way some men are—the court-injunctioned stalkers, the midnight phone-callers, the domineering fathers. I'd never be mixed up with men like that.

Would he want to live forever in Morocco? I'd have to think about that, but I knew my resistance to it was crumbling. I could throw myself into female literacy. How easily I could be melted into wifehood, that time-honored refuge and slightly unchallenging calling—I even yearned for it deliciously. I could even stay in my job, could tell him about it.

44

And once we accept the fact that intelligence cannot always supply us with one "right" answer, our efforts can be more productively focused on preparing contingency plans and counter-surprises for the moment when the inevitable occurs.

—Michael Handel, "Avoiding Surprise in the 1980s"

I'd left a message for Colonel Barka, and there had been a message from him to meet him at the Restaurant Sidi-Ali on Wednesday. I went straight there, without telling anyone at Ian's where I was going or that I wouldn't be home for dinner. When I got there, by taxi to elude Rashid, the colonel was sitting at the table we had sat at the day we saw Ian and Gazi there. He looked rakish in a conical red tarboosh with his usual military jacket, and rose slightly from behind the table, then sat back on the cushions, fatigued, it seemed, even distressed.

"My angel," he said. "What a trying time you've had. My colleagues are quite abuzz." His urbane tone didn't convince me.

There was little point in sparring with the colonel. "That isn't why I called. I have to know about the little girl who works at the Al-Sayads' and was arrested at the concert Wednesday night. Didn't you see it?"

"Yes, I saw you taking a young woman outside. What was that about? You went to dinner at the Franks' afterward; I supposed it was not important. Unfortunately, we did not get to the Franks'. My wife doesn't like late European dinners."

"Yes, I hustled her out, I thought she might be planning—there was something about her coat, I thought . . . anyhow the security guards took her away immediately, and now she hasn't returned home. She's a thirteen-year-old who works at the Al-Sayads' and watches their children. I have to find her, I feel terrible, the mother, everyone's upset, it looks like the girl was just dressed up for her first concert."

"Odd that such a one would attend such an event."

"I thought so too."

"I can't help you here, I'm afraid, but I'll inquire. I know someone who has contacts inside the *sécurité*. Dear me, you're rather the kiss of death, aren't you—in a manner of speaking, I hasten to say. I didn't intend a tactless reference to the fate of the Parisian visitor."

This was chilling. "How did you hear about that?"

"You know he was a—let us say, a valued person. Valued by *la belle* France."

Since I had heard that from Taft, I acted only a little surprised. Of course it had long occurred to me it could be the French the colonel worked for, but now I knew it must be so; otherwise, how did he know what they were thinking about Amid?

"Suma's brother, you knew we were interested in him. We talked about it." Had we? Had I told him about Amid? I couldn't thrash myself out of the tangled web in order to be sure. The colonel and I exchanged some recriminations like this, though he was growing more cheerful. Through his delicate allusions, I began to understand something else: Amid was not just a French citizen, he was a French agent.

What did that mean for, or about, Suma?

"Bourad's real allegiances with the French *sécurité* were not known to the DST, alas for him. If so, they might have picked him up before you did, thus saving him from the bungling for which your agency is known. In any case, one of my employers—I trust your discretion, Lulu—is in a position to mitigate your legal problems. They are interested in Lord Drumm, who has many Middle Eastern connections. It would be of enormous value to know someone who knew him well."

"I've only met the man once, I don't know him well," I protested.

"You have received a letter from him."

"No, of course not."

I saw he was surprised, betrayed by a tiny flicker of his eyelid. He knew I had told him a lie. Maybe he was surprised because I hadn't lied to him before.

"Perhaps you will," he said. Little bits kept falling into place. "My employers." Yes, the colonel worked for the French too. I was still trying to work out whether he was fishing or had actually opened my mail. He or someone could have opened my mail, and I'd never detected it. But only amateurs would be detected; we all knew how to do it properly.

"Suppose I do?"

"If you went to London, if you accepted his offer of . . . friendship, you could be sure that the French authorities would listen to suggestions that they not pursue the grave matter of the death of poor Bourad, illegally kidnapped on Moroccan soil."

"They'd want reports? Real intelligence?"

"Yes."

"Would my American colleagues know—could I tell them what I was doing?"

"Of course, yes. They'd have to know—you'd have to get yourself reassigned there. I would leave to your discretion how to do it." I thought of Taft's mention of *Notorious,* with Ian as the longed-for Cary Grant and Lord Drumm playing the Claude Raines part. In a good cause. America! I had to face facts. Obviously, because of Ain Aouda, to avoid prosecution I couldn't stay in Morocco, but I couldn't go back to France or California either, and I had to be somewhere. So I had to behave and take orders, like Ingrid Bergman.

It was through this frivolous film analogy that I could see the future, and what I saw was that I had plunged so deeply into the thicket, through the dark and tangled foliage, that I couldn't avoid seeing out the other side: there was London—a little flat in Chelsea or Canary Wharf, tickets for Covent Garden and the Coliseum, and tawdry, racy little West End plays, and the Royal Shakespeare . . . oh yes, I'd spent some time in London, it was very agreeable.

And, of course, I had signed on for this. Coming up, I could see, was the painful (for me) good-bye to Ian; in London, the pretty clothes and cultural events, and the weekly, or monthly, lunch with Taft, or the colonel, or some counterpart, and some time-consuming cover, crusading for female literacy. Beyond that, the view was obscured.

45

Then said I, Ah, Lord God! surely thou hast greatly deceived this people and Jerusalem, saying Ye shall have peace; whereas the sword reacheth unto the soul.

—Jeremiah 4:10

As the days continued, I would catch myself indulging in a self-pitying reverie as a sort of female Saint Sebastian being shot with new arrows at each moment, my heart totally disordered by guilt and confusion. Then a more normal state of mind would reassert itself. I heard nothing more from Taft about my legal jeopardy, and received no intimate visit from Ian, though the surface of things was as it had been, except for Posy's return home. To my relief, the happy excitement around this deferred serious talks with Ian. It was I who brought her home, in fact. One day on my visit, she was dressed and ready to come with us.

Ian happened to be outside in his courtyard as Rashid drove us through the gate, and he strode across the driveway, all smiles, to hand

Posy out of the car, clutching her bundle. Robin dashed down the stairs soon after, expostulating, "My dear! Is this wise? The doctor said . . . ," and so on, a mood that carried us through dinner with a minimum of awkwardness and an air of general congratulation, maybe except for Robin, who peered impassively at the baby, his eyes betraying panic equal to Posy's. I wondered if Marigold was still to be a great play-wright after all or if he would decide on a different career for her.

The week that followed showed Posy's growing exhaustion. Things didn't go well. She slept a lot, and the maids would walk in the garden carrying Marigold. I would hear the baby's thin little cry. I wondered if I should tell Robin about postpartum depression. Perhaps they didn't take it seriously in England. I talked about that with Marina Cotter, who had noticed Posy's fatigue too but dismissed Posy's gloom.

"Motherhood is a shock, that's all. It's normal to be a little de-pressed, tired and so on. She's better off than most women—all these people to help."

Since I wasn't a mother, I wasn't much of an authority, but I wished I could do something. "Couldn't she take some antidepressants?"

"Not when she's nursing, I'm sure," Marina said severely. "She has to think of her milk." Poor Posy. It wasn't my first glimpse into the way you burn your bridges when you become a mother.

I was aware—couldn't help but notice—that Gazi and Ian spoke most nights, maybe every night. Once he was with me in the dining room when his cell phone rang, and he answered, waved at me, and started to leave the room to talk privately. Then he realized he could hardly be wooing me and having surreptitious phone calls with her, so he took the call in front of me, in an affectionate but businesslike tone, no news of her children but no problems reported, some banking details.

"She's making some acquaintances in the building, it's a good sign, though it's probably the usual collection of American tax evaders and British retirees," he said when they hung up.

"I'll ask Suma about the children again," I said. "You should report."

Other nights, I would hear the low sound of Ian speaking in his room, late, after I was supposedly asleep. Once I tried to reveal that I knew this by asking how Gazi was doing.

"Fine," he said. "She's a brave girl, she'll get through it."

Another night, Ian came into my room after dinner, loosening his collar, the unconscious gesture I'd noticed before, one that always said to me that we would make love or that he wished to. I wanted to be in his arms, but I also thought it was a bad idea, prolonging something that needed to be over. Over, that is, if I was going to go to London as a London-based directrice of the Middle Eastern Partnership Initiative, the group for whom I was preparing the literacy report, or maybe the World Learning Project—which one had yet to be determined. Various thoughts descended on me simultaneously. Some were cynical thoughts; Ian/men just have to get it from someone, never mind that their beloved is off in Marbella. Desirous thoughts, since I was feeling quite hard up myself. Love for Ian, this powerful pull of his arms, self, situation; professional, competent thoughts to do with the always foreseen term of my stay with Ian. It was always going to end if we didn't prolong it, and now it was time to move on as my employers expected.

I should note that I didn't quite have the character to resist Ian this time, but at the climax, tears came, me knowing it was the last time. He, on the other hand, was passionate and relieved; we were back together, joined body and soul.

"That's better, Lu, now, right?"

. . .

"I know this is mad," Posy said one morning at breakfast. Her pink and white skin was dry-looking, with dark shadows under her eyes, and she tore her toast with fidgety fingers, quite unlike her pregnant, stolid self. "I recognize that it's bodily changes and all, but I can't seem to shake the idea that Marigold isn't safe here. Someone will kidnap her or drop her. I keep seeing it, a—well—a dark presence outside the window, all kinds of things like that that I know are mad."

"Oh, Posy," I began.

"I'm taking her to England; I will just feel better. Robin thinks I'm mad."

But I could understand, if you were in charge of someone so little, how the silence here, the creepy feeling the silent maids gave you . . . I could understand well enough. Even Ian could, though there was no danger, he said. "The Moroccans love children," he said.

"Let her try to find nannies in England," said Marina Cotter, sourly.

It was in the paper that the French had already asked for the extradition of a Walter Snyder in connection with the kidnapping of French citizen Amid Bourad. I knew I was procrastinating the real breaking off with Ian, the moving on, but now it had to be done. I had to let it be known I'd received a job offer in London, though its real nature was still being organized in Virginia. It would have to do with literacy.

I'd thought a lot about literacy. "What good does reading do them?" Marina Cotter had asked that question. Maybe she was unable to imagine—though I was able to imagine it—a world in which you had no way of finding out anything, and if some man, or your mother, or the imam, told you you were a low creature and a man had a right to beat you, how would you find out that wasn't true? You would be beaten because the Koran says that a man has the right, maybe the duty to beat you. If you couldn't read anything else, how would you know any better? Suma could read and must know better, so did her heart burn with devotion or with rage? Was I ever to know?

Of course I had to tell Ian I was leaving, but for a few days I procrastinated, maybe hoping for a miracle, something that would let me throw myself into his arms and say yes! our future! us! However qualified his hopes, I knew he meant them, the hope that he and I could rub along together and that I'd stay. The more fully furnished my imagination became with images of our future, of our happiness, our children even, the more miserable I became, until that very misery goaded me into making an end to it.

"It looks like I'll be going to London soon." I said this at lunch, in front of the Crumleys and Pierre Moment—a coward's way. They murmured, inquired; I explained about female literacy, the consortium of projects, the home base in London. Ian appeared startled, even dumbfounded. I knew it was cowardly of me to bring it up this way with others present.

"I think it's a great chance to operate on a more global scale—it's a huge problem, after all."

"You're doing so much here," Ian objected.

"I'm about finished with my report," I said. We'll talk about it, said Ian's glance. But we didn't. We avoided the subject pointedly the rest of the day. Then, at night, he came to my room, angry, as if his choler and disbelief had been growing all day and now must explode.

"I can't believe this, Lulu, how could you make a decision like that out of the blue?" And more in this vein. "We talked about this. We decided we could make it work."

"You told me what you hoped," I said, very resolute, steeled against this, gratified too, I suppose, by his chagrin. "And I've been thinking about it—whether we could get on, Ian. I didn't say I thought we could."

"But we do! Lulu, we have so much. . . ."

Of course I couldn't say those melodramatic things I wanted to say—"You love another, I am not your first love"—nobody has a right to say things like that. Life is full of compromises. I knew all that. I also knew I wouldn't like a French (or Moroccan) jail. Life is full of compromises, and I was going to try to be professional and not bitter.

He argued with me a little, then all at once, with a certain déjà vu expression, he said he understood and that he'd come visit me in London. I found this capitulation almost the most wounding thing of all.

"My father's company has a corporate flat—I'll see if you can use it while you get settled," he said.

For the good of her health and morale both, I was making Posy take walks with me each day. We could walk together on the road—it did her good to get out of the compound and feel a little free. The maids were in love with Marigold anyway and hovered over her basket with rapt devotion, so there was no need to fear going for a little walk, though the English child-rearing manual someone had given Posy suggested you were a criminal if you left your baby for half an hour. I would have to undo her bookish tendency to look up every child-care question in this misguided tract. Was literacy a good thing?

"Oh, you have so much experience, around babies your whole life," said Posy sarcastically, knowing I knew nothing about them, though

I did feel a swell of love for Marigold whenever I held the squirmy little bundle.

One day we tried going out together in Gazi's abayas, for she had left several behind, enormous squares of black rayon hung over the backs of a chair or on a peg in the hall. Sure enough, when men driving carts went by us on the road, they didn't look at us. Once, a truck would have run us over if we hadn't gotten out of the way; we were part of the landscape and had to throw ourselves into a ditch, invisible. It was up to women to get out of the way. "In some ways, I don't mind invisibility. It makes you part of universal womanhood," said Posy as we scrambled out again. "If it meant I could also tap into some realm of sisterhood and universality, I wouldn't mind. It might be calming." I wondered if she was being facetious or whether she had been co-opted in some surprising way.

"It would be a mistake," I said, thinking of the old, old women walking by us, who would turn out to be forty-five, their teeth knocked out by their husbands. "You wouldn't like it."

"It's just that I feel alienated from womankind. Why? Because I feel I was tricked. No one told me. They all pretended it was wonderful to have a baby and wear this lace nightie and smile. Other women should tell you the truth, how hard and scary it is and how you sign your life away."

"Well, I couldn't because I didn't know," I said.

"I'm so happy you're coming to England," Posy said. "At least we'll be safe."

And indeed, on these walks along the dusty Palmeraie roads, I found I was growing more receptive to the allure of London, to the idea of getting away from the repellent, skinny palm trees struggling for water in the desiccated landscape (while the Europeans' wells and swimming pools sopped all the water up) and the tumbling plastic bottles skittering across the desert, and even the poor, thin little girls whose only hope is in virginity—forget all this depressing disarray. Forget Ian. Brisk English problems appealed to me, never mind that English is no longer spoken on the buses up and down the Edgeware Road. Me, I'd be in Mayfair or Chelsea or Belgravia. But I wasn't leaving those women to their fate. I would have my work.

It remained in the next weeks to wrap up my Moroccan affairs and say good-bye to the people I'd become fond of here. Posy had left, Robin soon to follow. There were some drinks parties. The Cotters had a lunch, and Ian gave a grand dinner, for which Miryam oversaw a delicious *pastilla* of pigeon and raisin, and there were the drummers.

"To ensure you will come back. You won't get this in London," Ian said of the *pastilla*. "But I'll be coming to London for shepherd's pie." This genial formality had marked his demeanor in the past days and made my heart ache.

One friend I would miss was Colonel Barka. We had lunch at the Mamounia the day before I was to leave.

"I have something for you," said the colonel, pulling from a sort of man purse under the table a sheaf of papers. "These are copies of a notebook the Moroccans took from the luggage of the girl you are so interested in, Suma, Bourad's sister, at the airport."

At the airport? This was chilling news. "Go on."

"She was leaving. She has left, in fact. She had a flight to Nice. Apparently she plans to study medicine there, or near there. I read the transcript of the interrogation. They were interested in her connection to the little girl arrested at the concert the other night. Anyway, they let her go, but they'll be watching her. She apparently took this note-book, a list of donors to some cause, from the Al-Sayad household. I'm amazed it was lying around."

"It was probably in the safe," I said, seeing, of course, how she would get it, how she knew about the key, where it was, bath time. I was touched by her courage, but of course, Suma hadn't done it for me, she was taking it back to France. What for? Had she thought to filch Gazi's passport as well?

"Lists of donations, donors, organizations. This notebook is going to make your friends very happy. They will think of you very kindly, Miss Sawyer."

"Yes, thank you, I see that they'll be pleased," I said.

"A lesser man would exact a price for this from a beautiful woman" said the colonel, patting my hand. "But it is a token of my esteem for you and the hope we will always be friends."

"Thank you, Colonel," I said, at that moment adoring him. "We will always be friends."

"Not that it explains much—the notebook. It will keep your friends busy translating it and checking out the little donors Khaled so virtu-ously solicited *zatak* from. Probably your friend Ian's name will be there—who is so indifferent to human suffering as not to contribute something for the poor Saharawis, for the Iraqi refugees, for the dislo-cated of Darfur? You have heard the saying 'The bombs of Belfast were born in Boston'? It is a bit the same. The bombs of Baghdad are born in Marrakech, to be sure, though also in New Jersey, Cairo, Paris, London, Riyadh. It involves so many."

"She didn't say good-bye," I said of Suma.

"No? Maybe she believes her sojourn in our beautiful country was a mixed blessing. You'll hear from her again, doubtless, or of her."

He said again he would try to find out what had happened to Desi, but that such bureaucratic issues as the whereabouts of prisoners were often obscure.

Later, I looked at Khaled Al-Sayad's notebook in detail, pages and pages of names, in Arabic, so of course I couldn't read them. But the colonel had told me Ian was in it, giving money to Rashid for his brother. Habiba and her husband. Rashid was in it, of course Khaled was in it, Dr. Kadimi was in it. Lord Drumm? There were so many, I realized everyone was in it, the world was in it, paying conscience money, revenge money, compassion money—money that would end up as a bomb.

At the airport I was apprehensive, sure that the DST, or the Moroccan police, or some French undercover agent would prevent me, but such is the power of the organization behind me, or else the insignificance of my departure, that nothing happened at all. I presented my passport, my tickets, my carry-on, now innocent of any liquids or gels—and I'd given my gun back to Taft. I embraced Ian, showed my passport, boarded the plane. My tears were only inward. It was an outwardly cheerful, hard-hearted person Ian was seeing off.

On the plane, I opened a letter from Gazi, or so I assumed from the childlike, round hand; it was mailed from Spain without the name of the sender—it could have been from Taft or Snyder. But it was from Gazi.

> Dear Loulou,
>
> I thought I'd write—I have not much else to do, frankly—my life is so quiet, I might as well be in Riyadh. Just joking! What do I do all day? I swim and walk around. There is

shopping, time-honored pastime! But I do have to watch my pennies. It's worth it, to be here, though. One of these days I'm going to rent a car. I have a nice apartment (one bedroom) in a hotel in Puerto Banus, looking out on lots of yachts, you can imagine exciting for this desert girl! Well not exciting because the calm of life.

Do you hear news of my children? I have written Suma but no reply. I never thought she liked me. I think she liked Khaled a lot! News of Khaled? I don't care, I wish him in hell, but I don't dare ask Ian for news of him.

Sometimes I cry. Oh yes, we have feelings too, beneath our creepy black masks. (No, I do not wear the abaya at all here. I am supposed to be a Lebanese. Don't ask me how Ian managed that!) But the abaya did make me happy, cocooning inside!

I wanted to tell you, I do not resent you. You were always very nice to me, and I appreciate it. Also, I know how much Ian regards you. . . .

For the moment, I could read no further, exasperated at this childlike, self-centered missive. I stuffed it in my purse. I would keep it of course; it helped me understand what had gone wrong between her and Ian, if anything had: She was too dumb.

"I am glad you are going with me—well, I with you," said Madame Frank in the seat next to me. "I am not at home in *Angleterre* really, though now I must take into account their habits. The English are my natural market for the Palmeraie, don't you think? Just as Ian perceived when he bought the land in the first place. They love the sun, they can't afford Saint-Tropez—well, that's their own fault, it's the English that have driven up the prices in France, they've bought it all up already.

"I've thought of the name for my development, 'Les Arches d'Or,' or maybe 'du Soleil,' and for the logo, *tu sais,* the Islamic arch. Just the simple shape in gold on the letterhead. Palm trees too banal, I thought, idem camels."

"Are you just plunging into the English market, just like that?"

"*Non, non,* I am associating myself with Knight Randall, very reputable big firm who will represent Les Arches d'Or in London and Glasgow. I am going to meet with them. And you? You must be sad to leave the *charmant* Ian and his lovely place. Where will you be living?"

I was surprised to see that Madame Frank thought of the lives of others enough to fish like this. But real estate salespeople have to be good psychologists and good gossips, I suppose.

"We didn't really say good-bye," I said. "He comes to London. His father lives there, you know. Lord Drumm. Lord Drumm's been helpful in finding me a place. How about you?"

"I'm renting the flat of Sir Neil and Lady Cotter," she said. "It will be a little office and pied-à-terre. *Un peu cher,* I thought. The *anglais* are the most awful robbers. But I'm sure it will be lovely.

"You Americans are so impetuous," she added. "We hope you aren't breaking poor Ian's heart."

I said I doubted it, and anyway, we had sworn to keep up. So we flew off, not into the sunset, for we were flying east, but in the direction of dawn, agreeing it would be lovely in London, almost spring, probably rhododendrons already, and azaleas, or daffodils, but so hard to get used to driving on the left.